MEDIA VITA IN MORTE SUMUS

UNDER THE MOON IN ILLINOIS

STORIES FROM A HAUNTED LAND

KIPLING KNOX

A PRAIRIE STATE CREATION

Printed in the United States of America

First Printing, 2022

ISBN: 979-8-9871656-0-7

Prairie State Press,
Illinois
prairiestatepress.com

About the author: kiplingknox.com

Stories and illustrations by Kipling Knox
Cover and book design by Haley Knox
Edited by Elaine Palencia

CONTENTS

LETTER TO MY LATE HUSBAND

My dear Earl, it's about time I wrote you. I don't know why I let so much time go. I always feel better after I write, but I suppose there's something about people that makes them have to learn things over and over. The big news is there's been another storm, and this one was a doozy. The hens stopped laying two days before it came. Don't they just know better than we do? I think I told you: the hens are all that's left. The garden rotted in the rain, so there's no vegetables. Eleanor died of pneumonia, so we're out of milk. And the corn must be in the next county by now, due to all this wind, so there's no cash. Once the eggs are gone, then I don't know what. I could eat the birds but then we'll have nothing!

If you were here, you'd say Helen, we'll learn from this. Well I'll tell you what, Earl—I have learned something you won't believe, but I'm going to tell you anyway.

When the storm came, I had the hens safe inside their house. But the buildings aren't what they were. The barn leans so bad you might think it's a shipwreck on a sea of clay. So when the wind picked up, it ripped the henhouse door off, and sucked the chickens right out. It pressed them against the screen of the coop, like red, shaggy leaves. From the kitchen window I could see their yellow eyes, not blinking. I cried out (to whom I don't know), For God's sake leave the birds alone! And then I went out to see what I could do.

If you were here, you'd say Helen, your hands are shaking. You'd say you need to catch your breath. And you'd be right. But I haven't lost all my strength. I may be 5 foot 2 and half as wide, but I can still move, Earl. I got to the coop in two shakes and saw the river had risen almost to the floor of the house. Another foot of water, that henhouse might just float away.

There was garbage on the wind. Shopping bags twisted like jellyfish stuck to my legs. I had to swat pop bottles tumbling toward me. Cardboard boxes wearing smiles, food wrappers fluttering, and all this unopened mail. It all came on the wind and I didn't know whether to save my eyes or see what's coming. Well, I looked, and suddenly there was a big shelf!

I barely saw the plank of pressboard, with white lamination and peg holes, flipping end over end. Then my lights went out. When I came to, I was lying face-down in the mud, a little dizzy with a nasty throb in my noggin. I turned and looked for you, thinking it was over and this was it. But instead, I saw hundreds of wild birds, maybe thousands, flying on this river of air, wing to wing. I recognized these birds from pictures, with blue-gray bodies and red breasts, and I thought, they aren't supposed to be here! The last one died in the Cincinnati Zoo. I held up my hand to catch one, but it only passed through. Like it was made of wind. Or maybe it was the wind.

Earl, you know I'm a practical woman, not inclined to make things up. So hear me out when I say what else I saw. There came other creatures who perished long ago. I saw bison rumbling in dark herds, and their echoes made the heavens thunder. I saw wolves taller than me, loping on silver legs, who threw back their heads and howled lightning. And through the lightning came scores of pronghorn and hares and grouse, rolling across the land like the shadows of clouds.

I blinked against the rain, as the river rose closer to my muddy head, and I saw enormous armored fish whipping their tails to drive the flood. I tried to get up, but couldn't, so I turned and saw ground sloth on a distant rise, all in a line, pawing mounds of soil from the earth so the waters could wash it all away. And far beyond, along the horizon, where the bleak sun glowed white, I saw silhouettes of mastodon, marching tail to trunk, and the one in front—the great mother of all these beasts—reared back her church-bell head and wailed. But they weren't enduring the storm, Earl. They *were* the storm, all playing a part in some great communal tantrum.

My lights must have dimmed again, because when I awoke, it was just me and the hens and the weather. The flood had come, and river water lapped into my mouth. I spat it out and breathed deep. And then I thought, well, if I do nothing, if I let this river rise on me, let this water fill my lungs, I might just join those beasts. I might just join you, Earl. And then I thought, why weren't you there? If these were all the victims of 10,000 years of progress, shouldn't people like you be among them? Didn't you always do your best? And when you got ill, we knew where the illness came from. So why weren't you out on the plain, stamping your feet, making it rain? I reckoned I'd find out if I did nothing. I reckoned I'd let nature have her way.

But then I heard a croak behind me, a weak brawk. I turned and saw the hen we call Emily, still pinned against the screen. She shuddered and twitched and dropped an egg. It fell into the shallow water and rolled toward me, ushered by the wind.

The man you admire the most said, 'The hen never cackles until the egg is laid.' This came into my head as I lay in the mud. We are all a bunch of cacklers who haven't laid an egg. Except for Emily. And also, that great man 'resolved that these dead shall not have died in vain.' That also came into my head, which lay half in the river. And I realized that this wasn't much different. I heard myself say it out loud: Those beasts shall not have died in vain.

So I got up. As the wind beat my body, I peeled the chickens from their screen, like leeches from a bucket, and popped them into their hen house. One after another, I made them safe, and not a one has died. And then I came inside and wrote to you.

UNDER THE MOON IN ILLINOIS

I went to see the pastor because I was desperate and needed money. It was the second time he'd called me to do a job, and how he got my number I don't know. This guy, Pastor Yeshevsky, of the Most Redeemed Church, he's not the sort you'd expect to run in my crowd. But he had a job he wanted done and people around town know how to reach me when they need help with something that's, you know, less desirable.

There was a farmer hired me to watch the road while he dumped some bad-smelling shit on his neighbor's field. That went well for him, so then he hires me to follow his wife from her night shift at the hospital, to see if she's cheating. Not a week after that, a cop whose name I won't repeat pays me to sit in his squad car outside the high school so he can hook up with that farmer's wife! That's just one example.

I knew two things about Yeshevsky. First, when he took over the church five years ago, he added the word 'Most.' This struck me as funny, because aren't you either redeemed or not? I'm no expert on religion, being raised Catholic, but it strikes me that one guy can't be more redeemed than another. Anyway, the second thing I knew is that the pastor hired me to take some pictures of a couple coming out of the Good'n'uff Tavern late one night. The whole thing was handled through this lady realtor I met on a job. She said it was a birthday surprise, not that I asked. I never met the pastor, but he paid me well for it. So when he called again, I figured, why not?

It was a warm spring day, so I rode my little Honda 250 along the country road to the church. On the way, people waved. I like how people wave around here, much more than in other places. It helps, probably, to be a huge guy on a tiny motorcycle on a warm spring day. Still. Some of them knew me, but most not. They just wave because, I don't know. They just do.

The church sits right next to the river with an old cemetery in between. The secretary, Ms. Dalyrimple, had me wait in a comfortable chair in her office. She used to be the school nurse when I was a kid, and she was really good at it. If you had a scrape or if you'd been bullied or maybe just tired from not sleeping—she'd fix you up, sometimes just with a big, soft hug.

She says, Make yourself comfortable, dear, it won't be a moment.

I say, Well, it will, won't it? (Because it's a weird expression, right?)

She looks at me in her soft way and says, I'm so sorry about your mother.

And this is weird too, because that happened a long time ago, but people still say it to me. Nobody asks about Dad, but then neither do I.

Soon enough, Ms. Dalyrimple says, Pastor will see you now.

So I go in.

He sat on the edge of an enormous walnut desk, looking like an alert groundhog, with that round head and a nose-mouth combo that protrudes forward in a kind of muzzle. He has gray-speckled hair so thick it's like fur, cut short and brushed back. There's this matching goatee, and eyes so black you can't tell where the pupils start. He wore a red hooded sweatshirt with the words 'It's Not Too Late,' over a smiley-face that seemed sarcastic to me.

When he talks, his lips pull back from his teeth tightly, like he's trying to restrain the words as they come out. I don't know. Anyway.

I want to plant one thousand crosses, he says.

He leans forward from the desk and opens his hands, jazz-style, like he's just pulled off a card trick.

One thousand crosses, he repeats. All across the church yard, in honor of the unborn souls who die every year from selfish cruelty. You in?

He raises his eyebrows, which look trimmed.

Pastor Yeshevsky, I say, nice to meet you too.

I hold out my hand and make him shake. (Just because of my line of work doesn't mean I can't be polite.)

Can you do it? he asks. I'm thinking the night before Easter.

Oh sorry, I say, I thought you said *you* wanted to plant them. You want *me* to plant them?

He gives me a knowing smile and points at my face. He says, You're a funny guy, aren't you? I like that in a guy, sense of humor.

I pay attention to words, I reply. I think it matters what people say so I try to pay attention.

Fine, the pastor replies, and waves off my comment with a hairy paw. I would like you to plant 1,000 crosses. Can you do it?

Maybe, I say. I reckon I need to know a little more.

Ah! He says. Of course.

He jumps up from his desk and grinds a fist into his other hand as he paces to the window and back. He says, Here's the deal. God calls on us to condemn mortal sin and the wanton destruction of human lives, right? I mean, you can't just commit murder for the sake of convenience, you know what I'm saying. This! he yells and brings the fist down onto the desk, This will become the mission of Most Redeemed. I want everyone to know, and that's what this display of crosses is about.

Well, I say. That's your business. But actually I was wondering about things like: what are you paying and do you need me to provide materials?

He opens a drawer and lifts out a label maker—the kind that prints sticky clear strips. He fiddles with the thing and then out comes a label. With a weird kind of precision, he fixes the label to a sheet of paper—one of those donation envelopes they use—and slides it across the desk for me to see. I reach to pick it up and he pulls it back and says, How's that work for ya?

I pretend to give it thought and do some counting on my fingers and then say, Yeah I suppose that'll work.

But really it was ten times more than I'd usually make in a night. For a guy on my budget, this was life-changing money.

He goes on, I got some buddies from the dad's group who can make the crosses and deliver them. So you only need to show up the night before Easter and install them. Under cover of darkness, I should emphasize. I want this to be a ... oh, surprise is probably not the right word. Call it a modest miracle, in the eyes of our congregation on that holy Sunday. One kickass miracle for the re-invented Most Redeemed.

A thought struck me. Question, I say. Would it make more sense if we put down a thousand stones? Wouldn't crosses make more sense for Good Friday? I mean I'm no theologian, that's just what I remember.

The pastor didn't reply. He cradled his label maker and stared without blinking through those bottomless eyes and he held it for a long time. I tried to match him, because who wants to lose a staring contest, but in the quiet of the office I started to hear my ears ringing and that got unsettling so I blinked.

Then he came over to my side of the desk, perched his butt on it, crossed his arms, and leaned forward so his face was uncomfortably close to mine. I could see his pores and a few scars from chicken pox. He smiled, but his eyes were wild, like someone off their rocker.

A thousand stones, he says. You want me to put a thousand rocks all over my churchyard—the churchyard I just sodded, next to the beautiful church I just built? You think this is the way to celebrate Jesus Christ on resurrection day and to honor the unborn dead? Instead of a thousand beautiful white crosses? Is that what you're saying, funny man? Because last I checked, I was offering you a chance at some tidy money, not vice versa. So do you want to stand by that question?

This kind of irked me, so I crossed my arms too and made a little bluff, saying, Well, do you have anybody else can do this job?

Suddenly he laughed, too loud for the room, like a performance, and pointed at me with both hands, and said, Touché!

Then he said, Okay I think we understand each other. We got a deal. Can I show you around?

Technically, we did not have a deal, but I let that go and followed him.

He walked me to the new sanctuary, which went up just a year ago. He explained what a dump the previous church had been (which didn't square with my memory) and described his big expansion project with words like 'unprecedented' and 'blessed' and 'kickass.' His membership had doubled in the past year, he said, and people were driving from lots of other towns these days for the kickass worship service he put on. And now, he was ready for the next chapter, which began with the thousand crosses. On Easter, obviously. And then, just like that, he pulled a ringing phone from his pocket, and gave me a conspiratorial look like, 'I've got to take this,' and he disappeared. It left me alone in the sanctuary.

It was a huge, silent place. Everything was slick and clean and a lot of the seats up front were these fat recliners, which I had not seen at a church before. Also, two stages for rock bands apparently? And up along the vaulted ceiling were stained-glass windows. They were all sort of action scenes, things that might be R-rated in a movie: Abraham and Isaac, Cain and Abel, Jesus having a tantrum at the temple, the Four Horses of the Apocalypse. And then, as I stood there looking around, I got suddenly very cold. Not just a little chill, but seriously cold and shivering with goosebumps. I figured I probably needed to eat something. Also, my ear ringing really spun up at that point, which always puts me on edge. And then I heard this weird noise rattling up near the peak of the ceiling—like how cicadas would sound if they were as big as cats. I figured this couldn't just be my fucked-up ears, so I got the heck out of there.

Outside, I took a look around the job site. I needed to do some math—like how far apart the crosses would need to be and how fast you'd need to go to finish in one night. It was a big, sodded lawn that went from the front parking lot around the new building to the cemetery along the river. The cemetery seemed smaller than I remembered. I strolled over to take a look. Everybody knows that cemetery is haunted. Well, everybody knows it's supposed to be haunted. When I was fifteen, I paddled a canoe drunk with three friends down the river past the cemetery and we saw some smoky lights floating around and concluded that we saw ghosts, because of course we did! You always pick the best story at that age. But now, in the light of day, the cemetery just looked small and sad, all the Civil War era stones worn almost blank, covered in black mold, all kind of huddled together like that huge lawn was pushing them to the edge of the bank.

I jumped when I heard the pastor's voice behind me say, Andy! Yo! What are you doing over there? How about this lawn? Not a single weed, amirite? We're so blessed to have this beautiful sod.

What's up? I asked.

He looked surprised, like I had challenged him. Oh, not much. I just got off the phone with the mayor—we play cards, you know, Texas hold'em, anyway. You cool with the job? All set?

I felt like he wanted me to leave, and to be his buddy, all at once. I said, I'll let you know. I gave him a wave and walked to my bike. He followed.

Oh hey, I wanted to ask, he said. You know Sheila Fuglesen? She any relation?

I stared at him.

Because of the last name, he explained. I'm always trying to get to know families around here. Still a new guy, I guess.

Then he gave me the most silly, childish, vulnerable grin. It didn't match his face.

I had an idea in the back of my mind that Sheila wasn't a fan of the pastor. But she's not a fan of most people, considering her line of work. So I said, Yeah, she's my cousin. Like it was no big deal.

It seemed to be the answer he was looking for. Oh great, he said. Great. And he smiled and nodded, hands in the pockets of that sweatshirt.

I jumped on my bike and tore out of there, thinking maybe I would pass on the job after all.

Speaking of Sheila, she saved my ass again that night.

I was in my trailer eating ramen noodles when my ears started giving me fits. I don't know what brings this on. It's like your head is full of those gnats that swarm in the woods in summer, except they're inside your head making this tiny scream. If you listen harder, which you always do, you hear another gnat and another and another until it's a big raging chorus. You want to swat at your head, which sometimes you do, but of course nothing stops these gnats because they're not real! It's just a phantom sound coming from years of working a jackhammer and a chain saw and a tiller and the target machine at the shooting range where your dad works.

Well once it starts, there's no sleeping. When it's bad, like that night, there's really no thinking either. You drink of course, and then you walk around the neighborhood, or do projects, or read. But that night there was no relief so I just stood with my head under the shower until it went cold and then I dressed and got on my motorcycle and rode around town until the bike ran out of gas near the interstate, and then I just ran, like I could outrun the gnats, with my hands over my ears because of the non-stop whine of the semi tires on the highway.

Suddenly I realize Sheila is next to me in her tiny car with the passenger door open, yelling Get in! Come on!

Back at my trailer Sheila takes charge and makes me lie down on the couch while she fixes some herbal tea, which she serves me with a cookie. She also gives me a pill that kind of deletes the part of you that's freaking out, without making you feel high. It doesn't fix your ears, but it makes you not care. After a while, I'm feeling better. So we talk.

I tell her, You know I saw a doctor after last time and he said there are things you can do. There are these devices that don't make it go away but they trick your brain into not noticing.

Why don't you get some, she asks.

Why do you think? I say.

Maybe your dad could loan you …

I give her a look that settles that.

She says, Maybe I can scratch together something for you.

I tell her, No way. I can't ask you to do that. You're not much better off than me.

Sheila, I should tell you, is a journalist. She works for herself, publishing stories on a website, which has become quite popular—especially since our local paper was bought by some English company and pretty much got rid of actual news. The website also makes her some enemies because Sheila doesn't pull any punches. She's just out there every day finding out what's really going on and letting people know about it. And when people give her shit, she just stands straight in these high-heeled zip-up boots she likes and gives it right back to them.

So she's on that side of things, the good side. And I'm more or less on the other. But we're good friends, I'd like to say. And cousins. And we're just careful to not cross the line.

I say, I think I'm going to come into some decent money soon anyway.

So maybe I'll spring for those devices.

Who are you working for this time? she asks.

You're not supposed to ask me that, I say.

Her boots are off and her feet are up on the chair. We don't look related—Sheila's very pleasant looking, with penny-colored hair and blue eyes as serious as an eagle and freckles that trick people into thinking she's soft. She's the girl in high school that guys look back and say, why didn't I ask her out?

Suddenly, she says, You aren't working for Yeshevsky are you?

And I say, Oh for fuck's sake, how do you know everything?

And then she proceeds to tell me that I should stay away from the pastor. She says he's bad business, that she's giving me an inside scoop. And I say, yeah sure. And she says, no I'm serious. And I say, I know. And she says, Look I shouldn't say this but you're family, so: Some things may come to light meaning nobody's going to want to have done business with him, okay? So I ask, What's coming to light? And then she pauses for a long time and looks around my trailer, which embarrasses me a little, and then she says, You don't want to know. Trust me.

But I insist.

And she says, Fine. We've got him. We know where the money comes from, everything. We just need hard evidence.

Then she laughs and says, And a good lawyer.

The next morning I wake up before dawn and the ears are horrible again and I make some coffee and step outside and say, Sorry Sheila. Beggars can't be choosers. I call the church and ask Ms. Dalyrimple to tell the pastor that I'm in.

The night of the job there were three crates on pallets outside the back of the church, where I parked my truck, out of sight. I pried open the crates and sure enough found a fortune of white crosses in there, neatly assembled and packed, each one as tall as a standing cat. As I picked up a cross, I suddenly heard this loud croak, which startled me and got my heart pounding for no good reason, and I saw it was a blue heron flying like a pterodactyl toward the river. It made me pause and look around. There was a fog settling down on the river and over the old cemetery and rising to where I was working. Spring peepers and crickets were waking up, making a racket that annoyed my ears. There were little brown bats darting around in the foggy patches, eating a new hatch of bugs. And this whole scene was lit by the silvery light of an almost-full moon, which made long shadows in the churchyard. Jesus, I said (though not exactly to the dude himself), what a night.

But the clock was ticking, so I turned on my headlamp and got to work.

Just as a test, I took one cross and my rubber mallet out to the middle of the churchyard and set the base of the cross into the sod and gave the top a little whack. Well, it cracked just about as easy as a model airplane. I looked closer in the light of my lamp (which was a little harsh, like something medical) and I saw it was decent wood, maybe birch. So I gave the ground a good kick with the toe of my boot and god damn it hurt! That ground under the sod is basically concrete. No doubt it's cheap fill, packed with bricks and rubble and clay. This made sense because when they built the church, any decent soil would have been scraped and sold, probably to people in new houses whose topsoil had been scraped too. There's your Illinois prairie. Anyway, I digress.

No way I was going to be able to get those crosses planted without some kind of pilot holes, so I grabbed a shovel from my truck and stuck the point into the ground and jumped on the blade—that did no good either. The tip bent and the wooden handle creaked like it might snap so I put that away too.

Now I sat on the grass, on that hard ground, and turned out my headlamp, and gave it some thought. It was that point in a job where you realize all your plans go out the window and you have to do something drastic or quit. My eyes kind of wandered, past the cemetery and toward the crooked river, and somehow this thought pops into my head that Abraham Lincoln used to canoe down this river. That's what they say. So now I'm sitting there thinking about Abraham Lincoln, who died around the same time as the people in this cemetery, and it occurs to me that Lincoln must have felt this way a million times, with a plan that's doomed a few minutes after you start. And I think that Lincoln might have known some of these people who were buried here, and he might have asked them their opinions, while he sat pondering the nation's troubles. Because that's the kind of guy he was, supposedly.

Anyway, the crosses. I figured that if I could pop each cross into the ground in about 30 seconds, I'd have it all done in around eight hours, so no problem wrapping up by sunrise. Well, you're not going to drill a thousand holes in fill dirt in eight hours. But I can be a clever bastard once in a while, especially when it comes to basic tasks, and it dawned on me I had a piece of rebar in the truck and a small sledge. I got those out and took a whack at it and it punched right through. I had reached some softer layer beneath the fill dirt, like poking your finger through a pie crust. So that seemed all right. I took a fresh cross and poked it in the hole and it stood perfectly. I did a little math and figured that if I could repeat that operation, I could still make my deadline and get paid and get out. And then I'd have the money and could see about my ears and etc. etc.

But you know where this is going. It's never easy.

I had a couple rows of crosses planted. I had paced off the grid of holes and got into the swing of the thing. But then, as I'm walking back and forth with arm loads of crosses, I start to see a little wiggle in the first few I planted. I ignore it as a trick played by the light of my headlamp or the shadows of the moon or what have you. I'm thinking Please don't let that be groundhogs. But then, as I pause for a drink of water, one of the crosses pops right out of its hole. But gently, like when a beer bottle burps foam. The cross topples and from the hole seeps a bluish light, which drifts straight up like smoke and then expands out and takes shape.

It was person-shaped, but barely. I could see an outline of a man, with enough detail to show him wearing some old-timey clothes, but parts of him were torn away—the way an old flag gets ragged in the Illinois wind. His smokey shape bobbed and wobbled, and he flickered in and out, almost like he was losing power.

Now of course I'm a little flabbergasted by this sight. And some explanations are going through my mind, but they're all stupid—heat lightning, a gas leak, a trick of light, a hallucination. None of these add up. So while I'm watching this smoky guy, more of them appear from the ground, popping the crosses out of their holes. They all have the same bluish, ragged look, but they're clearly different people. A fat guy in a suit, a skinny soldier in a baggy uniform, a lady with horse-riding clothes, and another lady who looked like a chef. They just kept popping up, to the point where my theories are sounding even more stupid, until I'm thinking to myself, Okay. I guess there are ghosts then.

It suddenly didn't seem like such a big deal. The whole 'do you believe in ghosts' topic of conversation that might come up on a first date, say—it seems dumb all of a sudden, because the thing that makes a person a person has to go somewhere, right?

So fine, I've got some ghosts here. I mean, it's right next to a cemetery. But the problem is, they're popping all my crosses out and killing my schedule for the job! That's what I'm thinking now. To be honest, I'm also a little rattled, with these ghosts emerging. But they were far from scary in terms of their vibe. In fact, they were very calming and kind of warm-hearted to my mind. So ironically, their non-threatening vibe calmed me enough to get a little annoyed about what they were doing to the job site.

Shoo! I said, in the kind of whisper you make to a cat. Go on! I said, and waved my arms in the shooing motion. I made a little rush at them and stopped short, to scare them away like a flock of grackles. And that kind of worked, because the ones closest swooped away suddenly. This startled me, and I jumped backward, tripped on a fallen cross, and fell on my hinder. What the fuck? I said and ran back and shooed them some more, until they were all swarming around me. It was kind of a mess, and I was stepping on crosses and tripping all over the place.

While the ghosts were swarming, I could hear them talk. Their voices were ragged like their bodies, and only parts of sentences came through. But I heard enough bits and pieces like, Be still, we mean no evil, and Oh, the relief to be free! Enough that I got the gist that they were cool and wanted me to calm down. So I did.

I had a seat, right there on the ground. They stopped and just floated around me.

The fat guy in a suit, who looks like a mayor, asks, What do you know of spirits?

Well if you're talking whiskey—I know a lot. But if you mean ghosts—not a damn thing.

The mayor flickers and smiles, and says, We are the latter. And regard you with the most sincere approbation.

I know what that means, I say. I read, you know.

Certainly, says the mayor and bows. I realize I was a little defensive there, unnecessarily.

The chef lady floats closer and asks, So you haven't read of spirits in your study?

Well, I mean, I've read stories, I say. Every American kid reads those. But nothing true.

How do you know they're not true? The soldier asks.

I guess I don't, I say. You got me. But can I just ask, where are we going with this? No offense, but I got work to do.

And right when I say that, I notice something odd. The reason I'm so intent on working is that I need the money to buy some devices to help my fucked-up ears. But at this moment, with the ghosts crowding around me—my ears are completely silent! It's the first time in I don't know how long. So then I'm thinking maybe I'm not so eager for these ghosts to leave. Maybe I want to enjoy this, because when you've got what I have, a little relief is the greatest thing in life.

I say, Sorry, I didn't mean to be rude.

Not at all, says the mayor, not at all. It's disconcerting when mortals first encounter the spirits of unrest, and your composure is exemplary.

The horse lady comes real close and says, What he means is: thanks.

Oh, I say. Sure.

You released us from a prison of more than a year, says the horse lady. And we were already old spirits, fading away with every moment. Time becomes more precious at the end, when you still have promises to keep before your energy dissipates into the infinite fields of matter.

I say, Yeah, I can imagine.

Can you? asks the soldier.

I'm not sure what he's driving at.

Nevertheless, says the mayor, we leave you to your labors with profound gratitude and apologies for defiling your workplace. A year in subterranean prison has left us with a deep debt in deeds.

The horse lady says, What he means is, thanks again and we'll let you go.

No wait! I say, and I'm surprised by my blurt. Do you have to leave right away?

Because here's the thing: I'm afraid that the minute they leave my ears will go haywire again and I just want a little more of this relief, so maybe I can remember it in the future.

The mayor begins to speak, but the chef lady says, We will do whatever you like. You are only the second emancipator we've met.

The mayor adds, Tell us what we can do for you.

I'm not what you'd call prepared for this kind of question, so I just say, Maybe you could talk about what your deal is. Tell me your story.

So they begin to talk, often interrupting each other, or correcting each other, but eventually I get the picture. Apparently, they all died during the Civil War, due to causes that were not great. The mayor, for example, helped escaped slaves find homes in the North and he was shot by Confederate sympathizers down near Paducah. The horse lady was hung as a traitor for smuggling cotton up from Alabama to make soldiers' uniforms. The chef lady saved a little girl from getting hit by a horse and carriage, but in doing this, got run over herself. The soldier died from friendly fire during a skirmish along the Mississippi. And since they all died as troubled souls, they all persisted in these forms of light, which they call 'husks.' And they've spent the last hundred fifty years or so haunting around at night trying to help people who are taking a wrong path in life. So when I saw the ghosts while canoeing drunk down the river, it might have been some of these guys trying to scare me and my friends sober. Or something like that. You get the idea.

They were all buried in the cemetery by the church. They spent every night under the moon haunting people and returned to their graves during the day. (Hard to see the husks in sunlight, they say.) This goes great for a few generations, until our friend Pastor Yeshevsky shows up and buys a permit to expand his church. That permit must have cost a pretty penny, because the developer just bulldozed over half the cemetery, which is definitely not legal, and also not cool. My ghost friends were some of the ones covered up. And this rock-hard fill dirt—don't ask me how this works because I don't know—but it trapped the energy of their husks down in those graves. They couldn't come seeping up every moonrise, apparently, and meanwhile they weren't getting any younger as far as ghosts go.

So here comes me—I bust them out, and I'm a hero.

That was a good story, I say.

I'm realizing I have to get to work.

Can I ask you a question before we go? says the mayor.

You just did, I say. No, yeah, sure thing.

The mayor waves his arm grandly across the churchyard and asks, What are you doing here, assembling an array of crosses, under the light of the moon?

Just a job, dude, I say. It's for the pastor.

They all jump back a bit when I say this, and their faces are kind of horrified.

Hey, you do what you got to do, I say. We've all got our troubles, and we've all got our price.

The horse lady asks, But do you know why the pastor wants you to do this?

I give her a hand wave and say, Oh, you don't want to know. I think this shit was different in your day. It's just kind of his righteous cause, I guess.

Then they all exchange glances about who knows what, and the mayor comes close to me and crosses his arms and whispers, Are you certain his motives are what he described? Or … could there be something else?

I stand up, wipe my pants off, and think about it. Finally I say, Well, probably there's something else. But it's not my business, and there's no way of knowing anyhow.

Well, there could be, says the horse lady. And the mayor nods energetically and motions with his eyes and chin toward the church.

I'm sure there's more to learn, if that compels you, he says. He who talks loudest, hides the most.

No, man, I say. I'm keeping my nose clean. Finish this up and get paid and get on with life.

That seems good enough for my ghost friends and they swarm around me with more thanks and positive vibes and then they're off, like a silent squadron toward the river. But just one last thing—the soldier pauses near my shoulder and says, If you do go in, be careful. Not all spirits are generous. Beware the ones without the light.

Then they really are gone. It's just me, behind schedule, with my ears starting up again.

I was tired after that. It was hard to get back into my rhythm. So I got sloppy, and swung the sledge wrong, and brought it down on my hand, which slid down the rebar, which made a bad cut. I could see the blood all black against my palm. In two seconds, I realized this required some first aid. I tried tying it up with a bandana, but it soaked right through. And the worst thing was I was getting blood on the white crosses, which seemed like a bad idea.

So. I know there's got to be a first-aid kit in Ms. Dalyrimple's office, because she's a nurse, right? But then I really don't want to go into that church either, because things are feeling a little spooky, what with the warnings and so forth. But driving away isn't really an option—I can't just leave all these materials out, and I'm not sure any stores are open anyway.

I tie up my hand with my t-shirt, so as not to spill blood inside the church, and go to the back door and fiddle the lock with a credit card and next thing I'm inside. And oh man, do my ears start ringing. Probably because my heart is pounding like a trapped rabbit, but maybe because of the way it feels in there. Cold and damp feeling, the smell of concrete and cheap carpet, and then also this acrid smell, like someone's been burning plastic.

I make a bee-line for the office, but then I pass the sanctuary and

I hear—once again—that strange cicada noise. Curiosity gets the best of me, so I push back one of the double doors and slip into the gigantic room. Sure enough, there's that sound, loud enough to cut through the noise in my ears. The chattering sound moves quickly, above my head, all around the room. I look back at the door—maybe expecting some of the friendly ghosts have followed me? But no. Then, as my eyes adjust, I see what's making that sound. Or maybe I should say I didn't see. All around the vault of the sanctuary, there flies these dark patches where light just disappears. You can't say they're a color, because they're nothing. I mean literally, nothing. Just the absence of light, moving in swoops like swallows in a barn, chattering in some kind of rage.

I thought I might throw up. And then, weirdly, I thought I might start crying. And then I had this heavy awareness that I was alone. I ran out of the sanctuary and pulled the door shut. I went to the pastor's office. On my way, down red-carpeted halls, I saw more dark spirits passing across the hall from one room to the next. The chattering wound up, distant and then closer and then loud, and then stopped. I plugged my ears and shook my head, because who's heard of ghosts haunting a brand new church?

I find no first-aid kit in Ms. Dalyrimple's desk. The blood is starting to pool up, so I grab a bunch of tissues and stuff them inside my bandana. I'm thinking, Well maybe there's an actual nurse's office in this church—maybe I should be looking for that. But on my way out of the office, I look back and see (now really obvious) seven file cabinets lined against the wall. A person might put emergency supplies in one of those, right? So I look. Six of the cabinets are open and full of dull church business. No dice. But one cabinet is locked. Now, I realize that you're not likely to lock the cabinet with first-aid stuff, but on the other hand, who wouldn't be curious about what's in there?

So I take a paper clip to this cabinet and pull the drawer open. It's jammed with files, each stickered with the precision of the pastor's label maker. Interesting, I think, and forget a minute about my bleeding hand. I pull out a stack of files and have a seat at the pastor's desk and turn on my phone flashlight and take a look.

Each folder was labeled with a name—I knew of many of these people. Inside each folder was stapled a picture of that person in what you would call a 'compromising situation.' Some with people they shouldn't be with, some in places they shouldn't be, some doing things you'd rather not see. There was a lot of over-exposed skin, eyes partly closed, coats pulled up past chins, car doors opening, scenes in barns, in garages, in ratty woods, in dumpsters. I found the pictures I had taken of the couple outside the tavern. That made my heart feel swollen. I wondered why he hadn't asked me to take any more, and who took all the others, but who knows. I saw the mayor, the sheriff, city council members, farmers, cops, teachers, realtors. In each folder there was a sheet of paper with a kind of ledger. In strips printed from that label maker, it described a compromising circumstance (usually same as the picture but sometimes more) and then in another column, it described what the person was asked to do in exchange for their privacy, and in the last column, the amount of payment required. The pastor labeled that column, 'Contribution for Christ.' In most of the folders, stapled to the back cover was a donation envelope with a hand-written number for the cash received.

I wonder where all that cash is, I thought. Does he just stick it in the bank? But I didn't need to wonder long. Behind all the folders, wedged against the back of the file drawer, was a leather case with a zipper across the top. The case was fat and heavy and when I unzipped it, sure enough, it was stuffed full of a lot of bills. I mean, a lot.

The pastor had a file on me. It was a picture of the night I ran out of gas by the highway, not a week ago. It showed me in a full run, hands over ears, my face in a scream. A shitty picture. In the first column it said, 'mental instability?' and there was nothing in the other two columns yet.

There were files of young girls, just teen-agers, doing what they do, with demands made of their parents. These weren't the sketchy half of the town. These were decent people.

And then there was a folder for Sheila. The photo wasn't all that compromising—just a security camera picture of her looking through the window of the new church at night. She's shielding her eyes with her hand, her nose right against the glass, peering in with this amazing focus. Like a spaniel pointing. On the ledger, it was just notes scratched by the pastor. This file had been handled too many times, not so neat as the others. He wrote all over the ledger and the folder itself things Sheila might have done—all the usual things these guys say about journalists: taking bribes, making stories up, sleeping their way to the top. But there were other accusations—conspiracies, treason, sexual stuff—things you read about in the Bible, actually. And then, in the last column, there was just two words, underlined: Shut. Up.

So now I'm just sitting there, looking at this file about my cousin—the best person I know, honestly. She's looking up from her picture, through the dark window, squinting, like 'What's going on in there?' Only now she's looking from the picture right at me, through my eyes, you could say. And I'm hearing the same question, only now directed toward me. 'What's going on in there?' And I look at the other files, of the other good people just struggling through their imperfect lives. And I look at the pastor's desk, of his little framed picture of his wife and six kids at the ribbon-cutting ceremony for the new church. My hand is throbbing with my pulse, along with my head, and my ears are howling away, and I'm feeling really nauseous now.

And then I say, out loud, in that quiet room, looking at the pastor smiling in his picture. I say one word: Nope.

For a minute I think I'm going to vomit, but I hold it back, and pack everything up, and wipe some drops of blood off the floor, and walk down the hall toward the bathroom, where I do vomit (but just a little bit, no biggie) and on my way out, I see my reflection in the mirror and I say, That's right, you fucker. And then I see on the wall a white box with red letters: First Aid! And once my hand is properly wrapped up in gauze and tape, I march out of that church with the dark spirits chattering all around and burst back into the night.

The moon was high and the shadows were short. I got to work.

Next morning, I wake up on the tailgate of my truck with the rising sun in my face and a golf club poking my ribs. It's Pastor Yeshevsky, looking down at me in a way that makes his whole groundhog face droop, and I can't tell if he's mad or laughing.

I sit up and rub my head. I can see a couple guys putting up a small billboard by the street. It shows an 800 number next to a profile of a woman holding her belly.

The pastor says, You pulled it off, bro! It looks pretty kickass, right?

I squint up at him and say, A thousand crosses. You can count em.

I will, he says. But first we should settle up. I guessing you'll want to get going.

I hold out my hand. He gives me a fat donation envelope and I don't bother counting it.

He sees my hand and says, You hurt yourself there?

Just a scratch, I say. It's nothing.

Then he smiles and I can't tell if he's sarcastic when he says, Shall we say a prayer over it? And I say, What's that going to do? And he says, suit yourself. And I say, I will.

Okay if you just want to pull out your truck then, he says.

I stare at him, and can't help myself but say, I went ahead and let the ghosts out. While I was at it.

He makes a face like something tastes bad.

I mean, not from the church, I say. Just the good ones.

The pastor looks back toward the parking lot, and then at his watch. All of a sudden there's no eye contact, like I'm a nobody. He says, Your truck—it's blocking the way. So if you'd just please …

I didn't wait for him to finish.

I drive to the other side of the river and park in a dead end where guys poach deer in winter. I jog through the woods to the riverbank and tuck behind a big, leaning maple where I can watch the churchyard.

Sure enough, here comes the pastor. He takes a little walk through the yard, admiring his beautiful display of crosses. They're so perfectly arranged, so white against the new lawn, it's impossible to look at anything else. He's thinking about the sermon he'll give today, getting his congregation all whipped up and pissed, with a story they can repeat over and over, in any argument, regardless of the subject. From my perch across the river, I can see him walking proudly, coming closer to the old sacred ground where the Civil War dead rest, restlessly.

Then the pastor sees that one cross is shorter than the others and it's crooked in its hole. It irks him, this inconsistent cross. It's as if someone had broken it trying to pound it into the hard ground. So the pastor goes over and stoops down, wincing, to straighten it. And when he does, he sees something attached to the horizontal bar of that broken cross. It's a label! A label that the pastor himself produced, and pressed carefully on a folder. It says 'Sheila Fuglesen.' His first reaction is to be peeved. I can see him straightening up and looking around the church yard in a hard squint. But then, being a diabolical fucker, he gets to thinking. And he reaches out a furry hand to pull out the next cross. And sure enough, there's a label of a victim on that one too. He rushes to the next cross, and there's nothing. But three crosses down, there's another label of a person, whose whole life has changed for the worse because they were caught in some trivial act they were too ashamed to admit. A few crosses away, there's another label. And another, and another.

The pastor wanders around his churchyard as cars begin to roll into the parking lot, full of people dressed in their Easter finest. Colorful dresses and ties, coming out of those cars. Meanwhile, the pastor rushes among the crosses, stumbling sometimes, reaching down to tear off labels, spinning around to check the other sides. His congregation sees him. They give him a shout. He waves back, looking toward the church and the thousand crosses in between, pretending there's no problem. But then he snaps his slick noggin back to the ground, searching.

And me, I'm driving now, heading out of town, down the old county road where Sheila still lives with her folks, because a journalist doesn't do it for the money. I've got the stack of file folders on the passenger seat. It's all there except for the labels I peeled off. Plus the envelope of cash, which should pay for the lawyer she's gonna need.

People wave from the cars as I pass them. Sometimes it's a full wave, showing they know me. Sometimes it's a surprise wave, because they almost didn't see me and don't want me to think they didn't wave. And sometimes it's just one finger lifted from the wheel, to acknowledge that we're two people passing on a country road, each with our pain and our troubles and our secrets, but still human enough to say hi.

FOR THEIR OWN GOOD

My chickens are naughty and cruel but they love me so. I can hear their wicked cackling out in the hen house before dawn. The bullies tear feathers from the weaklings and the weaklings cry in terror. But when I step out in my nightgown and open the hatch door, they press against my legs with affection. I toss the corn widely, so no one goes hungry. Then I call the children with the old school bell that hangs in front of our home. The oldest two, Eli and Sarah, are already at the table with their workbooks. Noah puts wood in the stove like a good helper. Mary sings hymns while she fills the kettle. And Rebecca, my youngest, my dear angel, is still in bed with her rabbit. But when the bell rings, they come running to clean the filthy straw while the naughty birds eat. And when morning chores are done, we have prayers and breakfast and then, only then, may the children take their phones from the basket by my bed.

One day soon, when this trouble is settled, when Caleb gets home, we'll return to our routine. Oh! On those mornings, after breakfast, I would read one of the great novels—something 19th century and British, maybe, or perhaps some stories about life on the American prairie. One's morning is enriched by literature. And even the most tormented heroines never ask for help—they just ask to be heard.

But I was talking about the chickens! Well. I'm grateful to those hens for more than their eggs and their love. They sense when there's a threat, and if you watch them closely, you'll be forewarned. That's how it started …

A week ago, on a cold spring night, I was in the yard closing things up. Rebecca was with me, clinging to my skirt, dragging her rabbit, staring up at the moon with eyes of wonder. We noticed that the chickens were silent. There's not much spookier than a silent henhouse, and I'm not superstitious. When we shone the flashlight in through the doorway, we saw all the birds up on the roosts, pressed against the wall as high as they could be. Their eyes didn't blink, and their beaks hung open, like an actor faking astonishment. All the straw was pushed back along the corners of the house, and in the center, the floorboards were swept clean.

Must have been a fox, I said.

Rebecca motioned for me to lean down and whispered in my year, Foxes don't do sweeping, mama. It was invaders.

I shushed her then and said no such thing, but now of course I know better.

The next morning, the chickens were back to normal, except for one, who wouldn't leave the others alone. This big speckled hen with a royal purple comb chased one hen and then another, slashing at them with beak and talons. After the peculiarity of the night before, and a heart full of worry with Caleb on his mission, I lost my temper I suppose, and gave that hen a scolding and a swat with my shovel.

Eli was with me and he said, Mama it's all right. It's just that speckled hen acting up again.

Then he cornered her along the fence and tried to take her up, but she attacked like a fighting cock. I screamed to see him treated that way. And Mary, middle child and peacemaker, came from the side and got the speckled hen by both legs and lifted her upside-down, just like that, and the wicked hen struggled and flapped her wings wide and then gave up.

Eli said, Nice, Mary.

And Mary said, I'll toss her in the hen house—she'll calm down.

But I knew better. You can't just let a creature go around bullying everyone. A villain needs some comeuppance.

No, I said, give her to me. She's going in the cellar.

Mama, no, Mary said, and stepped away from me.

But I did what good mothers must do sometimes, and I took the hen from Mary and marched it right inside, with the children following me.

None of them wanted to help me get the cellar door open. We argued. Finally, I called Rebecca and showed her the upside-down hen, saying Don't be scared—she can't do anything if you just hold her that way. And then Eli stepped forward, saying Rebecca was too little for that (which made me proud, yes) and so he pulled back the old rope rug and grabbed the iron ring handle of the cellar door and opened it up.

We smelled the stale fragrance of wet clay and root vegetables and the children stepped back from the hole. I tossed in the guilty bird and dropped the door with a bang, and that should have been that. Except the children protested that it was dark down there, which wasn't good for a chicken or any other soul. So I showed my compassion and let Noah take down an LED camp light we keep for thunderstorms. I've rarely seen him move so fast.

That night the chickens went silent again just after sunset. Once again, we found the straw swept back and all the birds pressing up against the rafters, like prisoners cowering from a cruel warden. It made me wonder, then, if something more sinister than a fox were about. Maybe Rebecca had a logical intuition. A little child shall lead them, I thought.

Caleb didn't get the chickens to serve as watchers. He installed game cameras for that. When he came home in February with a cardboard box full of Easter-yellow chicks, he spilled them out into the new hen house and crushed the box flat under his boot. Together, we watched the tiny fluffs all huddled under their red lamp and Caleb said, Okay honey, now you and the kids will have protein. Then he told me he was going to Idaho to do his duty and keep the invaders where they belonged, which was not here, in Middling County, Illinois. His daddy and his friend Jeffrey were going too.

I lost my composure, to be honest. The news came so unexpectedly, and I dislike surprises. It was clear to me that the chicks were only a consolation for Caleb's abandonment, and I wasn't going to fall for that, so I climbed over their little pen and tried to stamp them—you know, just as a gesture of my feelings, not actually trying to harm them. Caleb stopped me with a hug that hurt—doing his job, you know—and held me and talked for a long time, saying

What do you think we been doing out in the pole barn all these months? We been getting ready. You had to of known that. It's time for me to man up, like Daddy's been saying my whole life, and now we're really going to do it. We can't just stand by while invaders infest the country, next thing you know they'll be all over here stealing and corrupting and putting notions in people's heads. Doing their voodoo tricks. Come on, that's a girl. You're plenty strong enough—No, yes you are too. Nobody's as good a mama as you. You got this. I'll be back before long. We got the gardens going, and the house all fixed up, and you got your books, and plus now these chickens so you'll have protein.

Caleb kept on like that until I came around and then, shall I say, we consecrated that hen house with love, my face up against the window looking at the trees budding out. So.

He agreed to stay for two more weeks. The house wasn't quite fixed up yet, and Caleb promised to finish the job before their mission. Jeffrey was there every day helping, and at night they went to the pole barn to do their prep and they were working so hard, burning the candle at both ends, that sometimes they just slept out there.

No one wanted this old one-room schoolhouse when we moved in. It was a day care, I guess, and then one day it wasn't. But now look at it!

The first thing Caleb did, dear man, was to patch all the holes in the wall from the shooting, inside and out. The so-called 'shooting,' I should say. Then we scrubbed the stains off the floor and walls and gave it a proper coat of paint. In a week you couldn't tell that anything had happened here—if anything had happened here. Caleb cleaned the chimney and lit a roaring fire and heated up the house 'to chase away the spirits,' he said, laughing. But we both know superstitions are nonsense. Just like the gossip in town is nonsense, the whole spooky story is probably mostly made up, if you ask me. How could we ever really know what happened? I say people want to believe in spirits and such things because it helps them avoid facing the world how it really is. But there is no such false comfort for Righteous folks. We live to a higher standard. They can talk all they want in town. That won't make them right. No one can question whether Susan Fallendini is a good mother and wife and homesteader. But enough boasting: He condemns the proud and shows favor to the humble!

As a final touch to the house, we put up a new post and painted the old school bell. And even though they groaned, everybody posed in front of the house in our matching outfits in the golden hour and I took the most perfect pictures—so grateful for them now—and posted them on HomeGround and so many people liked them, it was a bit immodest!

The next morning Caleb left early with Jeffrey and although I didn't show it then (having lost composure again) I admit it touched my heart to see my husband and his best friend walk down the gravel drive that last time, looking back at me with worry, then at each other with smiles, brotherly touches. A wren sang in the pale light of dawn. Caleb had the sack lunch I prepared and Jeffrey carried a box of canned pickles. When they drove away to get Caleb's daddy, the truck tires slipped on the gravel, like a stallion kicking up his heels.

The storm came that afternoon, just as Caleb predicted. At first the wind was hot, like a sweaty jacket, as we closed up the chickens and pulled the laundry off the line and tightened the bolts on the satellite receiver. Then the wind shifted from the west and the temperature dropped so suddenly it was like I had been punched in the stomach and couldn't catch my breath. Clouds formed a black wall as high as Heaven, sparrows flew scattershot away from the storm right past our heads. The trees bent sideways clinging to their tender new leaves, and the old school bell kept ringing. It tolled a steady rhythm with each gust of wind, as if it were rousing us from a stupor, preparing us for battle.

But it's cozy in a solid house during a storm! I had that feeling when we were all washed up and prayers were said and supper was eaten and dishes put away. Caleb would have been pleased. Eli stoked the fire in the stove because the wind was rattling the chimney and slamming the flue. Rebecca entertained us with jokes she found on her phone—these silly videos that made the other children frown but I said was all right considering the circumstances. Then I felt it was time for a story. When you have a love of literature, it's always with you. We collected the phones in the basket and I had a seat in my rocker and told Mary to go choose a book.

I closed my eyes and rested. I felt a child climb into my lap and I welcomed her, petting her hair and pulling her small shoulders close. I kept my eyes closed, just savoring the moment, the clover smell of the child's breath, the heavy warmth on my legs. I rocked and said, Little Rebecca, rose of the vine.

Who are you talking to, mama? I heard.

When I opened my eyes, I saw Rebecca sitting on the hooked rug, perhaps six feet away from me. I let out a cry and stood up. As I did, I felt the child slide off me. I heard a plaintive sigh, a kind of whimper, and saw footprints appear on the fluff of the rug and then vanish. I looked up to see if the children had witnessed any of this. It was hard to tell. They might just have been upset by my cry. So I carried on, as we do.

Writing it off as nerves and exhaustion, I put the phantom child out of my mind, and started to read the book. It was Mary's favorite, Last Battle of the Angels, which made Eli and Sarah roll their eyes. But I didn't get far.

After a page or two, we all heard a pop and then a persistent whistle in the room. I thought it might be the kettle, but Noah said No and pointed toward the wall where a hole that Caleb patched had reappeared. In a moment there was another pop, and then a few more, until all the holes had burst open, creating a chorus of whistles. It was the wind pressing through the holes.

Dear Lord, I said, that's a strong wind. Eli, can you help?

He found the small bolts of dried adhesive and put them back in the holes. But as soon as the boys were on the rug again, and I continued reading, the holes popped open again and the wind whistled into the room like a sad harmonica. It was perfectly explainable, but it put me on edge. Eli plugged the holes again and secured them with caulk and I said, Well! Let's hope that's the end of that! Now where were we ....

I could not blame the next thing on the wind, or on nerves, or weariness.

In the quiet of storytime, as the children sat at attention—a bit twitchy—there was a sudden slapping sound from the other side of the room. It was like someone clapping with mittens near my bedroom door. A cloud of chalk dust appeared near the sound and drifted toward us. There's no question it was chalk—the scent was unmistakable. Then, we heard the same sort of slapping from the other side of the house, near the front door, and the same cloud of chalk dust burst into the room. I heard a muted giggle and looked to see from which of the children it came, but they were silent.

I went quickly toward the cloud, with the book as a sort of weapon I guess, but when I got in the dust it was nothing. There was no trace of chalk on my skin, no sensation in my nose or mouth. And just as quickly, the cloud dissipated.

The four older children now sat quite straight and stared at me. They waited for me to respond to the weird incident. Rebecca saw it differently, though. She ran to me and put the mouth of the rabbit to my ear and whispered, Daddy said the invaders are coming. Now they're here.

I took a breath to reply, to dispel her fears, but then I paused to consider what she had said. It was a rare moment of confusion.

In that pause, Sarah said, There are no invaders, Rebecca. That's not what's happening here.

The other three waited for a reply. It was possible that they agreed with Sarah. I couldn't have them ganging up, but before I could say anything, Rebecca spoke.

They are too invaders, she said through the rabbit in my ear. And daddy says they put notions in our head with their voodoo tricks.

Come on Rebecca, Eli said. Come sit down with me.

Daddy doesn't know what's he's talking about, Sarah said. And he's not even here.

Then Sarah turned to me, her cheeks flushed, and blurted, How long are we going to go on like this? Can't we just try to be normal?

I kept my composure.

Hush dear, I said. All of you, hush. It's been quite a day with this storm and Daddy gone and everything. Time for an early bed. Bring me your phones.

That night from my bed I could see the trees bend under the wind in the moonlight. How could this not exhaust them, just resisting and resisting the wind, bent over from the force? And where does all this wind come from? How could there be so much air to come across the land at such speed for so long? Eventually I couldn't watch anymore and I got up.

Besides the steady shudder of the wind, the house was quiet. I made tea and sat in my rocker with a good book I'd bought at a library sale. It still had the shelf sticker on it. I thought I might just lose myself in that perfect world of ladies and gentlemen, and get some perspective on what was happening. I dozed off for a while. But I had no peace.

From down in the cellar, through the floorboards, the speckled hen began to scream. She seemed terrified, and the sound moved as if she were racing all around the cellar. I pulled back the door and shushed the naughty old hen. The light had gone out down there, but as soon as the glow came from above, she made a sort of gurgle from the shadows and was silent.

As I lowered the door, there was another sound coming apparently from within the room. It was a steady thud, very slowly at first. Then it grew to many steady beats, like people pounding on the walls, but weakly. Or with small fists. I went to the middle of the room, held my arms out for balance, and heard it on all sides, on all walls. This regular pounding and also (I hesitate to say this, but it's true) a faint chorus of plaintive yells. This combination— wall pounding and plea screaming—was just too much like what you'd hear from someone terrified and trapped and desperate for escape. That's what it sounded like.

It was the work of something mean and sinister. Or perhaps something clever and cruel. But either way, I couldn't deny the explanation any longer. They were taking advantage of Caleb's absence, thinking we were vulnerable, playing on the superstitions attached to this house—which we had turned into our lovely home. I couldn't explain how they were doing this—not yet—but it was plain enough who was doing it. I had to admit it, say it out loud.

Invaders! I cried. I know it's you!

It's not invaders, Mama.

I heard this from the entry to the loft. It was Eli. The other children huddled with him. He said, Mama you have to see that makes no sense.

Perhaps the lack of sleep gave me a temper. I scolded him, Be quiet, Eli! What do you know about these things?

I stood in the center of the room, still holding my novel with my arms stretched out for balance. I tried to see in all directions at once, to see where the invaders might next appear, to see how they were making these illusions happen.

Mama I think we should leave, Sarah said. She pressed past Eli and stood there, hugging herself in her nightgown, hair a mess.

She said, Let's go into town.

Enough! I replied. No one's going anywhere, and definitely not into town. Those people with all their gossip and their conspiracy stories, can you imagine? Yes, I know, something weird is happening in the house since Daddy left, and we need to get to the bottom of it. Maybe it's an attack, or maybe just pranks. But it's clear they've crept their way to this part of the country already, God help us, and we can't stand for it…

Sarah said, But you're not listening…

I am listening very well, I replied. And it would do you good to listen yourself, to me or at least your father and authorities who know a thing or two. Now I will call to see if they can come home, but meanwhile we need to handle this ourselves, like strong Righteous folk.

Mama, please, Sarah persisted. We have to get help now. Let's go and it'll get better. Think about Noah, or Rebecca!

Don't you Rebecca me! I said. It sounded foolish and ungrammatical the instant I said it, but the meaning was clear enough. My dear little one broke free of their huddle and ran over to me, hiding in my robe with her rabbit.

Mary cried, Rebecca don't!

Come back here, Eli commanded.

Well.

That was enough for me. I had to do what good mothers sometimes do.

I swept my youngest up in my arm, and with the other hand swatted at them with my novel. In the doorway they protested, they complained and argued, but ultimately, I subdued them with swats of the heavy book to their bottoms until they all saw sense. Then I shut their light and closed their door and brought Rebecca to bed with me.

Back in my room, the little basket was glowing and I saw that the phones were lighting up with messages from I don't know what. I couldn't hold them steady enough to read all that tiny print. So I took the whole lot of phones and stuffed them in the safe, where Caleb had left a handgun and some rum. After a thought, I took the rum back to bed. Spirits are a sin, I know, but only a small sin. I wasn't perfect, but I did my best. That's all you can ask. I just needed some comfort and rest. And in that way, with my little girl warm at my side, I finally fell asleep.

It's hard to say what I dreamed that night and what I witnessed as real. I know I dreamed that Caleb and Jeffrey stood at the foot of my bed, wearing those uniforms I made them, but without pants—or underpants. Why no underpants? It was a dream. Caleb was shouting something to me, but the room was full of wind so strong you couldn't hear. Jeffrey pulled at Caleb's sleeve to stop him from trying, but Caleb made a megaphone with his hands and shouted, convulsing his body with the effort.

What is it?! I cried, but my voice was also lost in the wind.

I love you! I cried. Come to bed!

I won't explain what I wanted, but you know. So badly. Then the wind stopped.

Caleb pointed at his friend and said, But Jeffrey's here.

It made sense in the dream, even if it doesn't now.

Later, the same dream came back, but got strange. Caleb and Jeffrey were crouched under the window, still naked from the waist down. From the bedroom I could see a chicken as tall as the pole barn, looking in through the window, bringing its rapacious beak up against the glass and tapping, making it crack. Caleb made military-style hand gestures to Jeffrey, but then the chicken smashed through the window and seized Jeffrey in her beak and hauled him away, his skinny legs kicking. I was glad—in the dream, of course—because now Caleb could come to bed. But when I awoke it felt like my heart had broken. I was ashamed and my head ached.

Then, in the hour before dawn, I might have dreamed I heard our bell ringing—tolling, I should say, as if someone were sounding it. And then I heard a crowd of footsteps across the floor in the living room. I heard a chorus of children singing a patriotic song. It was a lovely chorus but also quite sad. Lugubrious, as they say in the old books. I might have dreamed it. By the first light of day, it was over.

A neighbor came by after breakfast—Helen Pandowski, in her husband's white pickup. I should say late husband because I understand Earl died recently of a bad kind of cancer. The children were cleaning up, still somber from the night's events. I told them to wait in the house, and I ran out to intercept Mrs. Pandowski. One must maintain good relations with one's neighbors no matter how peculiar they might be. As I crossed the yard, the hens began to make a horrible racket—squawking like the wolf got in. I shushed them but it did no good.

The door of the truck flew open in the wind as Mrs. Pandowski stepped out. She carried a casserole dish. She wore a plastic hairnet and held it with her free hand while she crossed the yard, cowering from the wind. Once at church I heard one of the ladies call the Pandowskis 'adorable,' but I don't know—they seem judgmental to me. Though I shouldn't say that about Mr. Pandowski, now that he's dead.

I just wanted to see that you were all right, Mrs. Pandowski said. I brought you a tuna casserole for the kids—I remember they like it.

Oh that's very sweet of you, I said and took the dish. We're fine. It's a heck of a wind?

Making up for the mild winter, I guess, said Mrs. Pandowski. She was looking around the place with lowered eyebrows. She added, I couldn't help but see Eli scuffling with a hen the other day—I guess he's all right?

I crossed my arms and just looked at her.

She waved her hand, as if shooing a fly and said, Just with Caleb not here and all. Then she added, with a presumptuous wink, Not that we ladies can't manage on our own. And then after some silence she asked, Chickens all right?

They were still squawking in the house like holy banshees. I just shrugged. It was embarrassing.

I should really let you go, I told her. Thanks for the casserole.

Oh sure, said Mrs. Pandowski. I know you're busy with the children.

I noticed then that she looked very tired, possibly unwell. Her cheeks looked papery and her eyes watery and yellow. For a moment I thought maybe I should be looking in on her. But of course I banished the thought because I had my hands full of righteous work.

Finally Mrs. Pandowski said, You just let me know if you need anything. Help with the chickens, something needs mending, or what have you.

I told her, I sure will. You bet.

She said, Okay dear. You have a good day.

And she went back to their truck, leaning into the wind. You could hear the chickens screaming out of their minds, even over the gusts. Mrs.

Pandowski looked back at the hen house once before pulling herself into the truck. She waved as she backed out, and then she was gone.

She meant well, I guess.

Inside Sarah took the casserole from me and said, That was Mrs. Pandowski.

Yes dear, I said.

Why didn't you have her come in?

Oh, she was busy, I said. Just stopping by.

Sarah put the casserole in the fridge and said, Too bad. We like the Pandowskis. And now he's gone.

I'm sure you do, I said. The whole time she was here, the darn hens were making a horrible racket. It was embarrassing!

Sarah laughed quietly—perhaps sarcastically? She said, That's what you're embarrassed about ...

I didn't like her tone. This behavior—this insubordination, I guess you could call it—it had to stop. Get nipped in the bud. I could hear the hens outside screeching away. The house felt suddenly cold and uncomfortable. The residue of last night's dreams remained in my mind. And yet, despite all these obstacles, I had an idea.

We have to do something about those chickens, I said. They just aren't normal out there. And I think they could do us some good in here.

Sarah stared. Mama, no.

The other children had also come over and stared at me. They couldn't see the merit of my idea. They refused to help. I wanted to be angry, but I could see in their faces a childishness, an irrational fear, like a toddler on the other side of a fence from a barking dog. Sometimes you can only teach by example.

I went out to the hen house and, two by two, grabbed the shrieking hens and carried them into the house and dropped them into the cellar. They twisted and flapped in protest and nearly pulled my arms from their sockets as I hauled them in. But is there any safer place for them in these kinds of circumstances?

Once the chickens were inside, my embarrassment faded. Mary asked if she could read to them from the hatch and I said okay. Noah made me some tea. The house warmed up then and I was optimistic that having the hens inside would keep the invaders away. We had removed one of their interests, and the birds would sound an alarm if they came back. This was my hope. For a while, I thought it might be working.

We were having quiet time and tea. The wind had turned to cold rain, and it beat the metal roof in a soothing way. I was doing my counted cross-stitch and I let the children have their phones. Usually they complained about reception from our satellite receiver, which is the only way they can connect, but there wasn't a peep. Those five little screens glowed in various places around the room and up in the loft—almost a comforting glow, like lightning bugs or the tip of the tongue of deep sea fishes. But I was preoccupied. Even the faithful have doubts, and I was second-guessing myself—that is to say, I just had trouble explaining some of the things happening.

So I set aside my work and picked up my own phone to have a look at HomeGround and see if I could learn from some of my experienced brothers and sisters. Let me just say: all my doubts were erased.

The family of a pastor in Indiana took in a group of invaders living under an expressway bridge. The wife and children were found dead in their beds in a week, the invaders long gone.

A woman in Missouri picked up an invader hitchhiker and drove her car into the Mississippi River. When she was rescued, she said she didn't know why she did it—that these notions appeared in her head.

A man hired invader brothers to work in his lumber yard and in two weeks his cash register was empty. He had to claim insurance. What's worse, his daughter apparently eloped with one.

They can get in your house, I read. They can crawl through tiny spaces, climb precarious structures, drop from heights without a sound. They make you crazy with strange noises and illusions. They get in your head with voodoo tricks until you don't believe yourself, until you abandon your house—and then they swarm. They raid your garden, kill your pets, drain your gas tank, kidnap your children. And there are more of them coming every day, sponsored by the Earnest in the cities, coming to destroy our families and our way of life. This is what I learned on HomeGround. Thank goodness.

The children were still entranced by their phones. I watched them for a while, tapping away with their thumbs like chimpanzees engaged in some serious task. Every so often, they stopped and looked up at each other, meaningfully. How do they connect like that? I had no such connection with my brother. Neither did we have phones, I suppose. But my mother never arranged for quiet time like I do. She spent her time nagging my father until it drove him to drink. She must have been troubled, bless her heart, never even accepting my affection—the things she said to me, my goodness! But that made me stronger, a better mother, a better daughter to Papa until his body shook itself to pieces. My mind digressed in this way while I watched my children in their tranquility.

Then the bouncing started. The distinctive sound of a rubber ball began near the kitchen stove. It had the same rhythm every time: a 'bounce-bounce pop,' just as a ball might go off a floor and then the wall and into a child's hands. I looked up when I heard it first and saw that Sarah and Mary were already staring toward the stove, their phones in the laps of their dresses. There was a short break from the sound, and I prepared to file it away as jitters, but then it started again, now right across from me in the great room, where the plugs in the wall strained against the wind. Bounce-bounce pop. Bounce-bounce pop. Noah leaned his head out from the loft and looked toward the sound. Eli sighed sternly from the corner where he read, and now we were all listening, watching.

Then we heard the ball drop, bounce rapidly, and roll across the floor. In the next moment, the old bell outside rang—once, twice, three times— and then we heard the sound of a dozen footsteps across the old floorboards and right out the door. Then a heavy silence, except for the drumming of rain on the roof.

My heart rate accelerated to an unhealthy level. It was unmistakably an invader inside our home. Or outside, throwing the sound somehow. Bounce-bounce pop. On it went, moving around the floors of the old schoolhouse.

A blessing came down to me then. A moment of clarity. I had read on HomeGround that the first action must be to secure your dwelling. Clearly—despite all Caleb's efforts and despite the vigilance of the hens in the cellar—our dwelling was not secure. Action was required.

Action was required.

All right, I said to the children. All right, it's time.

They looked at me with open faces, expectantly, hopefully.

Let's have your phones first, and then we'll get going, I said.

They came over and dropped their phones into our basket. I took the basket into my bedroom and locked everything away in the safe, with the handgun and the rum.

When I returned to the room, the children had dressed with jackets and boots.

Oh my dears, I said, almost losing my composure. Look at you, always ready to help!

Where are we going, Mama? Mary asked.

Well, to board up the windows, of course.

Board up the windows?! Sarah exclaimed. What are you talking about? I thought we were going into town.

Sarah! I said, Of course we're not going into town. That's exactly what they want us to do, so they can occupy our home and steal us blind and who knows what. No! We're going to secure our dwelling!

Eli said softly, Why are you talking like that Mama?

Like what, I demanded.

Like, 'secure our dwelling.'

Because action is required, dear heart. Action is required. Now if you aren't going to help, I'll do it myself.

There were boards piled up behind the pole barn. I carried them through the rain and took a hammer and some 16-penny nails and climbed on a paint bucket turned over and began to seal off the windows. A physical barrier is the most important, they say. Physical defense is the only real defense, Caleb always said. You can talk until your face turns blue, but words don't compare to a fist. Or a gun. So Caleb says. And since Caleb wasn't there, it was my job to secure the dwelling.

Eli came out first, and then Noah, and finally Mary, and they helped me. No one said a word. But Eli held the boards and Noah brought a stepstool when the bucket cracked, and Mary held up an umbrella as best she could. And then it was done, and we all felt so much better. The rain was heavy and cold and it was delightful to get inside the warm house and shake off our coats.

Sarah was on the couch with Rebecca on her lap.

You can't do this, she said to me. You can't just lock us all in here. People will see the boards and wonder. If all you care about is what people think, you're making it much, much worse!

It broke my heart to hear her talk to me this way. But one must rise above such challenges and take the high road.

I explained: People will say, Oh, the Fallendinis are taking care of their home during a major storm. That's all. It's not unusual to board windows in the country. During a storm. Plus, anyone who's well informed will know that we're taking measures against invaders, who are now here and gaining strength. It says so plainly on HomeGround.

Sarah appealed to the others, You guys, let's go. We have to go, right now. She's lost it.

And that was just too much. I had to step down from the high road. I went to Sarah and pulled up her lovely hair in a pony tail and held it, firmly but fairly, until she released Rebecca. She swatted at me, just like those hens, while the other children pleaded for us to stop, but soon Sarah came to her senses and just cried and the trouble was over.

Now, we're going to bed, I said. And they all did immediately, without supper. That was a shame, but it happens. I tucked each one of them in, and when I saw that Rebecca was under the covers with Sarah, I didn't object one bit and tucked them both in. Forgive us our sins just as we forgive those who sin against us.

The rum helped me get to sleep but it didn't last. The pounding began again just after midnight—the sound of a dozen little fists striking the walls and plaintive cries more chilling than coyotes. I went out into the living room and witnessed it all, now so plain and riotous. In each direction, the walls echoed with the desperate thumping. There was nothing to see, but everything to be heard. And there was a strange scent, like perspiration and dirt and the sweetness of clover.

I had to raise my voice, to let the invaders know they were dealing with a strong woman.

Go home! I cried. Go home!

I yelled it at each of the boarded-up windows, down into the floorboards, up to the roof. I yelled it everywhere I could imagine the sinister invaders crouching, making the sounds, inflicting their pranks on my poor family. That didn't work. So I explained to them, as loudly as I could muster, My husband will be home soon and I warn you he's well-armed! For that matter, I am well-armed now! Don't make me come out there! I'm warning you!

Then it was quiet. Even the rain had ceased and all you could hear was the pop of the last embers in the wood stove and the ticking of the antique clock. I stood in the middle of the room and closed my eyes. I breathed. I lost my composure just a bit and wiped the wet from my cheeks. And then I felt the children come around me. I just kept my eyes closed and appreciated the feel of their hands and arms embracing me—Eli and Sarah and Mary and Noah and dear sweet Rebecca, all in one embrace. It was all over, I thought, just like in the novels and although it's sappy, I'm not ashamed to admit that more tears came.

If only it were all over.

When I opened my eyes, I saw none of my children around me. Instead, I saw them across the room, dressed to go out, a suitcase on the floor. I felt the phantom arms release me and I went very cold. I screamed. Just as anyone would in such a situation.

Mama, come with us, Eli said.

Please, said Mary. You have to come.

How many times do I have to tell you, I replied, That if we leave we will lose everything—our home, our reputations, maybe our sanity! We can beat these invaders, they are not too much for us.

They aren't invaders, Mama, said Noah. Everybody knows something's happening here. The people in town will be nice to us.

They will pity us! I explained. They will look down on us and condemn us as a Righteous family who failed! That's what! I will have no part in that. That is not how my papa raised me. Do you understand? That is not what Daddy would want us to do.

An idea came to me.

I said, In fact, I'm calling Daddy now. I wasn't going to bother him, but it's his right to know.

I picked up my phone and struggled to unlock it, my hands trembling.

He won't answer, Eli said softly.

How do you know? I asked. I dialed the number, put it on speaker.

We've tried, said Eli.

He's off the grid, Mama, said Mary.

Or just not answering, spat Sarah.

The phone rang and rang and finally went to his voice mail and I hung up.

We stared at each other.

Sarah said, We really are going, Mama. Would you please just get dressed and come with us? I'm asking one last time.

Mary added, almost in a whisper, You're not right, Mama.

So. That is what they thought, I realized. I wanted to scream at them, to yell over and over the truth, that I wasn't the crazy one. I wasn't mad. I was the one the invaders hadn't got to yet. The children, poor dears, and half the town—they were the crazy ones, who believed in the conspiracies and spooky fabrications. But screaming would only make it worse, because a mad woman screams. A clever woman schemes.

Wait! I said. If you have to go, you should have your phones.

The children looked surprised, eager.

Yes, I said. I'll just go get them. Okay? Don't leave just yet. I'll be right back.

I went to my bedroom, unlocked the safe, and took the phones. I also, of course, took the handgun. I had a carrot and a stick.

When I returned to the room, the children stopped discussing something urgent and looked at me.

Please open the cellar, Eli, I said.

What? Why?

We need to check on the chickens. Just help me out before you go, okay?

Eli looked troubled, and exchanged glances with Sarah, but he obeyed.

He moved the rug and pulled back the cellar door. The chickens below began to croak and flap about.

Eli turned to me and said, They seem fine?

Then I took their phones, all in one fist, and tossed them down the hole. Go get them, I said. All of you.

Oh, Mama, Eli said.

That's enough, we're out of here, Sarah exclaimed. She took Noah and Rebecca's hands and pulled them toward the door.

I drew the handgun.

Sarah sneered, Like you even know how to use that.

I flipped the safety on the gun, raised it to the ceiling, and discharged it. There, now it had gone off.

I gave Sarah a hard look, one I never wanted to use, and said, A mother does what's required.

Eli held a comforting hand toward me and said, Okay Mama, it's going to be fine, no need to shoot. I'll just go down and get those phones.

All of you, I said, and used the gun as a sort of pointer to encourage them. It sounds bad—the whole scene—now that I'm saying it. But the moment called for it. It was a desperate time.

Sarah began to argue, but I yelled, Quiet! Not one more word.

The children exchanged looks as they had earlier. It was their peculiar communication again. They went down the ladder of the cellar, oldest to youngest, helping each other. All except for Rebecca.

As Noah descended, I heard him say, Rebecca, remember.

She gripped her bunny and stood on the top of the stair. She held up her rabbit to me and whispered, Mama, tell me about the invaders again. Why are they bothering us?

It was a decoy. A distraction. She was buying time. It pains me to say this about my dear littlest one, but she was part of a game to deceive her mother.

I squatted down and looked at Rebecca, balancing in the cellar door. She smiled at me and tilted her face. In that moment, for some reason, into my head popped the memory of her putting on too much makeup, like a clown, and combing her hair out wildly, and waiting for the milkman so she could greet him and ask 'Do you like my dress?' And I thought My God, you poor dear. And I helped her down the stairs of the cellar with a sort of love pat and the door dropped shut. I put the rug back and pulled a bureau on top of it and that was that.

Then, to action, quickly. I sent one more emergency message to Caleb and then I grabbed the hatchet and ran out into the night and cut the cable to the satellite receiver. There will be no calls from the cellar.

My children are safe.

Now I wait in the pole barn for Caleb to come home. I couldn't bear to listen to the children or the chickens calling to me, so I had to leave the house. I know he'll come soon. Now I have to content myself with waiting, sitting on this double bed in the back room of the pole barn, looking at pictures of my husband and Jeffrey on their adventures.

When Caleb comes home we'll sort this out. He'll be proud of me for protecting our children and our dwelling. People will say I was brave, a great mother. And that's comforting. I can't hear sounds of the house anymore. I can't hear the wind, or the rain. It's quiet. Now all I can hear is that chorus of children, which might have come in a dream, which might be a dream now, singing in harmonies like flowing bands of colors. Singing, O Beautiful, for spacious skies, for amber waves of grain.

A DATE THEY WON'T FORGET

Felix Fuglesen arrives five minutes early for his first date. He sits in front of the Lincoln Mall on the rim of a planter that holds trash, rather than plants. He wears a collared shirt he borrowed from Dad and ironed himself. For ten minutes, Felix looks around—at the neglected brick buildings, a few trees choked by sidewalk grates, and maybe ten people who walk by like they're eager to be someplace else. He resists the urge to take his phone from his pocket. Once you do that, you're no longer present, and if this date is going to be a success, Felix will need to be present.

Five minutes late is pretty late, isn't it? Or is that a rounding error and it's not until, say, fifteen minutes that you can be annoyed? At 20 minutes, you just give up, because there are many places Felix would rather be. For one thing, the river would be great today. You could sit under the trestle and wait for trains. He'd also rather be at the sculpture park, where he had originally proposed they bring frozen custard and take a walk. But Jess won't be at those places—she will be here, at the mall, where she wanted to meet. And Felix agreed because, as Dad says, compromise is the grease of human machinations.

Places are weird, because in reality they're pretty static, but in your memory they can be completely different. Looking at the Tudor-style façade of the Lincoln Mall in this bright sun, it's obvious that the window trim is split and curling, the stucco is crumbling, and weeds grow from the pavement. But it's the same place Felix came with his family one Christmas to hear the choir and admire the yule-tide displays. It can't be that long ago. But he yearns for the Lincoln Mall from those days and this is not that place. It seems weird to be seventeen and yearning for something lost. You'd think that would come when you're older.

Fifteen minutes and still no Jess. Felix stands and puts his hands in his pockets and walks, but there's nowhere to walk to, really, so he makes a circle around the bronze sculpture of the 16th President, whose nose and privates are polished from people touching. On the other side, an old man lies against the base of the sculpture, hugging plastic bags stuffed with plastic bags.

Felix nods at the man and says hello, which seems to wake the man from a trance, to provoke a slow smile. It's like the old man recognizes him. He raises his arm and points a finger at Felix and laughs, silently, and his eyes are watering. Felix pauses longer than he means to, because maybe you're supposed to give the old guy money? Or probably food would be better?

Then Jess appears at the mall entrance with three friends. Eighteen minutes late. Well, that's not so bad.

However, they had not agreed that there would be friends! If Felix had known that, he might have brought his friend Conor, although Conor would have been scared to hang out with girls of this level. Now Felix will have to re-factor his plans, for four girls, to make things fun and worth doing again.

But holy mackerel Jess is beautiful! Why is this a new discovery each time? You get a strange sense of weakness that's unexpectedly nice and your legs feel heavy and it's hard to keep your head up. She runs toward him and on tiptoes makes a kiss beside his cheek without touching (but still, it's a kiss! Is that the first kiss, officially? Hopefully not) and grips his wrist and pulls him toward the mall. Striding after her, he catches his shoe on a crack in the pavement and trips. When he recovers, he remembers Dad reminding him of posture, and he stands straight before the group of girls, because it's best even if it makes you feel conspicuous.

Jess says, So… this is Ashley, and that's Ashleigh, and that's Neveah.

Felix raises his hand in hello, although he recognizes all of them. How would a clever guy—or even Dad—how would they start this conversation?

Felix takes a breath and says, Well isn't this my lucky day? Four lovely ladies for the price of one!

The girls stare at him. Ashleigh is chewing gum.

Ashley says, I didn't know you were so tall.

I like your teeth, Neveah says, Do you use whiteners?

Sometimes when a joke falls flat you double down, so Felix says, I mean, we could field a basketball team with this many, right?

Jess says, Find your own tall boy. He's mine.

She puts her arm around his waist and presses her hip against the side of his femur. This is a lot of contact, starting from no contact ever, but it would be rude to just stand there without reciprocating. So Felix cups his hand around the bump of Jess's shoulder. It feels like a pose, which probably needs some correction to be natural. But Ashleigh, apparently inspired, leaps in front of them and points her phone camera, exclaiming, Adorable!

To which Jess says, Okay! Enough! Enough!

She makes swatting motions toward her friends.

Ashley and Neveah study their phones to see what Ashleigh has sent them.

The double doors of the mall these days have a dark film over the glass so you can't see through. But the old ornate logo, an elaborate, cursive *LM*, remains. The sight of it brings back that yearning for old times.

Jess pulls him inside.

When Felix was young, there were bronze sculptures of bison in the atrium of the Lincoln Mall, enormous and bright under round skylights. Your hands tasted like pennies after you played on them while Mom bought socks and books. Now the bison are gone, along with most of the stores. There's a place that sells plastic bathroom supplies. There's an acupuncture place. There's the arcade, where nothing good happens. And there's the teriyaki restaurant, where Felix is taking Jess for lunch.

They are still holding hands, but as they approach the center, where bison once roamed, they tug in opposite directions. Felix turns toward the hall with the teriyaki restaurant, and Jess turns toward the hall that leads to the arcade.

Ope! Says Felix. We're going this way!

Jess drops her hand and looks at him, narrow-eyed and puzzled. Um, no, she says, the arcade is down here.

The three friends are coming down the hall now.

We said we were getting teriyaki, Felix says.

Well whatever, Jess says, the arcade is amazing! My dad says it keeps this place afloat, which is good for the economy. Come on!

Felix's dad says 'On the world, take action, lest it act on you.' He painted that on a smooth river stone and keeps that stone on his desk. That's how Felix achieved this date—by taking action on the world. The hardest and most awesome thing he could think of was a date with Jess Hollerman, and so at an optimal moment during passing period, he set his intention, and pushed upstream through the crowd of students and books and backpacks until he reached Jess's locker and, seeing that she must have been crying, nearly lost his nerve, but kept it, and asked the question, which took her by surprise, but then after a moment of thinking and looking first one way and then the other down the hallway, she accepted and they called each other's phones right then and the deal was done.

Now there is no way Felix is going to see all that effort go right down the drain, with a sudden change of plans, to visit the arcade of all places, where nothing decent happens. Dad says you can judge a place by its people (especially when arguing against vacations in Florida) and by that logic, the arcade should be judged very severely. The kids who go to the arcade are not honor students, let's just say. They don't ever get out of Middling, either. But you don't change a person's mind by just contradicting them—you need to provide alternate paths. Life is an infinite web of alternate paths, each suited to an array of possible scenarios—Felix says this. Needs work though; not quite ready to paint on a stone.

The three friends are just strides away, though still studying their phones and bumping shoulders. On the world Felix needs to take action again, and pretty quick.

Let's go to the river! He says. I know a great spot. Way better than the arcade. It's so peaceful …

No that won't work.

He tries again … There are ghosts! Under the train trestle. There's this amazing story …

Jess is looking at her friends. She looks back into Felix's face, and once again narrows her eyes in puzzlement. But then she laughs and hits his chest with her open palm, saying, You are so random!

The friends look up and witness this. Ashleigh takes a picture.

Jess presses her bosom against Felix's ribcage and looks up into his face. He can see the pink of her tongue and smell the mint of the gum beside her teeth. The whites of her eyes are just white, with no imperfections, but her irises have flecks like a stained-glass window.

She whispers, This is our first date! Aren't you excited?

It's as if the reality has just sunk in, and Jess is not having second thoughts. Wow, unexpected.

An alternate path will present itself. Felix follows her into the arcade.

Inside the music is deep and repetitive and you can feel it in your stomach, and after a while it's as if your heart has modified its beat to the rhythm. This is where the old movie theater was—you can tell by the sloping floor. But otherwise, everything in the arcade is new and unlike anything outside. Vague blue light comes from bulbs strung just above their heads, far below the vaulted ceiling. There are rows of the vintage machines their parents used to play, muttering and exclaiming like droids. And there are rows of densely-packed consoles and gaming PCs with curved monitors. The vintage machines attract the crowds, though. Why? Nostalgia? But for a time when you weren't born? Doesn't that contradict the definition of nostalgia? Or maybe that's not exactly what it means.

Jess turns suddenly so Felix bumps into her. She holds out her cupped hand in a way you might admire a bird's egg. Jess is holding a triangular pill.

Do you party? she asks. She has in her eyes a look you would call sultry. The blue light enhances it. So this is the arcade.

Felix deflects the question, Well. I can see you have only one, so I wouldn't want to …

Yeah, no, Jess says. I did one earlier. I'm good …

She holds her cupped hand up to his mouth, like how you might offer an animal water, and her eyes are still sultry but also sparkly and mischievous. Also, coming from her wrist there is a fragrance of perfume like bunches of delicate flowers. This is how it happens. Certainly an unexpected path among the infinite paths. But who's to say?

Then Jess's eyes switch away from him, over his shoulder. They switch twice like this, and then she pockets her hand, stiffens her body, and says, Shit!

Felix turns to look. Jess says, Don't look! Okay now look.

Here comes Donnie Martin. There is no mistaking Jess's usual boyfriend. He already has the face of a middle-aged man, with the bulging brow and the skin creased around the mouth. As he marches through the arcade, with two friends flanking him, people move aside. This happens despite him being probably the shortest guy here. Rumor says he stacks insoles inside his boots to gain an inch. Rumor says he missed his junior year because he was in rehab and another rumor says he was in the Marines but got kicked out because he lied about his age. That rumor doesn't hold up to scrutiny, but people don't care. They say he once stole a boat in Wisconsin. They say he sold half his dad's gun collection and bought bitcoin. They say he's double-jointed, that he had a twin who died in utero, that he had intercourse with the crossing guard.

As a peer tutor, Felix once reviewed one of Donnie's essays, 'Making My Personal Brand,' which was actually a series of paragraphs copied from career help websites. Felix rewrote it for Donnie, and changed the title to 'Cultivating A Unique Identity,' and Donnie turned in the re-write, but kept the original title. Plagiarism or not, Donnie did have a brand—quite literally. In the true meaning of literal. That is, Donnie has a logo. He took his initials *DM* and mashed them into the outline of a mean-looking eagle, or some bird of prey. You see the eagle from the side, and it looks prepared to obliterate something. This logo seems to be in motion wherever it appears—on Donnie's flat-brimmed cap, on patches on his friends' jackets, on stickers on people's laptops, in spray-paint on dumpsters downtown. So maybe the essay doesn't matter. On the world Donnie Martin is taking action.

We should say hi, Felix says to Jess. He looks at Donnie, who hasn't returned the eye contact. In fact, he seems to keep his gaze pointed just over everyone's heads. He talks to his friends with a side-mouth, without looking at them.

Jess stands behind Felix, in the leeward side from Donnie's wind, you might say. She's gathered her arms and wrists like an insect in a cocoon and presses Felix.

Are you freaking crazy? she whispers. We have to go right now.

Felix turns around. Well I don't think so, Jess. We're on a date, aren't we? No need to be weird or secret about it. Didn't you break up with Donnie?

Jess compresses her face, clenches her hands, and has a kind of convulsion, which ends in a fierce but almost silent scream. Then that's done and she looks at Felix with weary eyes and says, It's complicated. You don't need to … Come on let's go.

Well just hold on a second, Felix says. And he begins to explain the principle of the matter, but Jess interrupts him to say

Show me the ghosts!

Sorry, what? Felix asks, though he has heard her plainly. You do this sometimes so you can think.

Take me to that place—the river. I want to see your ghosts.

Jess puts a finger through his belt loop and pulls. As she stares up, he can see her pupils are the size of dimes.

Together they slide through the rows of the arcade, down the sloping floor, and burst through the emergency exit into blinding sunlight.

When Jess sees Felix's dad's car, she says, Oh let's put the top down!

Felix knew this would happen, and almost decided against taking the Fun Car, because what's the point? The top is not to be put down because it's maple seed season and those whirlygigs are a bear to get out from in between the seats. So Felix says,

I thought you didn't want to be seen. This car is kind of conspicuous, you know, with the top down?

As Felix drives away, Jess rolls down the window, puts her face in the wind, lets her hair flow backward. Oh man she's so beautiful! Why is this a surprise, every time? The air currents whisk her hair so that sometimes he can see all of her neck, but then it curls her hair around like a scarf. Briefly, Felix sees a mark just behind her ear. A birthmark? Then it's covered again, secret. But now there's a sudden awareness that Jess is a real human animal who needs oxygen and has to eat and processes that food with the same organs as everybody else—the organs are right there, inside her—and just like everybody else she needs to ...

You can just take me home, Jess says into the wind. I think maybe Daddy will have the pool open. You know where my house is?

Felix swallows. Is this an invitation? What about the river? How do you clarify this. Casually...

Oh I don't have my swimsuit, he says. We could swing by my place?

Jess turns her face into the car, her hair still in the wind. She says, No need.

She says this as if it's an obvious answer to his question. But what does it mean? Felix tries again. Joking...

Oh, so I can just borrow your dad's trunks?

Jess sits back against the seat and studies the side of his face. You're funny, she says. You're one of those funny people where almost nobody knows they're funny? But at the ten-year reunion or somebody's wedding you make a speech and everybody's like, 'I didn't know he was funny!'

Jess appears pleased with her anecdote. She looks through the windscreen nodding in a slow rhythm.

So ... Felix says. Are we going swimming at your house or the river? You wanted to see the ghosts?

Hearing himself say this, he realizes that if she were to choose the river, he would need to produce some ghosts. No, no he wouldn't. Just a story would work. Just a walk along the river there (and maybe a real kiss?!) Just an interesting experience like she's never had, given her lifestyle—that would be enough. That would be fair and honest, mostly.

Jess shudders as if coming out of a trance and laughs loudly, once. Okay, funny man. Yeah, no, I really appreciate this time with you, okay? If you just take the highway, that's to my house. Drop me off at the corner or something and then you can go to the trestle and maybe tell me about it some time?

Maybe he should have put the top down after all.

Then Jess makes a gesture of remembering something suddenly, and Felix anticipates her reaching into her back pocket to retrieve her phone, and he swerves the Fun Car just enough that she grabs on to the dash and says, Easy! Geez.

Felix drapes one hand over the steering wheel and lets the other rest on the seat between them, as the cool guys do. While driving straight, he looks at Jess, and holds eye contact.

He asks, Do you have a medical issue, or a legitimate concern about how this date is going?

Jess pulls her chin back and says, Excuse me?

Felix's question sounds weirder when spoken than when just thought. But now he has to persevere. You don't let a little setback ruin your plans.

Felix replies, Well because those are justifiable reasons for why we'd end our date early—if you were sick or not happy with how it's going. But if that's not the case, then I'm assuming we're still going to hang out. We're going to have this date like we said we were.

Now he wonders if that was too harsh.

He adds, Does that make sense to you?

Jess blinks a few times, as if to clear her vision. She combs her hair with her fingers and then shakes her head to settle things in place. Then she looks at him, now again with the puzzlement, and asks, Do you have anything to drink?

Funny you should ask, Felix says, still draping his hand but now looking down the road that will take them to the trestle. There's a cooler in the back seat.

Jess turns and pulls herself between their seats and now she's very close to him, her waist against his shoulder and her hip just inches from his chin.

You call this a back seat? She says. Then, Oh sweet!

She brings forward two damp cans of hard seltzer and opens them and hands him one.

Can you hold mine? Felix says. Just till I'm done driving? We're almost there.

Jess shrugs and sips from one can, and then the other.

They park the Fun Car along the shoulder of County Road 1250, where on one side there's the woods and the river, and on the other side, as far as you can see, fields of ankle-high corn in gray soil. The rows come almost to the road, as if the farmer had crayons and obsessed about coloring right up to the line. All that's left is a strip of weeds, littered with plastic grocery bags that rattle in the wind blowing across those fields. Probably tomorrow that farmer will come with a mower and shred those bags and some animals will eat them and die. Didn't someone in town try to ban those bags?

Felix knows a trail, and he shows Jess how you push through the wall of honeysuckle bush and then suddenly you're in the woods. They behold the scene. This is better than the arcade, right? Water maples, white oaks, and hackberry trees soar up to a new green canopy. On the forest floor bluebells are still in bloom and mayapple creates this kind of stage of giant green leaves. And there are the tiny white and pink flowers he can't identify yet, all tucked into secret places like somebody planned it. Woodpeckers swoop beneath the canopy in parabolic lines, chattering. You can hear other birds sing but you can't see them. Dad would know what they are, by what words they make. What says 'teacher-teacher-teacher?'

Jess stands with her arms hanging loosely, jaw slack, a slight frown.

She says, What is this place? I didn't know this was here.

Felix shrugs, It's the woods. Wait til you see the river.

Now's the time to take her hand and Felix does and she holds on. But Jess doesn't move yet. She asks, How do you know about this place?

The truth is Dad took him here first, but instead Felix says, I like to explore, you know? Just get out and find interesting places, outside Middling.

This is also true.

Felix leads them down the path, with Jess a step behind, gripping his hand but looking in one direction and then another.

Weird, Jess says. It's like some kind of nature show.

Felix affects an English accent and says, Then I shall be your guide, here, in the remote riparian woods of Middling County!

He looks back to see how his bit landed and sees only the puzzled face.

At the top of the bluff to the river, he says, It's best if you just run down.

Felix demonstrates, in basically a controlled fall and stumble, and grabs a willow branch to stop himself.

Jess hesitates at the top of the bluff. If I fall, she says, that's on you.

Felix stands at the base of the bluff and holds out his arms, and Jess stumble-falls down gracefully and stops in his embrace. How perfect! Felix lowers his face and prepares for a kiss.

Jess places her forearm in his chest and pushes herself back, finding balance, and says, Okay, now what?

The river is high and brown and carries loads of fallen trees that snag and make dams at the curves, where trash piles up. It's not as scenic as he was picturing. But a kingfisher darts past, makes its distinctive rattle, and perches on a dead limb.

Felix points and whispers, inviting Jess to share the sighting. But she is slapping her calves to brush away some insects. Then she looks up and says, You didn't bring the cooler did you?

Well you drank it in the car, Felix says.

Yeah, Jess says. She takes a deep breath, as if suddenly overcome by exhaustion, and says, Okay let's see your ghost and then we can go.

Now what? Felix had rehearsed topics of conversation for a teriyaki lunch. None of that will work now—he's not going to ask her if she remembers the party after their first communion when she dropped her jello cup and he got her a new one. He's not going to ask if she still goes to the used book sale at the library with her mom like he saw her once. Or how funny it was when they had to share a seat coming home from the district meet and they had to triple up and he kept falling off. Those topics will have to wait for date #2, which is definitely going to happen, somehow, along one of the infinite paths.

People sometimes laugh at Felix's watch, because it's an outdated relic, but who's laughing now as he glances at it with urgency and declares, We better hurry! The train's coming soon and that's when they appear!

He begins to jog down the dirt-and-sand beach, and turns to call back, Come on!

Jess raises both eyebrows, shakes her head no slowly, slips off her sandals, and sprints after him. Felix turns and runs, now more quickly, and hears her steps coming rapidly, rhythmically, like a metronome set too high. He wills his knees to rise faster, but Jess passes him easily, tearing away down the sand toward the trestle. As she crosses the shadow of the high railroad tracks across the river bank, she throws her arms into the air. He lumbers in a moment later, and they stand, hands on hips, breathing.

Felix says, Now we sit and wait quietly.

He drops to the sandy bank beneath the tracks. Jess sits beside him, not as close as he'd like but all right, and looks across the water. She's still breathing, with renewed energy it seems, and there's a shine of sweat along her hairline.

They wait. The river makes a trickling noise as water flows around a massive block of concrete and rebar. This is peaceful, right? Better than a mall?

But Jess is not reading his mind. She says, This place is kind of creeping me out. It's like you can hear your thoughts.

Felix continues looking toward the other bank and says, That's good, right? You gotta let yourself think.

Jess says, Most of what I do when I'm not sleeping is whatever it takes to not think. Thinking is what makes people crazy.

That's a good line, Felix says. Though he would not recommend it for painting on a stone. Still, it's better than his.

It's not a line, Felix. It's just the sad truth. If you think hard about it, everything is shit. So, don't think.

There was a thrill that came when she said his name. It came as kind of a surprise, that she knew it—well that's stupid, or silly rather. Of course she knows it. But still.

When's the train coming? Jess asks.

The shadow of the tracks moves with the sun, marking time, and now they are sitting just barely in the shade.

Pretty soon, I think, Felix says.

I hope so, says Jess. Hey do we have service here? Let's play some tunes or something.

Jess leans to the side to get her phone. That must not happen! If that happens, the date's over. Effectively.

No! Felix says. He reaches over and puts his hand on her knee. She looks at his hand, puzzled again. But at least she sits back and leaves her phone in pocket.

He says Service is shit here—don't bother. I'll tell you the story. The story about the ghosts!

Okay, sure, Jess says. She lays back and cradles her head with her hands and looks up where the tracks make dark hash marks against the sky. Make it good, she says.

That's a weird thing to say, because Felix is just going to tell her what the story is. There's no real making, just telling.

Back in the 1880s, he begins.

No, no, no, Jess says. That's too long ago. Make it like the 20s.

Well but it happened in like 1887.

Who cares? The 20s have flappers and Prohibition and like Al Capone. He used to come down here right?

Yeah but that's not the true story. Not this story anyway.

Fine.

Felix continues, Around here, in Illinois, there was a terrible drought that year. It was super hot and no rain.

Jess sighs, Oh god. Can you make it a little less depressing?

Felix's rare temper flares. He turns to face her and says, Can you just let me tell the story for a minute? It's not polite to interrupt like that. Okay? Can I tell the story now?

Jess rolls her head to the side to look at him. Her eyebrows lower and the fine corners of her mouth turn down. It's a joke sad face, mostly, but her eyes are complicated and her cheeks are flushed. Felix ignores his instinct to apologize and goes on.

They had just built this trestle, he says, especially for excursion trains. A lot of people then paid to just ride these trains for fun—to get out of their towns, to go to Chicago. Lots of them went to Niagara Falls.

Jess lets out a breath and whispers, That sounds nice. Now her expression is kind and soft. Felix moves a little closer as he talks.

Well in that drought, they were trying to give people things to do and one thing they did was burn weeds along the railroad tracks. Some guys were right here, on that day, the day before it happened, burning weeds. And in the heat and the dry, these beams and what do you call—ties, railroad ties—they caught fire and burned all night. But nobody knew.

So the next day the excursion train was completely full of people. You can imagine ladies in long dresses and hats and gentlemen in gentlemen's clothes and the long jackets and hats too. They all crowded into this excursion train, which was made almost entirely out of wood, you know, and they were partying and leaning out the windows. This train was going to Niagara Falls—probably some people on honeymoons.

Now Jess is just listening.

Oh and one thing, Felix says, is that there were two engines pulling all the wooden cars full of people. There were so many people—hundreds—that they added a second locomotive to the front. And they were coming fast along these tracks, the big party train, blowing smoke and tooting the whistle, like chugging along, coming toward this exact bridge over the river—this trestle.

Felix pauses to let that soak in. He decides to improvise on the story and says, Places are weird, because it's hard to imagine them any other way than the way you see them now, so when you hear about some big event happening right there—it's hard to process, you know? In this place, where you and I are lying, that train full of people came. On this sand, with some of these big trees here. Under this sky. Sometimes don't you think about this—all the layers of people and what happened in places?

He looks at Jess and she looks back at him.

He continues, The first engine made it across the bridge. That was Engine 21. That engineer saw the bridge smoking, he said later, but couldn't stop. He felt the bridge sag and sway when he went across, and knew it was bad but couldn't do anything about it. So the next one, Engine 13 (totally true) wasn't so lucky. The trestle collapsed right under it and it tipped off the tracks and fell into the river, right here. And you can see the huge dent it made in the bluff right there—can you see it? And all the cars, the coaches, slid right off the tracks into the river and on the banks here. They were all just smashed terribly—those wooden cars with all their people. Hundreds of people. It took like just a few seconds, from having a party headed to Niagara Falls to lying crushed between benches and roofs and wheels and other people and suitcases and ...

Okay, I get it, Jess says. She has turned on her side. She whisks her hand for him to go on.

It took weeks to sort it all out. Even then, some of the bodies—the people—were never recovered. Specifically, seven people just disappeared. They looked and looked and never found them.

Jess says, And now those seven ghosts haunt this bridge!

She lies with her head on one forearm, her other hand massaging the sand. Did I get it right?

Well, yeah, Felix says. That's kind of the punch line—I was just getting to it. But yeah, there are seven ghosts of the seven lost people.

Okay cool, Jess says. Keep going.

Well, that's kind of it. That's the story. Felix's enthusiasm is suddenly drained. It's hard to get momentum back when this happens.

Right, but what about the ghosts? You just told, you know, the setup. Now what happens with the ghosts?

Well, at least she's interested. Felix resumes,

Sometimes, when the train comes, you can see the ghosts under this trestle. They are up there, under the tracks, with their arms in the air and their hands on the beams—just holding the thing up, you know? Helping trains make their way. They say they light up and flicker in their places while the train goes across.

Jess turns her mouth down. Sometimes? she says. Like how often?

It depends, Felix says. Now an opportunity presents itself to him. A little deception is okay, every once in a while, right, if your intentions are good?

It depends, he says, on how the watchers do. If you're very quiet and respectful. You have to sit close together, to show respect for the people who loved the ghosts and the ghosts loved. Then you're likely to see them.

Then Felix adds, My folks saw them on the day they got engaged.

This was true, but also, maybe not a good idea to bring parents into the conversation?

Jess's phone rings from her pocket—a melody from a children's movie he can't remember.

That's weird, she says. Who calls?

She rolls on her back and looks at the screen and says,

Shit.

What? Asks Felix, but somehow he knows.

It's Donnie Martin. He's been messaging me too. Oh my god.

Jess sits up.

He saw us. He knows. People are talking about it. We have to go.

No we don't.

Um, yeah. We do. You gotta drive me home. Or drop me off and I'll walk.

Felix feels his pulse in his temples. There's pressure everywhere and he can't swallow. That old man by the statue pointed at him and laughed. But he seemed nice, didn't he? What is he doing here? What the mind should be doing is saving what's left of this date ...

Felix says, Why? I mean, seriously, what will that do? Nobody knows we're here. And isn't it better if we wait until he chills out anyway? The best thing we can do is stay here. The best thing to do is to keep having our first date and spending time together like we said and that's what we're going to do!

With this last statement, Felix drops his fist on the sand. And then he adds,

I mean, as far as I'm concerned.

Jess looks at him, her eyebrows up. It takes some time for her to speak again. Felix waits.

Then she says, quietly, Okay. But what are you going to do if Donnie Martin shows up?

I'll tell Donnie Martin that he had his chance and he blew it. Too bad, Donnie Martin. You didn't know what you had. Because now I'm with Jess Hollerman, and I appreciate her. And also, you're a cheater, and if you don't back off I'll let people know how you got an 'A' on that paper. How's that?

This all seems a bit extra. But Felix had said it anyway and Jess watched him intently the whole time.

She lets out a long breath and says, Come on over here.

She pats the sand beside her hip. Come over and we'll wait for the train and the ghosts.

Felix holds out. He says, Turn off your phone first.

Jess shrugs, and turns it off.

Felix crawls across the dirty sand of the riverbank and sits beside Jess so that they're touching, and he leans on his hand behind her back. Jess lets her arm rest on his knee. The river trickles around the block of concrete and rebar. A bird goes 'teacher-teacher-teacher!'

Carolina wren, Felix whispers.

What?

That bird, it's a wren.

Oh.

It's hard to know how much time passes. They are still sitting close, their sides touching, their ribs moving in and out together. A sound comes from the train tracks. A high, metallic hum—you can barely hear it. Felix turns to Jess and she looks in his face, very close, and he can see she hears it too.

The sound grows louder, gradually. But there is only that sound, and nothing more. No train whistle, no rumble of wheels at junctions, no chug-chug-chug. Just the high, metallic hum, getting steadily louder.

Jess says in Felix's ear, You think there are ghost trains here too?

Felix looks down but keeps his face close and says, I've heard of them. So maybe.

Then a silent, mutant vehicle appears on the track above them. It has the body of a truck but the wheels of a train. The body is white. The wheels are silver, polished from rolling down the tracks. When it's overhead on the trestle, it just looks like a single coach. It might be an old wooden coach. But from an angle, you can see its truck body, mounted too high, weirdly. There is no sound except for the high hum on the tracks and now a gentle 'clunk' as it rolls over joints of the bridge and then the mutant vehicle vanishes and the high hum fades away.

A cloud passes over the sun and a breeze comes down the river and the temperature drops. The breeze is strong, and it ripples the surface of the water and shakes the trees like applause. Then the air is still, but the shadow remains over them and it's still cool. Felix can see bumps rise on their arms.

Did you see them? Jess asks.

He looks at her face. It's an honest question.

What? He asks, buying time.

The ghosts, silly! Jess whispers. Did you see them? Was that them, what happened then? When the ghost train came through?

Her lower lip is damp and he can see her teeth. He can smell her breath, a little sour from what she's had that day, but also nice like cut hay.

Felix looks away from Jess and now at the river. The water just keeps coming, from all the drainage ditches and field tiles, carrying the soil, day after day, year after year, down the river and into the next river and the one after that and finally the sea, and then what? They say that most of the original topsoil is gone, they say it's going to run out, and if someone doesn't stop this at some point, well then.

Jess waits. Felix swallows.

No, he says. To be honest.

You didn't see them? Just under the bridge when the ghost train came over?

Sorry. I thought that was probably a maintenance vehicle. But weird for sure.

Now Jess looks down at the sand between her legs. She picks up a stick and flicks it.

When she looks back at him her face is like it was at her locker. It makes him want to do something. To take away that suffering.

Jess says, Is it too much to ask to have a few ghosts? I mean, is that gone now too?

Just because I didn't see them doesn't mean they aren't here. Who's to say?

Jess says, With everything else, and now we don't even have ghosts.

She lies down now, rests her head on her forearm. Our parents, she says, they had all kinds of cool spooky shit—like your parents and their engagement? And our grandparents, they had ghosts all the time, they just lived with them, like one haunted story. That's where all the stupid stories came from. And now those stories are all we have, which are dumb to be honest. No ghosts. It's pathetic. I'm so tired.

Jess closes her eyes. Felix watches her for some time. Her nostrils dilate slightly as she breathes. There is a slow rhythm to her breathing, now. A breeze returns and lifts some strands of her hair, which shines backlit in the late afternoon sun. The breeze lifts more hair and Felix can see part of the mark behind her ear. It looks like a soft 'v,' like a seagull you'd draw by a sunset. He reaches out with a finger and lifts her hair away to see all of it.

That is not a seagull. That is an eagle. A tattoo made of initials mashed into the outline of a mean-looking eagle, on the delicate skin on the bone behind Jess's ear.

Felix holds his breath. Maybe there aren't infinite paths. Maybe there's only one.

He draws Jess's hair back over her neck.

He unbuttons his dress shirt and takes it off, so now he's only wearing his white t-shirt. He lays the dress shirt over Jess's shoulders and tucks it under her arm so the breeze won't take it.

Then Felix stands and walks down to the river. The brown water just keeps coming. Why doesn't it run out? Well, sometimes rivers do. This one might. The breeze stirs up the leaves of the tall trees along the bank. And he stays here, in a cloud of whirling maple seeds, waiting for the next thing to happen.

RESCUE

My son is buried somewhere on a western slope of the Cascade Mountains. The officers told me they can't find his remains because the avalanche that consumed him and seven other volunteers was too massive. They said it happened during the same storm that doused the wildfire he was fighting, out there in the mountains, far from the comfort of his family. His family—his wife and two daughters—they were with me for a few days after we got the news. They're gone now, because I'm miserable company.

None of this would have happened if I hadn't moved us away from Middling, Illinois, so many years ago. But I guess you could say that about any decision, looking back.

My son, Ron, hasn't come to visit me yet, in the spectral hours, to explain. Probably because he's floating among his family now, trying to make things right. Or maybe he's looking for his mother. Lately, she's appeared in my room at night. She stands encased in the wall—neither inside nor out—and tells me to be patient, that they'll find him and we'll have peace. His grandmother comes too, usually just before dawn, only her head above the lampshade, saying that they'll never find him and it shouldn't matter anyway.

Why do I believe in these things? What is it about tragedy that leaves us groping for superstitions we know are absurd?

I sleep so much these days I've lost common sense. For a week I couldn't get warm. I piled on every cover in the house—down comforter, wool army blanket, tattered quilts. I felt the tremendous weight of all this fabric and filling, but still I shivered, old bones and loose ligaments clanking like kindling.

I only got up when I heard the thump of a bird hitting the window. Not long after the fires, the varied thrushes came down from the foothills and found refuge in scraps of forest spared in our village for the dying. There are too many clean windows here for these quiet forest birds. They fly when the light is most deceptive. When they hit the glass it makes your heart jump and you imagine you can feel the shudder of the house.

The days are long and wet but the smoke still hangs among our rooftops, carrying the stink of the smoldering mountains. Everyone is irritable. My elder neighbor Earl says don't worry what people are saying. This makes me wonder what people are saying and he obliges me. He tells me that they are asking, What was Ron doing out there? He wasn't a proper firefighter. These do-gooders, these radicals, they just cause trouble. And think about his family! They say these things about my son, according to Earl, who says he disagrees.

What is it about tragedy that brings out the meanness of people? As if the loss alone isn't enough, we coat it with judgment. Then I wonder whether I brought all this on myself, with my irascibility and heartlessness, and now I'm back to superstition.

So the birds got me out of bed, and I'm grateful for that. One of the thrushes didn't fly away after it hit the window. I knew it was bad immediately. The concussion shook the shabby frame of the house and in a brief flash, my wife and mother appeared in their respective places, as if the bird conjured them in the impact.

So I got up to see what I could do.

I froze at first, seeing how exotic the bird was. Most of us never witness the wild world close up. The thrush might have been painted—precise brush strokes for an orange throat, black necklace, blue shoulders, discrete tufts that lay delicately scalloped under its belly. And then I observed the bird's suffering, as it lay splayed on its side, eyes shrouded by nictitating membranes, feathers puffed in shock, panting.

This bird would die without some intervention, however unskilled. So I found a shoebox and lined it with a kitchen towel and set it on the stoop. I lifted the bird, whose weight barely registered, but whose softness I felt even through these aggravated joints, and set him down with his feet under him.

The bird didn't topple over. But its feathers continued to bristle as if electrocuted. It was cold, in the way it can be cold here in the shade even on a mid-summer day. So in a burst of ingenuity, I retrieved—behind rows of medicine bottles I just can't throw away—an old electric blanket. I slid that under the box and plugged it in, and covered the bird gently with the corners of the towel, and hoped for the best.

Earl came by to encourage me to ignore the latest gossip, which I had not heard. When he saw the bird, he began to speak, but stopped and instead just shook his head for who knows how long. It was long enough to create awkwardness between us. As his lower lip trembled and he blinked, I wished he would compose himself. That kind of outburst does no one any good.

Finally Earl said, He's a goner, that bird.

And, because Earl makes me argumentative, I replied, We'll see.

After blowing his nose, Earl tucked away his handkerchief and asked, You don't suppose it's Ron, do you? Like, come back?

Meaning, my dead son.

I'm gonna have to let you go, Earl, I replied. I'll let you know when the bird dies, okay?

He looked at me with his watery blue eyes, and held the gaze painfully long, because he knew he had misspoken and I wouldn't forget it for some time. You try not to make mistakes at this age, because amends are never certain. But I said no more and let Earl leave without comfort because who says things like that?

The bird didn't get better and it didn't get worse. I kept checking, wondering. Had it moved? Did the towel fall on its own? Had those neck feathers flared so? I couldn't tell, but still the thrush held its squat posture and panted, blindly, instinctually.

During the night I dreamed of the bird, of course. Not true dreams, but the visions you have when your body and mind won't let go, more common for me than true dreams these days. The bird was larger than the house, tipped on its side, stinking like a late-summer beach. I could feel tremendous, salty rushes of air from its blowhole. Then it was Ron and he was panting, having just pulled himself from a frigid river, having just rescued a kid on a toy raft, and he was only nine. Later, my wife came and said, Let it go, honey. And my mother looked from her perch on the other side of the room and said, Pay no attention. Nurse the bird if it makes you feel better. Then I turned on the light to flush the room of all this nonsense.

I must have fallen asleep. When I awoke, I went to the door and saw a thrush now perched athletically on the edge of the box, just a corner of towel over its tail, eyes clear and alert, beak closed. I wanted to grab a camera but didn't because I could tell the bird was about to take flight. And it did. With no warning, it launched into the air and stretched its exotic wings and glided through a stand of hemlock and vanished into the dark embrace of a dwindling forest. If I see it again, I probably won't recognize it. But its flight looked strong to my untrained eye.

Now. Surely this can't be where my story's going. Surely it's not some allegory about the resurrection of the bird. And surely, I assure you, it is not. Because Earl doesn't know the difference between a male and female varied thrush. The original thrush—the male—is almost certainly decomposing in the scrap of forest behind my house. And his replacement—the female, more subtle but no less exotic and beautiful—may still be flying back there, or perhaps farther up into the smoky, charred foothills.

I can imagine Earl now, in pajamas and robe, stepping warily into my back yard, peering into my window to make sure I'm asleep. He fumbles with his phone to make the flashlight work. He illuminates my dead male thrush in the box. Drawing from his pocket a female thrush—probably stunned but in fair shape—he sets her down where the male had been. I can imagine his unshaven lip trembling, his moist eyeballs reflecting.

When I see him next, when he comes by pretending to have no purpose, I see the dirt under his fingernails, which I do not mention.

Instead, I say, I told you that bird had a chance.

He smiles, barely able to contain his secret, and says, You sure did.

And now Earl feels that he has earned forgiveness. And my son is buried on a western slope of the Cascade Mountains.

RESURRECTION MARY

In freezing rain, a pickup slides to a stop where I stand ready. The wind comes horizontally, painting white ice on fields, roads, fenceposts. Dark spirits, sensing vulnerability on such a night, rush in chaotic flocks over the land, chattering and obscuring. Before the pickup window opens, I appear in full view, framed by the door and hazy in the wet glass, my smile cheery as a daisy in winter. Two young men sit in the front seat, blowing warmth into their hands. I chose these two when I saw the headlights up the highway. But I am surprised to see there is a another one, in the back, an old man. He thrusts his fists into his jacket and holds his eyes forward, like a child accused of cheating. I am unprepared for three.

The driver says Where's your car? His name is Caleb.

I have no car, I reply. Usually it's fine to walk here.

Jeffrey, the passenger, says, You must have walked a long way. Nothing around.

I look up the road, squinting, contemplating. The longer I hold this moment, the deeper I set the hook. But should I? I've attempted three only once, and failed. I look back and see Jeffrey study me—not my body but my face. The fear is heavy in his eyes and on his breath. It manifests as sadness, resignation, but beneath that he is terrified. Like black water rushing beneath pack ice. I have to try.

I say, Storm just came out of nowhere.

Well, says Caleb, do you need a ride?

I look at him and hold it. He is inscrutable, with the fierce face of an owl feeding chicks, delicately. I look at Jeffrey, whose eyes water in the cold, whose mouth is soft.

Would you mind? I ask.

Course not, Caleb says. Get in.

I turn to the rear door, but the old man doesn't budge. Neither does he move his head but I hear him say, Leave three hours late, now you want to pick up stray women. This rate I'll be dead before Wisconsin.

Jeffrey says, I can scooch over. And so he does, straddling the drive shaft lump. The truck is just as cold inside. The hole for a radio is stuffed with rags. The cab must reek with the odors of mildew, petroleum, and men. But I am spared of this sense.

I arrange myself on the seat, taking half a man's width, and hold my hat in my lap. Jeffrey excuses himself, reaches across me, pulls the truck door shut.

All set? Caleb asks.

The old man strikes the back of the seat and says, For Christ's sake, drive! We want to make Montaner by morning—it ain't gonna happen pickin up whores roadside.

Caleb works the shifter until the truck catches a gear. The tires spin and the tail drifts out as we take to the road. He looks at me around Jeffrey's solemn profile. Here comes the unavoidable question.

Where you heading?

I wince. How many times have these three words spilled out on a highway in America? A triptych of words that bear all the images of possibility, promise, tragedy. For ten generations, the phrase endures without improvement, a tired formula that signifies for so many a pivot in their course, whose simple question marks the interminable movement and collision of people across this continent, helping and hurting, saving and killing, inspiring a thousand dreadful stories of a folklore drawn down by its coarseness, its banality, its weak chicory facsimile of the European masters. It's a sorry phrase, but it's our phrase, and I seek it every night.

Just to the cemetery, I say. And so we are off.

Under pressure of the wind, the truck begins to drift across the shoulder line, and Caleb corrects it. He says, What cemetery? Nothing for the next fifty miles but corn and Casey's.

You'll see it when I show you, I say. It's easy to miss. I can walk from there.

How far?

Not far.

I could just drive you home—it's no problem.

The old man interjects, Take the lady where she wants, all right?

Caleb lets out a breath and adjusts his rear-view mirror. Jeffrey balls his fist and bounces it on Caleb's knee, just once.

Are you traveling far? I ask. Are you from around here?

Jeffrey says, We're going to Idaho. He hovers his hand over his mouth when he talks, surely because he feels we are too close.

Driving straight through? I ask.

Naw, stopping in Montana. He adds, If this storm don't blow us off the road.

And you started where?

Middling County, basically, Caleb says. Not far back. But it was a heck of a lot warmer down there, I'll tell you what.

They laugh together awkwardly—although it wasn't quite a joke, it was good enough.

I nod. And now it's time for me to be quiet, and let silence fall over the cab, let their minds begin to work until their energies betray them and I grow familiar with their particular fear. All of it will come. It feels heavy and oppressive, like a cold fog in a river bottom. Each man has been nurturing this fear, what they feel necessary for survival, since their memories began. They are artisans of the material, turning fear into rage, bitterness, hatred, contempt. It destroys their perception and deprives them of tranquility. A person at peace would have mentioned my dance-hall dress, my impractical pearly shoes, my rakish bonnet unaffected by sleet. But they see none of it, so bright are their fantasies. We sit in silence and hear the tires howl and the windshield wipers snap and the tailpipe rumble. They clear their throats. From the back seat the old man snuffs his nose repeatedly, a bloodhound blasting a scent.

Ordinarily it's just one man. Take last night. A bald, bearded man somewhere in the disoriented middle of his life, towing a boat. His vast vehicle, black as a water moccasin, swallowed up his small form. So much car for so little man.

I could use some company, he said, and cleared lunch wrappers from the passenger seat. He expressed surprise at how easily I climbed into the car.

I told him I was lonely too, to measure his excitement and vulnerability. He dropped his guard and began explaining how badly his wife disrespected him, for his priorities, his taste in entertainment, his political views.

He confessed, We both knew I was a consolation prize when she married me. The other boyfriend, her so-called 'great love,' got religion one day and said she wasn't good enough. So she gets me. I guess I made it worse cause of all that. Anyway. She hates my dad because one Christmas she made him a sweater and he put it on his beagle. But it's my job to hate that old bastard, not hers.

He turned and smiled at me, whitened teeth behind whiskers. He said, Not sure why I'm telling you this. After a moment's reflection, he added. She's pretty, though, I'll grant her that. Even now, after everything.

Then he looked at me, one wrist draped over the wheel, and said, Not as pretty as you, though.

I told him I thought we could talk more easily if he pulled over. He glanced at me with eagerness, his thumbs tapping the steering wheel. He guided the giant vehicle to the shoulder with intense concern for his boat, craning his neck and checking mirrors. But once he parked, he dropped out of his door without a word and came around the car. By the time he reached my door, he was readying parts of his clothing—buttons, zippers, all the gates that restrain our wild impulses. And when I said no I really just wanted to talk, to just sit still together along the road for a while, he said he knew better, he knew that game, and he came for me through the open door. He missed the running board with his small western boot and stumbled. He glared as if it were my doing. Now his fear had grown to a lopsided mushroom larger than himself—fear of embarrassment, of public shame, of the cruel voice that condemns him with almost every thought. And the fear transformed to aggression and he made a little hop up to the cab and lunged for me.

When he seized nothing, when his stout arms collapsed on themselves, the aggression melted and there was nothing but unadulterated fear. A boy who's seen a ghost. Now I could commence my promise.

It all happens in less than a second.

First, the scene of my demise unfolds before me, and at the moment of impact it blackens, and my awareness shifts to the heavens and I breathe deeply. I reach in all directions, past the moon, planets, farther out into nebulae where stars are born, into undulating mesh of dark matter—I open myself to all this energy and let it fill me from the balls of my feet to the crown of my head. And then, empowered by such a charge, I pounce on the man.

He feels nothing but the impact of the energy—no flesh or nails or hot breath—just the overwhelming force flattening him backward and crushing him against the road bed. I fly at him like a great cat, muscular and beautiful, and thrust my heart-breaking face into his, blasting energy so his eyes stick open and dry and he has to witness my control and determination. His face thus open and his spine flattened and his skull shocked, he becomes as tender as an orchid petal. Holding my terrible, dazzling gaze, filling his field of vision, I sap his amygdala until it ceases to function. I seize the hippocampus into a trembling suspension. I flush the man of adrenocorticotropic hormone and epinephrine and norepinephrine and corticotropin-releasing factor. He becomes, in moments, physiologically incapable of fear.

Then I release him, my remaining fury dissipating into the night. He rolls to his side and hugs his knees to his chest and begins to sob, gently.

I stood with my arms crossed and my chin lowered, smiling like a sister. There's no need to be sad, I told the small man. I extended my arm and hand as you would to help someone up. But just far enough he couldn't reach it.

The man sat up, elbows on knees, eyes looking beyond the road with an expression of simple wonder.

I don't know why, he said. He wiped his cheeks with flat palms and said, I don't know why. This never happens.

Through his eyes, now, emerged his four-year-old self. The self who nursed a wounded toad in a box beneath his bed until his father found it. The one who searched for his lost classmate in a straw maze in the barn and hugged her when she was found. Who cried when he saw his grandfather's shelf of medicine. Who escorted a caterpillar from the street to a milkweed in a school lot where older boys chased him down like a rodeo calf.

Temporarily depleted of his anger reserves, drained of the fear he had cultivated since the sap rose in him—now he could listen and receive.

Why are you wearing that dress? He asked. You look so old fashioned.

I came from a dance, I said. Thank you for asking.

Did you enjoy the dance? Do you like dancing? Were you with a boyfriend? His questions came urgently, earnestly.

I did. I do. I was with my husband. We are both gone now.

His face fell into concern, but before he could ask more questions, I said, I want to show you something.

I led him down a tractor road along a drainage ditch and up a gradual slope until we could see the horizon curving in the arc of the planet. Lights dotted the night—distant grain elevators, wind turbines, cell towers, urban glow from crossroad towns.

Just wait, I said. We're patient.

The man stood with arms hanging loosely, shoulders curved, chin up.

Car tires cried shrill on the highway, the lights of industry glowed, a breeze carried agricultural dust.

But then, all that faded, and the phantoms of the lost prairie emerged. First a flock of a thousand pigeons, feathers of light in gold and blue, rushed overhead. A ghostly avian aurora. A herd of tiny deer, whose translucent legs glowed fine as silk strands, bounded from the ditch. A troop of purple hairy men came just after and chased them with ancient weapons. A wagon train of prairie schooners rumbled from beyond the horizon toward us, steel-wrapped wheels sparking against the stones of the field, the driver a pink smear of light, drooping in exhaustion, barely able to lift his whip against the draft horse, whose eyes glowed white and rolled back like enormous eggs. And along the distant ridge, in silhouette from an unseen glow, marched a line of mastodon. They might have been cut of art paper, but they shone deep blue, like ocean water at dusk, a blue so dark it only appears against black. One mastodon lifted her trunk, rolled back her head, and bellowed a note of doleful horns. The last of the herd, a small one whose curling tusks outsized his head, stumbled, fell back from his position, then ran to catch the others, and then they all disappeared beyond the horizon.

We saw spectres from all ages, walking in solemn luminescence across the molested land. But it was no mourning. Only witness to existence, the evidence of everything. I explained things to the man. He listened, asked few questions. I let him see my vulnerability, admitted that I wanted the respect of the mastodon, because they're the elders of the phantom world. He looked at me with pathos, and then let his gaze drop to the ground, unfocused. I gave that man a brief respite, so that he might see the world clearly, without the fog of fear, so that he might believe in a future of kindness and security. I fulfilled my promise, as best I could.

Dark spirits came then, as magpies to a carcass, chattering and circling, sensing the man's vulnerability. I swatted at them, shooed them. They formed a bunch between us and the man's vehicle, obscuring it, erasing light. I flew at them and they scattered.

I stood by the roadside and waved as the man left. He used his turn signal and accelerated up the road delicately. He returned my wave and was gone. Then the mustard seed of fear began to take hold again in his acid belly, and I will never know if he gained what he needs to control it. But we made the effort. We resisted the inevitable descent.

These three men—Caleb, Jeffrey, and the old man—they won't be so easy. They are comfortable riding in silence. By now most men would have started conversation. Some men joke, some confess, some flirt, everyone talks, eventually. But not these three. They sit like prisoners, wholly preoccupied. This impermeability makes them so much more difficult. And there are three.

Caleb points to the glove box. Jeffrey gives me a polite glance and reaches over, taking a pack of cigarettes. He lights two and gives one to Caleb. He passes the pack back to the old man, who grunts his acceptance. We continue riding.

In earlier days, when I felt my most capable, when legends of my practice had spread among the living and the dead and I believed the stories they told, on a humid summer's night, I attempted this many. Three MBA students in a German sedan drove home after a wild night in the city. They saw me in their headlights almost too late and slammed the car into a slide, then reversed wildly and greeted me through open windows.

I thought they would be simple. The one in the back seat feared he would never be loved. The front passenger feared the others would recognize him as an imposter to their elite caste. And the driver feared the disdain of his parents, where even a scratch on that car would represent his hopelessness. They were polite at first, giddy, speaking in a slang of their invention. But inevitably the one in the back reached out to try the seam of my dress and found nothing there. He began to scream, 'What the fuck are you?' and the driver pulled violently off the road.

Even then, I didn't give up on my promise. I had never endured failure. I beckoned them out of the car, but only the front passenger came, to prove himself to the other two. His fear of me was over-ripe and reeking, but his terror of embarrassment was stronger. Encouraged by his vulnerability, I flew at him. But in my eagerness, I used too much force and passed through. My advance hit the car and I imprinted hand marks on the door frame— deep impressions in the steel that would later appear in testimonials of my legend, identical to those in the gate of the cemetery where I was buried.

I turned and got to the fallen man, and I reduced him to his boyhood and made him wait—just for two seconds, I said, while we got the others.

Sometimes the burst of energy manifests as light, a pop and flash visible for miles, and the phantoms of night pause and look toward me. In those days I savored their attention. People are the most interested and amazed. The common animals skitter wide-eyed and respectful. They see something extraordinary has happened in the fabric of space, in the membrane between corporeal and ethereal. It fueled my legend. Only the most ancient creatures ignored my concocted events. The mastodon showed the least interest.

Such a blast of light came from inside the sedan as I rushed at the driver, who I considered the most difficult of the three. But he also ducked in time—not a reaction to my move, which isn't possible, but rather a premeditated act already in motion when I pounced. And so I glanced off this man, knocking some of his senses askew, but not all of them. As I repositioned, the dark spirits arrived in a dense flock, and burrowed in the vulnerable man. By the time I chased them away, he was sick.

I finally admitted failure, and didn't attempt the backseat man who had originally groped me. He was screaming, pressing himself down into the crease of the seat, as if he might push himself into the safety of the trunk. His face was distorted, his eyes pathetic—now, another kind of child, but one filled with absolute terror, rather than compassion. I had broken the fundamental tenet of my promise, leaving more suffering in the world, not less. Adding more fear to men, rather than taking it away. All three were compromised. I retreated and drifted around the fields aimlessly for nights, until my resolve returned.

By the time they reached their home down state, the boys had recovered and invented a story that would make my legend vulgar. I had been their willing servant, and they had completed their rite of conquest. How many friends and sons will they infect with this fable? It's possible that I'm still making up for this cruel math, in every promise that follows that night.

So what makes me think I can manage these three men after such a failure? Every point of reason suggests I should leave them immediately, spring that rattling door open and drop into the night like a scarf in the wind. But I can't give it up, yet. It would be another wasted night and although the debt of life can never be repaid, I believe it can be reduced. This keeps me in the seat. I think, Perhaps if I try to understand…

What are your plans in Idaho? I ask.

Caleb grips the wheel with both hands and says, We have a duty, ma'am.

Call me Mary, I say. What duty?

Patriotic duty, ma'am, that's all. We have a situation at the border. Intruders.

The old man erupts from behind, Caleb can you shut your trap and turn the goddamn radio on?!

Radio's broke, Dad. Broke since we got it.

I feel the old man kick the back of the seat. What kind of man are you, Cal, can't even get a radio in your truck. And you can't keep your mouth shut, neither, telling every whore comes along our plans.

Then the old man's face is right behind my ear as he says to me in a low tone, Don't you breathe a word of this to no one, ever. You hear me, girl? Not a god damned soul. You never seen us, never had a conversation, nothing. Or we come for you next.

Caleb glances in the rear-view mirror. His voice grows tauter, fiddle strings tuned tight. That's enough, Dad. Have a drink.

Jeffrey puts his hand on Caleb's thigh. Caleb pushes the hand away quickly, but leaves his on the seat. They both look ahead. I smile at them, but they won't meet my eyes.

Have a drink, the old man mutters. The kid tells me to have a drink. Like that's all I got left in this life. You have a drink, you wuss.

He snuffs outward again, bloodhound. His voice tails off, muttering, You have a god damn drink.

I am still thinking this group may be wrong for my promise tonight. I am considering leaving the cab of the truck while it blasts 70 mph down an icy highway in Illinois. They will argue about what happened for the rest of their lives. But come Idaho, it will all fade in the urgency of their crusade.

But there is Caleb's hand gripping the wheel as if to wring it dry. There is Jeffrey's right knee pumping up and down like a mad oil derrick. There is the old man snuffing and snuffing and kicking, a toddler in an airplane seat. There is sickness to be healed. They feel sorry for me, that is plain, and they are not seduced. But there is a greasy smoke of fear from them that will yield no good in this world. And the bed of the truck is full of weapons, I can feel that too. It would have been easy to surmise this, but I didn't have to. So it continues.

In the sleet beside the road I can see phantoms. A woman in bare feet and a summer dress peers into a drainage ditch, alone. She glows light green, frets her hands against her dress, glances up at me as we pass. A family of coyotes radiate in slack-limbed rust-colored form, heads below their shoulders, all in a file trotting the highway just as we pass through them. Another woman hangs over the guard rail of a bridge, her body bent as a sapling—legs in the road, head hanging over the side like squash on a vine. A man comes on all fours up the embankment onto the shoulder, dragging a limp child. He and the child glow orange—their faces follow as the truck passes. A translucent whitetail deer bolts just beyond the weak headlights and runs, springing from yellow line to line, then vanishes in the dark. A family of long-legged raccoons, barely visible in the dark red of pomegranate, swim through the young corn where in life they gorged themselves.

The men beside me see none of this. I don't know why. I never saw it either while I was mortal. I search for the mastodon, for the bison, the older beasts. They are not here tonight.

Jeffrey looks at me, smiles, then looks away. Hand over mouth he says, I love that vintage dress. If you don't mind my saying. Must be cold though. You lose your coat?

Thank you, I say. You notice things.

He waits for me to answer and he gets no satisfaction.

You're married? He asks, pointing to my ring finger.

I was, I say.

Oh I'm so sorry.

Caleb glances and clears his throat. He shakes his head as condolence.

The sleet turns to heavy rain, overwhelming the wipers. Caleb slows the truck.

Can I ask, Jeffrey says, what happened? If you don't mind my asking?

I tell them the truth. They won't remember it anyway, so long as I fulfill the promise.

We were in Chicago. A night like this, actually, and the sleet made a rime on the rooftops, the cars, the railroad tracks, umbrellas. The whole city sparkled, white lights on icing. We were out dancing. We were always out dancing. The only time we didn't fight was when we danced, and then we were perfect—two vines as one trunk, swans in a lagoon, hands in prayer. We barely spoke but only danced and drank until the club thinned out. Word spread that travel was dangerous. I wanted to stay. He wanted to go. He called me a drunk; I called him a monster. We glared at each other and danced another number. Finally, I agreed to go. I had my shoes in my hand, like I do now.

My gosh, you do, says Jeffrey. I totally missed that.

Me too, says Caleb, with a whiff of unease.

I continue.

It was easier to walk on the ice in my bare feet. I felt nothing. I slid and danced. My husband barked at me. He tried to catch me but slid on the sidewalk and fell hard on his side. As he pulled himself up, he slid and fell again. I laughed. Eventually we got in the car. He was furious with me. He called me a tart. I called him a coward. I felt the back of his hand crash my mouth, tasted blood, but felt no pain. I hit back, a fist to the fleshy ear. He kept bringing the back of his hand, weighted with his class ring. The car slid and drifted on the icy pavement. With the sudden loss of traction came a disorientation I had never felt—a nauseating, total loss of control. Cars honked, as we drifted in our ton of metal and glass. People called warnings. I cursed him until I didn't know what I was saying—brutal, hurtful words that erupted straight from my gut. He reached over me, driving his shoulder into my head, unlatched my door, and pushed me out. I tumbled into the street, sliding on my dress, felt the wet cold and the asphalt pebbles on my hands and thighs. I belonged to the night, the weather, the careening cars in a horrific dance in an ice-clad city.

I pause my story, waiting for one of them to draw a breath—the sign that someone is about to say something. None of them did. The old man snuffed, but I could feel his attention. I continued.

While I tumbled down the street, followed by my husband, another car raced toward us. It was one of those new, enormous sedans, with bench seats you could sleep on. From where I slid, splayed like a lizard, head up observing—I saw three people in the front seat. A man and two children. So plain in the streetlights, in all the glamorous reflection of the avenue. The man's face was compressed in anger. But the children just stared without judgment. A boy and a girl, chins just above the dashboard, looked out at this lady in a dress in the street, at this reckless man swerving a car with side door flapping. The boy, the girl, whose faces were painted with wonder, seemed to ask 'Is this something that happens?' My sight grew shockingly keen. I could see the wet of the girl's lip around a crooked lower tooth. The boy's delicate nostrils flared. Their eye color was identical, a golden-brown around dilated pupils. The steering wheel was enormous, thin, light blue, crenellated. A toy elephant stood on the dash, unprepared for the crash.

Then I lost their faces behind the great chrome bumper and the car bounced over me and demolished my husband's car such that the motor rammed through his ribcage.

I end the story, without explaining the moment I made my promise to those children. Because that would be showing my hand, of course, to tell these three men that I committed myself to that girl and boy, to combat the source of violence in their world. It's strange, I suppose, that I made this promise while I had only moments to live. Did I know I would have a chance to fulfill it, after dark, for as long as we can comprehend? How could I have known? I had no faith in any existence after death, which is why I danced, why I drank, why I spent my nights with that thrilling, talented, awful man. But I made the promise anyway, and remain just as committed to it now, to drain the fear, drop by drop, night after night.

We listen to the highway noises for a while. I wear a thousand-yard stare, as if in a trance. I await their reactions, to see if it helps me understand.

Jeffrey says, So you were... you're okay now?

Oh yes, I say. I'm fine.

The old man says, You should of listened to him. Should of gotten the fuck out of that club when he said so.

Jeffrey says, That's not fair. It's not like he's the boss of her.

Caleb whispers, Dude.

The old man strikes, quick as a snake. He stiff-arms the back of Jeffrey's head with his flat palm. In that instant, I see his fingernails, wooden and yellow.

Just as quickly, Caleb whips his right arm around the back of the seat, swatting at his father, but makes no contact.

The old man seethes, No fairy's gonna backtalk me. You keep your opinions to yourself. Better yet, you get yourself some proper opinions. Afore they eat you up in Idaho. I may be dead by then so I won't be able to provide protection and Caleb ain't worth a shit …

Caleb yells, Shut the fuck up! Just shut up! Right? You fucking hear me?

The old man flicks Caleb in the parietal bone—a practiced flick that makes a sharp rap. Caleb swings back again, the truck swerves across the center line, and his hand glances over Jeffrey's forehead on its way.

Oh I'm sorry, Caleb says. His face is suddenly compassionate. Then he lectures, Dad if you don't behave yourself I swear I'll turn this truck around and cancel the whole mission. I'll do it. Seriously, I will.

I have no business taking on these three. If I think I can control this situation, I have learned nothing these many years. They aren't worth it. Then again, if I could fulfill the promise with these men, how much suffering might I prevent? It could be my greatest night, could reverse the damage I've caused. But no, it's no good, this situation.

I say, Can we pull over? You can drop me off here. It's fine: I can walk.

Caleb studies me. I can see he's about to argue, to point out rational objections. But he refrains. He says, Sure. Just let me find a spot.

The old man shouts from the back seat, No one's stopping this truck! You think I got time to kill? We let her out next filling station. That's what.

Caleb sighs, That doesn't make sense, dad. We didn't give her a ride to just take her to some random gas station.

Then Caleb says to me, quietly, Don't worry.

Jeffrey raises his hand, almost drops it to my knee in reassurance, but stops just short.

The old man continues yelling, Who you telling not to worry? Some god damn tramp you don't even know? How about my worry? Sitting in the back of this truck worrying about one last chance I get to do something decent, worthwhile? For once! Just one thing before I keel over. And you messing it up over some god damn girl. How about that worry?

Jeffrey turns in his seat to give the old man a look of understanding, of calm. Look, he says, it's gonna be all right. We'll just pull over quick and drop her off and then we'll be on our way. It's the right thing to do.

The old man spits his reply, punctuating each word, Who... are.. you to tell me what's all right or what's not? You prancing through life like a girl with a pecker putting notions in people's heads, notions in my son's head? I've told you before and I'm not warning you again to not backtalk me. You shut up. You follow orders.

Caleb shouts, a sudden eruption, Nobody asked you, Dad! Nobody fucking asked you!

The old man punches Caleb's headrest, I don't need permission. When I say we don't stop, we don't stop.

Guys, Jeffrey pleads. Can we just...

Don't bother, Caleb says.

No, says Jeffrey, listen guys. We're going to make it to Idaho just fine. Emotions are just running high. Everybody take a deep breath.

The old man is silent now, but I can feel his raging anxiety. He is overwhelmed with it, speechless. Perhaps I should take him on right now, in the moving truck. I could subdue him in two seconds, probably. But that could be too much for Caleb. It could cause a crash. I just need to get out of the truck and let this one go.

Could you crack the window? I ask Jeffrey. Just give me a hand with this crank?

Sure, says Jeffrey, and he begins to move.

But suddenly the old man punches and kicks Caleb's seat, a tantrum. Keep that god damned window closed! Freezing enough in here! This girl's got some spell over you two fairies and it's about to ruin our mission, you doing everything she says.

I begin to consider again taking the old man on now. But I want to calm the situation, bring some net of control over it.

We don't have to pull over, I say.

That's right, listen to the fucking whore! The old man screams. She knows who's the god damn boss around here. Thank you, you fucking whore.

That's too much. I turn to face him over the seat.

He stares back, bewildered, furious. What the fuck are you looking at?!

Caleb reaches out a hand toward me. It's gentle but I retreat instinctively. He withdraws his hand and says, Sorry.

Jeffrey puts a hand on Caleb's shoulder and says, Just keep your eyes on the road, buddy. Just drive.

I see the old, twisted car bumper on the road as we speed toward it. Caleb does not.

Dark spirits have gathered outside, flying across the road like torn shingles in the wind, as if they sense something is going wrong here. They obscure Caleb's vision, though he doesn't know it. To him it's just one of those strangely black nights.

The line of the wheel draws over the bumper precisely, and the explosion of the tire jolts their hearts into racing.

Caleb grips the wheel against the sudden pull of the truck. We're fine, we're fine, he says. Just a flat. Goddamn old bumper—I didn't see it.

He slows the truck and searches for a wide spot on the shoulder.

The old man lets out a sob and drops his face in his hands.

How could you not see that, you dumb shit? he cries. You can't even drive right, for fuck's sake. Now how much time are we gonna lose fixing this wheel? If it can even be fixed? All this because you pick up some girl and get distracted? You dumb shit. You dumb, fucking shit ... I might as well die now, with not a god damn thing to show but a dumb shit son doesn't know how to drive.

He moans, his head still down.

With remarkable speed, Caleb retrieves the jack and puts it in place. The rest of us are out of the truck now. Jeffrey crouches to help. The old man puts his fists in his jeans pockets and thrusts his face toward the scene, his cap low over his brow. I prepare to leave, considering what I'll tell them that might be plausible but so subtle it vanishes from their memories soon.

The old man says, It'll fall, you set it up like that.

Caleb is under the truck now, looking for damage to the axle. He looks up at his ranting father. Would you just shut up for a minute? Seriously, can I just fix this without you going on like a fucking idiot?

The old man kicks the fender and the truck sways uneasily on its jack.

I want to get away from this man. He is unsalvageable. He just needs to die, preferably somewhere far from others, where his hot energy will decay toxically, like spent uranium. When this man dies, no one will want to be near what manifests.

But Jeffrey stabilizes the truck, offers encouraging words to Caleb, who takes short breaths, straining to pull off the wheel. The tire is a shredded bloom of rubber. A black peony.

The old man stiff-arms the truck with both hands. The truck sways again, dangerously.

Jesus! Jeffrey yells. Fucking stop it, dude!

The old man takes a long step toward Jeffrey and puts his face close. Don't you fucking call me 'dude.' Call me 'sir,' or better yet, don't say nothing.

Jeffrey looks him back in the eyes and laughs. You sad, little man, he says.

Without warning, the old man jerks up his knee and rams it between Jeffrey's thighs. Jeffrey folds forward and drops.

Caleb is up on his feet now rushing toward his father. He grabs the old man's shoulders and slams his back into the truck. The old man releases a bellow of air and Caleb stands back, surprised by what he's done.

I am wondering what would happen if I unleash my promise on them now. I am concerned but also curious. Could they survive? In all that clash of energy, would I survive?

Caleb goes to help Jeffrey. The old man drops to all fours, pulls in a wheezy breath, and then scrambles to the back of the pickup. He opens the hatch and retrieves an assault rifle. He turns to face all three of us, gun hanging from both hands, chest heaving. I am thinking, Now that gun has to go off. It's inexorable.

But Caleb moves as lithe as a ferret, snaps the rifle away and strikes his father in the head with the butt. One, quick, well-practiced jab of the gun stock to the super orbital ridge, and the old man's skull splits like a dropped pumpkin.

He falls, dead.

I know this before the boys do. They are on their knees trying to revive him. They are both sobbing, not for the old man but for the shock of the moment. All the rest of their lives will be defined by this one act, and every decision made thereafter will cascade from Caleb's act and they both know it. There are no reactions equal to this event, so they do the best humans can do—they cry. They shake the old man. Caleb attempts CPR but only manages to crack a rib.

For a minute they sit back on their knees and pant, looking at the corpse. They turn and look at me, and then at each other.

Jeffrey puts his arms around Caleb to console him. Don't shut down on me now, he says. We'll get through. None of this matters. Only us, right?

Caleb looks at me with embarrassment.

Jeffrey continues. We can go to the border, do your duty—do it in your old man's name. Anything. Just don't shut down on me, Caleb. Don't go away.

He's shivering now, his lower mandible trembling visibly. Saliva drips from Jeffrey's lower lip but he is unaware. He stares at the other man.

Caleb is weak, leaning to one side, his gaze swaying like a willow branch, to one side and then the other, without purpose.

I wonder: Have I caused this? If I hadn't chosen their truck this dark night. If I hadn't entertained the possibility I could manage three this time. If I hadn't turned around and looked at the old man. If I hadn't made the promise in the instant before that boy and that girl disappeared from my sight.

Then I realize they are watching me. Caleb looks with curiosity and perhaps a slight malevolence. I am a witness. Jeffrey considers my incongruity—my vintage dress and pearly shoes—and wonders how I came to be involved in all this. The dark spirits gather in a spiral high above—you can hear the chattering. Across the plain the phantoms emerge in shifting light, a palette of pale radiance. They lift their heads and stare. They wait to see: will there be a flash this time?

Caleb asks, What will you do?

I have no choice. I tilt my head back and begin the practice, filling with energy drawn down from the fabric of everything, and then I fly at the men.

It's easy and explosive. Their fear is immense and ready—as sharp as quinine, as rich as lily dew. And the blast of light comes like a thunderclap, rumbling in waves across the dark and wet fields. The specters have never seen such an emergence as this. They lower to the ground as it passes.

With placid smiles and moist eyes, Caleb and Jeffrey follow me down the steep bank to a path through a hedge, ground too depleted to plant, where wicked honeysuckle taps what nutrients remain, where dead osage branches grasp at a dull sky.

The young men see the specters in the field now.

How are they so beautiful? Caleb asks.

Are they always there? Jeffrey asks.

Seven children made of silver light dance in a circle. A pale yellow mother lifts a baby in one arm and a cat in another and stares. Crows, black on the outside but illuminated in blue from within, flap a lazy path around us and continue west. Long-legged raccoons of multi-colored light scatter up the trunks of dead trees. A farmer stands at the rise of a hill, arms down and fingers curled—he just looks away and away and away.

The mastodon come up over the distant rise, from where the farmer looks. They walk in a line, trunk to tail, electric blue beasts along the horizon, making their migration across the spirit of grasses and the memory of savanna. A bull rolls his head back and calls, a chorus of foghorn and brass, an exaltation of the wonder of things, and then turns toward the place where I stand. Our gaze meets, for the first time. But even so, the beasts never stop marching. Their tusks nearly touch the ground and sweep up, a repeated curl, same as seashells, same as galaxies.

All phantoms, near and far, watch the mastodon pass.

When I explain it all to the young men, they barely need to hear the words. On nights when we see mastodon, my promise is easily kept. In the sight of such a thing, who needs reminder of their mortality? Who needs to hear that every action prompts a reaction, continuously through time, that none of us are exempt from the balance of forces? Who clings to fear, when it's so obviously irrelevant?

Then the young men, Caleb and Jeffrey, work together like classmates as I watch from the guard rail. They repair the truck. They wrap the old man's body in a faded nylon tarp. They struggle him into the truck bed, working his stubborn corpse, its arms falling out of the shroud again and again.

They look at me and say nothing and leave with a short spin of the spare tire on gravel.

And although the old man's body speeds away down the highway, tucked in a bed of weapons, his energy remains behind. I feel it coalesce and rise. Soon it will gather in his form. It may be a color of light, it may be the absence of light. But very soon, he will be here. He will haunt the same highway that I rule.

He will come to know Resurrection Mary.

ALL I'VE GOT FOR YOU

All right kids, I hear you coming up the trail through the woods to my cemetery. You think you're being quiet, but you're not. You trip on roots and giggle, shushing each other. Any old geezer could hear you. And I'm no geezer—I'm a spirit in the prime of my afterlife with excellent senses plus an inexplicable intuition. And although I just barely remember your voices from when you were young, say around fourth grade, my intuition tells me exactly who you are. You are the Trundle twins, Greta and Ada, with your boy friend for life, Felix Fuglesen. All grown up and about to graduate. You girls are like sisters to him, sometimes like mothers. And poor Felix is torn between loving your attention and wishing another dude were here. Well, Felix, that may be the least of your worries. Soon I'll learn what kind of people you three have become, and what kind of terror you deserve.

Up here on the hilltop there's an empty grave. The edges are as eroded as an abandoned gravel mine. The bottom of the grave is deep and as black as the pupils of the owl who calls from the bluff across the river. Did you like that? When I was teaching I would have called that a 'tortured metaphor' or maybe 'purple prose,' but these days, who gives a shit? My point is: The night is perfect. See how those trees, those hickories and hackberries—see how they encroach the cemetery, reaching to join the tips of their branches against the purple sky? In their tangle of branches, in the confusion of the wind, you see glimpses of the moon and Mars. It's god-damned perfect. Hawthorne would love this. I wonder if his old soul is still wandering around Concord? He certainly had issues to work out. One day I'll take a vacation from this gig and head east and see if I can find him.

But back to you kids.

You were nice when you were young. In second grade you joined my soccer camp and played for two years. Greta, you're a lefty; that's how I told you apart. Ada, you played goalie so you could sit in the grass and read. You laughed at my tiny hoop earring. And Felix, you were a natural striker, but you passed to the girls anyway, when you could have scored yourself. Are you still so kind? Or did this country beat that out of you, like it does to most young men? And girls, you might be surprised to know I remember that sweatshirt you made for me, which your mom insisted was your idea, which said 'World's Greatest Coach,' which I thought was a little trite when I first saw it, until Ada said, That is our opinion, so it's undisputable! And Greta added, in that laugh-talk of hers, You better wear it, Mr. Dudek— we'll be watching you! And I did wear it every time I changed the oil on my motorcycle, or cleaned the gutters, or raked mulch on the prairie flowers, or fixed a kid's bike. And sometimes you walked by with that enormous and terrified greyhound of yours, and you cheered.

But after that we lost touch, because I got killed.

I might have spoken at your commencement last week, as I did for so many graduating classes. By popular demand, I might add, because there's no point in humility now. I would have worn my tiny hoop earring, despite your teasing, and worn my hair a little too long in the back, and quoted rock musicians you don't know but will look up now, and told you there will be 40 million minutes in your life, if you're lucky, and they're ticking off even while I speak (so I probably should wrap it up and get off the stage, which got a laugh every time) and then declared that I would like to thank the extra special kids and proceeded to name every one of you, pointing at each one, without breathing until the end, when I took a comically long breath, and then whispered thank you right into the mic, and walked off to emotional applause. You missed that performance. So tonight, perhaps, I offer a performance of a less celebratory nature. I don't know yet. I hold that decision like Poe's pendulum on an upswing. First I must decide if you deserve it. I must determine whether you've turned into cruel little shits, brainwashed by their Righteous culture. The nicest kids often turn into the most wretched adults. Maybe because they're the most vulnerable? As if that matters now. Let's get on with it. Come on up my hill.

My goodness, you talk loudly. It echoes through the chill air of this hardwood forest.

Greta says, Come on, Ada! Keep up. We got to stick together so ghosties don't catch one of us alone hahaha!

I'm coming! Ada says. She is panting, and adds, You guys are going too fast. You can't enjoy this whole scene if you just run through it.

Greta trots back down the hill to her sister, her feet thumping.

She says, You need to start working out, sheesh!

I do yoga! Ada protests.

Felix has been running up and back on the trail, like a border collie, scouting the approach and returning to his girlies. Mostly he just listens. But when he comes back to Ada, he asks, Do you want a piggy back ride?

Ada stops and leans against a burr oak. She breathes hard, laughs, and says, I don't know if you're joking, but yes!

Greta says, You can't do that—what if you break your back, L'il FX?

This must be what they call him now. L'il FX. He's actually quite tall.

Greta says, What will you do if a ghostie shows up and we have to run?

Ada lets out a 'whoop!' as she jumps on Felix's back, and he groans theatrically, but then they continue up the hill at a brisk pace.

Look out ghosties! Ada cries, having caught her breath. Here comes the Terrible Trio!

Felix says, seriously, Do you think it really is Mr. Dudek? It could be true, you know.

I hope so! Says Greta. Plus lots of other ghosties!

Some people don't come back, says Felix.

Most people say they saw nothing, says Ada. It's not about the ghosts. It's about a night like this. Can you believe this night?

Then Ada says, L'il FX I'm slipping!

Sorry! Says Felix and he adjusts and they continue.

After a brief silence, Felix says, It is kind of spooky, TBH. I mean, the wind, and these branches, and it's getting dark. People have died, you know. Or disappeared.

Greta says, I don't know if that's true, haha. People say all kinds of shit. But if it's Mr. Dudek, how can that be bad?

They march up in silence again, watching their step, considering this. Oh Greta, if you had any idea. It can be bad. It can be very, very bad for some of my guests. But the question is: How do you define bad? Bad can be nothing, can't it—an utter disappointment? Expectations dashed—just to find that the world is plain and uninteresting. That seems pretty bad, in my world. But there's also the other kind of bad, the kind we see in the movies. That's what you want, isn't it? Well, we shall see.

Felix says, There's an empty grave up there. Supposedly. People fall into it. Nobody knows who the pit was for.

Not true, Felix. Many people know, but they don't talk about it. I'll tell you. My great uncle Nicholas once rested in this pit. He fought in everybody's favorite war, the war that spawned all the sentimental movies, the literary gift that never stops giving. Nick was a lieutenant under Patton.

He commanded the team who identified the dead after battles, who loaded up the bodies. One of his privates stepped on a mine nearby and Nick earned a purple heart. See, there's your story. But it gets better: Not long after he died, some rascals of Middling County dug him up. Why? For the metal in his teeth? For the war bonds he supposedly clutched? Because we are Poles, papists? Who knows? What I know is that it's in my god-damned cemetery now.

What you kids know is that it's after sunset under a crescent moon that cups a fiery Mars, and you have to use your phone lights to see your way through woods that might ignite at any moment in this drought. You hear the owl (an actual owl!) calling from the bluff. Crazy breezes lift the hair on your arms. Parched leaves fall down your collar. It's perfect.

And you do remember me. But do you know how it ended? Probably you've heard that Mr. Dudek was killed in a hunting accident here, and now he haunts the old family cemetery. Fair enough—that's a lovely tale. But if I had the privilege of teaching you AP Lit, I would ask: Does it make sense? Critical thinking is so hard these days. Reality is what we make of it! But does it make sense? An English teacher hunting at dusk? On land his family donated as a conservancy to the county? Hunting with a farmer who sold weapons and flags from his root cellar?

It does not make sense. There's your answer. It's a lovely tale, but a stupid story. It's out of character for me, and for the farmer who killed me. We were not hunting together. First of all, it was spring, when there is no hunting. Secondly, I was following the year's first yellow warbler through the woods near the property boundary, where the Fallendini farm borders ours. I hid in the brush with my camera and 700mm lens, hoping to use the last light of the day. Sonny Fallendini spotted the disturbance while patrolling his property on his four-wheeler. He yelled for me to come out. I did not, because he is not the boss of me. He accused me of being 'an illegal.' I ignored him. So he shot me. With buckshot that scattered across my torso, and I might have survived if one stray shot hadn't ripped a hole in my femoral artery. Recognizing the urgency, I ran back through the woods, spraying blood across the brush and forest floor. But very soon, I ran out of blood, and then there was nothing, just nothingness, and then I was back, as the wonderful illuminated husk I am now.

Sonny said we were hunting. His son Caleb backed up his story. The other neighbors shrugged. The school did not pursue the case. For a while, my brother Milo, the professor, tried to prove the crime. But he's a philosopher, and not very effective at life, and after his wife died, he gave up. And so the hunting story became reality. Not that I'm bitter. Not that I'm angry! Fuck those fuckers! I'm better off now. I have a purpose now.

Actually, I have two purposes. First, if the conservancy ever runs out of money, if some new Righteous politicians get on the county board and decide to sell this place to a developer or some rich fuck looking for a retreat to play with weapons—if any of those things come to pass, and they probably will, no one will want to buy land as haunted as this. Secondly, and probably more importantly, I get to assess how kids around here have turned out, and then give them what they deserve. You understand? Because the thing is, I'm almost as popular after dark as I was in life, with the young people, and so I can keep on giving, in my way. I mean, a person's death has to be worth something. Right?

Ah, now you're almost here! At the crest of the hill, where the trail ends at this small clearing of tall grass and lopsided headstones, I see you three pause. Girls, your legs are so long and skinny! All three of you—your pale skin glows in the dim moonlight. Your hay-colored hair flies outward on the wind. Such northern Europeans, you might be ghosts yourselves!

Aw, it's hard for me to look at you. I feel badly already, but that won't stop me. It must be done. A judgment must be handed down to you. The passive voice absolves me of blame. Oh screw that. Take your seats, kiddos, class is in session!

Greta asks, Is this far enough? We can say we got up here now, haha. Who votes for going back?

It's so cool, says Ada. She begins to walk forward by the light of her phone, and says, Whoa this person died in 1857! That's before the Civil War!

I wish I brought some paper, Felix says. We could have done a rubbing of these stones.

Oh my god don't touch them! Says Greta. She holds out her hands but doesn't follow the others.

Felix laughs. He holds his phone light under his chin, to light his face ghoulishly, and moans the cry of a cartoon ghost.

Stop it! Greta cries.

Oh come on, says Felix, it's just an old cemetery. Look, they're all Dudeks! Well, mostly. Over here there's a Hinrick. There's a Knox.

He draws a breath, then says, Oh shit—that one was just a baby.

The wind has picked up. The tree branches rub and groan. I'm grateful for the help. I wish I could get more help around here. You'd think there would be other spirits, but I've never seen a one. It makes no sense that all this family would have gone so peacefully. At least there should be some tasteful husks bobbing among the stones. I assume Uncle Nick would be here but he must be chasing his body across some other county. So this cemetery is totally dead. Ha!

Felix is the first to spot the empty grave. He says, Guys! Look. It's the pit they talk about.

Oh man, says Greta. Okay, I think that's enough.

Let's just check it out, Ada says. Come on, Greta, I'll hold your hand.

Ada reaches back, and Greta approaches slowly, with her hand outstretched, nervous, giggling, her phone light sweeping the ground.

Felix raises his phone, points it toward Uncle Nick's grave as he walks, and begins to record.

This is not allowed!

The show must begin immediately. I summon the energy I've learned to wield.

A harsh whispering insinuates from the darkness beyond the trees. It comes from all sides and grows in volume. The three kids stand still, eyes drawn, mouths just open. The whispering closes in toward them, becomes a static chorus like a plague of insects, and descends on them. When it arrives, a force tears their phones from their hands and it's dark! It's silent. Except for the wind and the knocking of the trees.

Oh shit! whispers Greta. Something took my phone!

What the fuck was that? Ada hisses.

Don't move, says Felix. Someone must be here.

They stand still, their knees bent, their arms held out as if they're balancing. Greta's legs are trembling. Ada makes an exaggerated frown and appears on the brink of crying. Felix stares hard at the edge of the woods, and then back at his friends.

Kids, before this ends, I want to apologize for the world. It is cruel, and it is trashed, and I know that it seems like all the bright mornings have been used up and crumpled and thrown away, like fast food garbage along the interstate. My generation made a lot of this mess, but that's nothing compared to what Sonny Fallendini's generation did, those selfish fucks, with all their bullshit idealism—it turns out they were just having a big god damn party and now it's over and here we are. So I'm sorry. This world is not for you. You are too kind, too thoughtful, too good. My intuition tells me this. So you qualify for the full haunt. The pendulum drops.

Frigid air creeps across the weedy ground and envelopes your ankles. You feel it rising, like walking into a river. No one says a word now, and you each feel horribly alone. As the coldness rises to your torsos, it compresses your lungs and it's hard to breathe. Then it rises to your chins, and over your mouths and noses, and now you can't breathe at all. You begin to know what it feels like to drown. Felix wiggles like an emerging fish, like he can shake off the pressure. The girls grasp at their throats, then flap their arms. When finally they all let go, and look at each other with desperation, sadness, love—the pressure stops. All three gasp.

Greta pants, That was totally fucking uncool! Seriously. Not acceptable!

Ada starts punching the air around her. Fuck you! she yells. I'm gonna punch you fucker, whatever you are, so get out of here!

I like their spirit.

Felix says, Girls, come on. Let's get in a group and look for our phones.

Don't tell us what to do, FX! We're pissed! Says Greta.

Yeah, let us be pissed! Says Ada.

Fine. Be pissed. But can we be pissed together and find our phones and get out of here?

They walk toward each other. Felix holds out a hand to each girl. When they touch, there is a devastating shock and a flash of blue light. They fall on their butts on the ground.

Why'd you do that? Ada accuses.

Do what? I didn't do anything, says Felix.

Guys let's not fight, says Greta, quietly. She is hugging herself now looking up at the trees.

She says, I don't feel so well.

Ada crawls to her. Greta says, Don't touch me! Something is wrong.

Now the ground begins to quake. Dirt sifts and rises above the leaves and sticks, the weeds and derelict grass. It's as if the earth is suddenly alive—and it is alive! Up from the dirt come insects of many forms, worms and beetles and larvae, dead and alive. The layer of insects rises up, buzzing and humming, and this blanket sweeps toward the kids, gaining in depth, until it's three feet high, approaching steadily like a wave.

No! Felix shouts. His voice is high. He searches for a weapon, or some defense.

The girls say, in a terrified whine, No … no … no!

All three run, but it's not nearly fast enough.

The wave of insects hits them and submerges them and the bodies of the kids thrash in a terrible, involuntary way—just the vague outline of human forms beneath this collective monster. It's not the insects' fault. Insects are good. There is no life without insects, and I still love life—that is the point of this place, this conservancy—to preserve what we still have of life. So it's not the insects doing this. I am doing this. It is being done by me.

The girls' thrashing becomes deliberate. It's clear they're fighting, sweeping their arms and hands at the insects, batting them away, emerging from the wave to catch their breath. They aren't giving in. Felix emerges with his shirt off and surfs the layer of insects to get to the girls and uses the shirt as a kind of net to uncover them.

I admire these kids. They have mettle. They have sand, as they used to say, when there was still hope in the world.

The insects disappear more quickly than they came, and return to their subterranean residence, to play their role in the cycle. The kids pant and hang their heads between their knees.

Enough, Greta says, holding up a hand. She keeps her head down, raises that hand in concession, and says, I've had enough.

Ada, her eyes closed, shouts, We're sorry! Okay?! For whatever we've done, we're sorry we did it.

Then Ada adds quietly, Just let us go and we'll do better.

Felix looks at the girls like a boy seeing a puppy, flat on the road. The wetness of his eyes reflects moonlight.

It is quiet for a while. Why would these girls apologize? Just because they're midwestern? Or is something else going on here? Why would they say they'll do better, like they had any hand in this terror? I would expect them to be angry, to be defiant and resentful. But when they are completely beat, instead, out comes this earnestness. This sincerity.

So …

My light appears at the edge of the cemetery—pale blue, softball-sized, hovering at eye level. When it has their attention, it darts—first to the mausoleum great grandpa had made, then to a hollowed tree trunk, and then to the open grave. My light hovers, so bright blue it's white at the center, just above Uncle Nick's grave.

Oh my god do you see that, Greta says.

Uh-hum, says Ada.

Felix says, Whaaat …

My orb begins to pulse. A plane of light radiates outward, then inward, with each pulse. It respirates like this, growing larger each time. The plane is bright and thin, like a great, circular blade. The kids remain on the ground, watching. With each pulse, the plane gets closer to their faces—to their necks.

Felix draws in a deep breath. Then he whispers, Okay.

He springs up and, remaining in a crouch, runs toward the girls with his arms outstretched to embrace them.

Come on! he says, We're getting the heck out of here.

The girls agree, and pivot to lift themselves up and begin to run just beyond Felix's embracing arms. It takes them a few steps before they realize he is no longer behind them.

A length of Virginia creeper rises from the ground and whips around Felix's legs. It tightens around his ankles and drops him with a thump. Then it begins to draw him back, toward the open grave, under the globe of light.

Felix grunts, claws at the ground with his fingernails, thrashes at his waist. His efforts make no difference.

Greta and Ada stop and look. No! They scream, and prepare to run.

But another Virginia creeper rises like a serpent in front of them, arching with its leafy tip at eye level. Both girls stop. Ada takes a small step and the vine lurches closer. They look at the vine. They look at Felix, who's nearly at the grave.

Felix sees this now. He struggles to hold his chin up and yells, Go! Just go guys! Don't worry about me! Seriously!

Greta looks at Ada. Ada looks at the vine.

Fuck you! she says, and runs.

Greta follows, pointing a finger at the vine, saying, Yeah! Fuck you!

The vine, of course, is in my control. I am the animation of the vine. So in a sense, the girls have just said Fuck you to me. They have a point.

Felix continues to plead with the girls to run away. The girls run toward him at full sprint, stumbling and tripping, still gaining ground. But the vine pulls him faster. The blue light descends into the depths of the grave and extinguishes, and the vine follows.

Then all three of you are at the edge of the grave. Felix hangs into it. His legs dangle into the darkness where my great uncle once rested. His fingers pull at the turf. Then his fingers join with the pale hands of each of the girls. These hands are so delicate, so unspoiled. They're like ice cream hands.

The wind halts.

The trees wait.

I release the vines.

Felix scrambles to his feet and helps you girls up too. You stare into the grave, then back at the cemetery, the trail where you arrived. You wait for something to happen. Nothing happens.

Okay, so...? Says Greta.

Do we just go now? Asks Ada.

Slowly, says Felix. Walk away slowly.

After one step, the whispering begins again in the woods. It rises in volume quickly, and surrounds them, and shrieks like a thousand locusts until …

Your phones return to your hands. You grip them but don't dare move.

Then there are bells. Deep bells toll from within the grave, like a clock tower ringing midnight. You see the blue light arise from the pit. It expands into a shimmering form, the spectral form of a human, who you once knew, and that form is me, who says,

It is I! Mr. Dudek!

And you kids, you see the opportunity. You just understand, your instinct tells you how to make the most of this awful turn of events. You turn away from me and you form a group, shoulder to shoulder, and you lift your phones at once to frame yourselves, your fresh and uncorrupted, terrified, delighted faces in those forward-facing cameras. And into the frame I appear, with my little hoop earring, and you get it: the perfect, perfect shot.

That's it, kids. You passed. That's all I've got for you.

Then you run.

Down the hill, in wild strides, to the gravel patch where you left Ada's car. And when you're inside, you are laughing, and crying, and hugging across seatbelts, because the thrill was harmless but terrifying too. What a gift! What a delight, to have a trouble that goes away and leaves a souvenir! And for a moment, you forget all of it, the whole mess we've left you, and for just a little while, you are unburdened and happy.

And I rest. I hang limply over the grave, the light of my husk diminished with exhaustion. I rest, in the light of the moon and Mars, in the murmur of the forest, held aloft by the possibility that this night's thrill may in some way inspire you to keep your heads up, and resist the decline, and remain kind. Please, remain kind. And also, I hold the possibility that this piece of land may survive a while longer, and that one day you kids may return.

THE CORRUPTION OF TIME

Ms. Dalyrimple says the neighbors want to know what's going on in the garage. To Milo, her husband, this is the beginning of the end. Now he and Arnie must finish soon, and see the thing through, because it's just a matter of time before their project is revealed and they're forced to stop. It must be serious if Ms. Dalyrimple has raised the issue. Ordinarily Deloris (he must stop thinking of her as Ms. Dalyrimple) ordinarily, she absorbs this kind of thing, soothing any kind of rancor with a slice of banana bread and coffee and a little innocuous gossip. But that must not be working. So this night, for the first time, Milo steps out into the street to see how bad it is.

It's winter in Middling. The brick houses of Campustown are solemn-faced, and their porches sag under the burden of snow. Through the windows, lamps glow weakly where Milo's colleagues read magazines nearing extinction. Oak trees reach crooked limbs over rooftops in a protective embrace. He hears a piano playing Debussy down the block. A dog barks and a door shuts. It's all peaceful. Sadly beautiful. But Milo's house is another matter.

Clearly, something peculiar is happening in the garage. For starters, there's this steady, throbbing hum, the cadence of a heartbeat—that's the magnetic stabilizer. Then there's the chuff-chuff-chuff of the oscillating vent, and the periodic growl of the compressor. Although Milo and Arnie have papered over the windows, light escapes around the edges. It also comes out the exhausts along the eaves and up through the sky vent. It's an antiseptic white light, the sort you see in hospitals.

Then Arnie fires the welder and Milo can hear the crackle and spark. The lamps dim in the windows of all the houses. The streetlamps go down, too. The Debussy piano stops. There is the whiff of molten metal and solvents. Then there's the clang of Arnie dropping a piece of angle iron, and as he releases the welder, the street lights return to their yellow glow.

The neighbors have a point.

In the garage, Arnie hands Milo a can of beer and they sit on folding chairs in the middle of the makeshift lab. Well, Arnie asks, how bad is it?

It's bad, Milo says. He looks at his friend with a kind of guilty mirth and drinks half the beer. He says, We really need to speed it up. No way they're going to put up with this much longer.

Arnie laughs and reaches out to put a heavy hand on his friend's shoulder. Just speed it up, you say! Like we're putting together a set of shelves in here!

Milo pulls away. When people touch him like that, he expects there to be pain, even though there rarely is, lately, but you never know when the wrong touch or twist might set off a crippling wave, from spine to limbs. Dude, I'm serious, Milo says. We'll get shut down, and I can't live with that. I mean, sorry, not to be selfish, but really.

Arnie clicks the tab on his beer can nervously. He is always doing these things, because of all the extra energy, but you can't let yourself be annoyed.

Finally he says, We're going as fast as we can within the constraints of safety.

Milo replies, I don't give a shit about safety. I've told you that. I mean, for myself. I totally care about your safety and Deloris and everything.

Okay, says Arnie. He drinks the remainder of his beer thoughtfully. There's also the matter of budget. We still need liquid helium, panels of graphene. That shit's expensive.

I've got the money, Milo says.

Arnie looks surprised and amused. What? From where? How much?

Enough to cover whatever we need.

Well gosh, friend, Arnie says, this seems like something you would have told me.

I'm embarrassed. The two words just come out, before Milo can add nuance. But at least it's out there.

Arnie goes over to the little dorm fridge to get two more beers, and as he walks, he says, Embarrassment may be the biggest obstacle to success. It's an irrational emotion.

So says the physicist, Milo says. But of course, Arnie is right.

Arnie opens both beers at once on his knees and hands one to Milo. He says, Well come on, professor, out with it. What explains this sudden windfall?

My book is selling again.

You mean *Dreams Manifested*?! Arnie pronounces the title with incredulity.

Have I written any other books?

Well, I don't know. I thought that was out of print.

It was. But now it's back. I guess the library copies circulated and it caught on again.

After what like 25 years? So what's so embarrassing about it?

Well have you read it?

Arnie shrugs and sips his beer with lowered eyelids. Eh, he says, I prefer nonfiction.

It is nonfiction you dick.

Milo's stomach tightens as he explains. It's like he's talking about some other person who wrote that bestseller. He says, Well, let's just say that most of those ideas are no longer in fashion. Since you didn't read it… It basically presented the whole notion that our success and happiness is controlled intrinsically, that falling short of your desires is unnecessary deference to society—that was the idea, in a nutshell—everybody has the seeds of triumph, and we alone, as individuals, allow those seeds to die, because we give in to culture or genetics or whatever—but really, you're ultimately entitled to success and pursuing it at all costs is how things will just magically go right for you. It's kind of a riff on Schopenhauer's Will, but saying it's actually our greatest gift, our superpower. I can see I'm boring you… Anyway, it's not exactly *de rigueur* now. It's what they call privileged thinking.

Arnie laughs and points at Milo. He says, Well, not unless you're one of those dickheads, one of those …

Righteous, Milo says. That's the thing. That's who's buying the book now. They don't understand it. To be honest, I still believe the core precepts are true, I mean, the base philosophy is incredibly inclusive. But then I added the self-help shit, unfortunately, which did great in the 90s, obviously. And now those people have distorted and embraced it.

Ha! That's so fucking awesome! Who would have thought that Milosz Dudek would become the guru to the Righteous in this country! Awesome. Arnie pauses, thinking. Well, at least it's money.

At least it's money, Milo says. But I only want to spend it on this. And of course Ms. Dalyrimple, if she needs something.

Deloris, Arnie says.

Right. I need to stop thinking that.

That night Emily comes to Milo again, as he falls asleep in his reading chair. She is herself from the days before she got ill, sitting in the window box with her bare feet pulled up to her seat, arms hugging her knees. She has a rolled bandana holding back her dark, unruly hair. Her hands are stained with pastel dust, as if she's just come from the school. She smiles, and that compresses her eyes in the warm, familiar way and she says,

I miss you. I wish I had told you that more. I missed you sometimes when you were right there. All I wanted was to be with you and when you weren't, it was like that side of my body was cold, as if the blankets were pulled back in early morning, just half-way, and I couldn't pull them back again. Just this total cold and it ached. It ached to miss you.

Milo is too overcome with emotion to speak. He knows he's in the study, and it's nearly midnight, and Ms. Dalyrimple has given up texting him from bed, and the ice has melted in his glass, and his eyes are closed. He can direct his thoughts, but can't control his actions. There's just a tremendous pressure building up inside, a yearning to reply, to walk to her, but he can't. Is it just a dream? Are they dreaming together? If so, how is that possible? Or … are they each poised on top of a peak, on a symbolic landscape draped in an irregular grid, seeing each other across a valley imposed by the idiosyncrasies of matter, action, and time? He and Arnie are betting on this last one. They will flatten that landscape, or bring those peaks together, when the system in the garage is working.

But now there is no patience for that. He says, I'll come to you. How hard can that be? You're right there.

Emily puts her hands down on the windowsill and shakes her head. She says, Don't try that. I know. I've tried and it's too much. Like walking into a crazy headwind. You push and you lean but you just feel like a toy.

She looks down where she's left pastel dust on the molding. Oh gosh I'm sorry, she says.

Milo laughs, Well it's your house, too.

Emily looks away. He's expecting her to say something like 'it was my house,' or 'not any more' even though she never says things like that. So he says, have you just come from school? How were the kids?

But now she is vague. There is the study, and the chair, and window well, and the glass with melted ice. Emily is there and not there simultaneously. How do you describe this? That yearning dissolves into melancholy. But that melancholy is pleasant—why?

Then a fog rises in the room from the floor. What is this, some dark smoke seeping from the vents, carrying a stink like burning tires? He can't breathe. He can't move. He wills himself to move, throws his torso forward …

The fog is gone. It's after midnight. Milo becomes aware of the continuous pain from his spine—a hot, yellow pain—and so realizes he is present. He is fully awake.

The only thing is, pastel handprints remain on the window sill.

In the morning, Ms. Dalyrimple is in the kitchen, along with bowls and mixers, sacks of flour and sugar, spent eggshells oozing on the counter. Milo stands in the hallway and watches her. Could it be two years since they were married? Every year in your life is proportionately smaller than the one before so, at Milo's middle age, maybe it's not strange that two years seems so short. Maybe it's not so strange to think of your second wife by her last name. No, that is strange, and Milo should stop it. But for fifteen years, before they were married, he knew her as Ms. Dalyrimple. So it's not crazy. She was the nurse, for everything. She was there after his botched surgery, and she was there during all of Emily's treatment, and she was there at the end, the warmest and most compassionate nurse you could ever want, with those soft, consoling, competent hands that she's employing right now in this chaotic kitchen. She has since left the hospital, and that is a pity.

Deloris carries her weight athletically, reaching down into dark cupboards, climbing up on a step stool for an obscure sifter. She has a tulip-print dress, bound tightly by an apron that says 'Bakin Babe.' It was a gift from her church friends, along with a matching hat, which she also wears until it 'drives her bonkers,' and then she'll toss it on the table for later.

Milo hears her say, Oh for Pete's sake, it's true! I get it now. Makes total sense.

What makes sense? Milo asks from the doorway. He puts his hands in his robe pockets and smiles.

Well look at you, sleepyhead, Ms. Dalyrimple says. She comes to him, arms wide and substantial, and hugs his sore and creaking frame. For a moment, her embrace dissolves his pain like butter in a saucepan. She kisses his neck with a smack and he pats her broad back. He is no more used to this affection, and with each passing day feels less deserving of it. But Ms. Dalyrimple only seems to give more. She grabs his shoulders firmly and says, You were up puttering all hours again, Mr. Absentminded Professor. Not healthy! Let me get you some breakfast.

What were you saying is true? Milo asks.

Oh, that! She replies, and looks back at the counter. Well, math!

Yeah, you can certainly say math is true. It might be the only true thing, objectively.

No, Ms. Dalyrimple protests. What I mean is that it's true that math isn't true. I just finally got it this morning. What Pastor's been saying …

You mean Yeshevsky? Your boss?

She snaps Milo with a towel drawn from her waist. A puff of flour coats his robe. Yes, of course you silly goose! What other pastor?

What has he been saying? About math?

Just that it's all made up! she exclaims. Her face is ecstatic. She pulls Milo by the elbow to the counter. See, look, she says. Like, recipes—some use ounces and teaspoons, some use the foreign measures like grams and liters. It's all made up!

Sure, Milo says, but the underlying math …

She rests her fists on her hips and tilts her head, looking at him. Think about it, she says, you'll get it. Some of the measures are divided by sixteenths, some by twelfths, and the metric ones use tens … Just random, you know? As made up as a fairy tale.

Milo's head is not yet clear. He considers whether it's helpful to untangle these ideas. Ms. Dalyrimple is clever enough to understand, if she chooses to.

The units of measure are sort of arbitrary, that's true, he says. But ultimately they serve as integers and the mathematical principles we use to manipulate them—that's universal. That's like the definition of true.

Manipulate! She says, and Milo instantly regrets his word choice. That's exactly the word Pastor used. People keep inventing math to serve their purposes, and it just keeps changing, so we need to be smart and question it. Especially when people use it to manipulate each other.

She hands Milo a coffee. Looking over the brim he says, How, exactly?

Well in any way they please, she says. But just think about math that doesn't serve you, all around you! Like, is your bank account the number you want it to be? No. It's not. But bankers use math to make it that way. Same with taxes. Also, do your votes always count the way you want them to …?

Oh, Deloris, no, Milo says. He sets down the coffee cup. Please don't go down that path.

She turns back to the stove and begins cracking eggs for breakfast. This means the discussion is over. She has one last word: Choose the math that serves you, the Lord says, and you'll be happy. I like this cooking math, so I'll use it. But not every soul on the block has to.

Milo picks up the coffee and finishes it. He feels the draw of the workshop in his garage, the gravity of the miraculous machine they are building. This could be true, physically, because it has electromagnets so powerful they tug at the plates and screws along his vertebra. But the circuit is off now, so the draw is in his mind. Also, he is still haunted by a sweet residue of last night's yearning and melancholy.

Hey, he says, I'm just going to pop into the workshop for a few. To check on a few things. I teach at ten today.

Like you do every Tuesday, Deloris says. Now be sensible and eat this.

Suddenly there is a plate of eggs, muffins, orange slices in front of him. Milo pulls himself loose from his distraction, blinks, and sits at the table. Deloris joins him and watches him eat, her hands working the tie of her apron.

Speaking of Pastor, she says, he's coming by on Thursday. With some ladies from Session. We thought you might join us?

This is not a request. He looks at his wrist as if it has a watch. Thursday? What time?

Whatever time suits you, she says.

Well, the meeting's not for me… he says, and then realizes that it is.

The ladies love your Dreaming book!

Milo winces to think of what they're getting from it. Would he remove that book from his past, if life worked like that? Would he erase that part? He would still have married Emily. He would still have made tenure, probably. He would have been kinder to Emily, probably. But life doesn't work like that, so.

Well, can you come? Deloris asks, waving across his unfocused eyes.

And Pastor Yeshevsky? he asks, What does he think of the book?

Ms. Dalyrimple stands up and lifts his plate and fork primly. I couldn't say. There's only one book for him.

So why's he coming?

To talk about some other things, I suppose. We are all his flock.

So now it's not just the neighbors Milo has to worry about. Now it's also the notorious pastor. He and Arnie have no time to lose.

When Arnie arrives that night, Milo is lying in the titanium tub in the workshop. Hands behind his head, he contemplates the pipes, ductwork, conduit, transformers, and circuit boards that decorate the ceiling. It's complex but perfectly ordered. Everything is labeled.

Arnie drops his backpack and exhales, Did you stay in here all night?

It's the most comfortable spot in the house.

Arnie starts the console on the laptop and, without looking up, says Well it's definitely the most dangerous spot in the house.

Don't start with the safety business again, Milo says, because I've got another reason we need to hurry up.

Arnie looks over his glasses. He says, quietly, Did you see Emily last night?

I did. Thank you. I don't want to talk about that. But I feel like she knows what we're working on.

Well even if she doesn't, Arnie says, I don't think that matters. We'll get you two together. She'll be psyched. And you can find some… you know, peace, I guess.

But that's not what I meant about hurrying.

Arnie looks at Milo and waits.

They're planning an intervention for me, Milo says.

Who? For what?

That god-damned pastor, Yeshevsky. And some church ladies, though I doubt they're scheming. My guess is they're going to scold me about spending too much time out here when I should be with my wife. Which honestly, dude, is true. Clearly I'm not a good husband or a good person, really, but I can't help this thing, so we need to finish.

Milo pulls himself out of the tub, wincing, and sits on the edge.

Arnie says, Yeah but what stake does the pastor have in it? He doesn't give a shit about your marriage.

I think, says Milo, he doesn't like how his congregation are into my book. I think his goal is to scare me off somehow, or embarrass me.

Arnie compresses his lips and looks down.

Milo says, Don't laugh, you asshole! It's paying the bills.

Speaking of which! Arnie says. Help me unload!

Arnie has brought some military-grade graphene panels, with lower conductivity than anything they've used before. He's also got a tank of liquid helium. If his formulas are correct, this will be the last alteration to the system. With these supplies, they'll reach absolute zero.

They get to work cutting the panels to fit.

This will drive the sci-fi guys crazy, Arnie says. He holds a titanium screw in the corner of his mouth. The time-travel loonies too. It cracks me up.

Milo hands him a torque wrench. How do you mean?

Oh, they're going to find all kind of perceived 'holes' in the science, and problems in the continuity of time, and blah blah blah. They love it. They live for that shit—trolling message boards with their superior analysis.

Yeah, but how will they ever learn about it?

When I publish my paper, obviously. And then when I get my own best-seller out there. And when they make a movie out of it. They'll all be chattering like chickens while I—while you and I—have the last laugh. And then the university will have to explain why their most famous physics professor was never promoted.

Well, you will if this all works out.

No I won't.

Why?

Because this is all totally illegitimate, man! Remember?! I'm not going to get promoted. I'm going to get fired.

You're kidding, right?

I don't know, maybe. Hand me that epoxy, will you?

They work in silence for awhile. Milo understands why Arnie would rather not rush the work. You become unaware of time in the workshop, you settle into a therapeutic flow, and the instinctive partnership with another primate gives a sense of purpose and meaning. If you sit on a beach and think too long about how things are, your soul will collapse. If you pick up a soldering iron and begin to assemble something, your soul rests and recuperates. The inevitable disordering seems to pause for a while. So why wouldn't we want to remain in that state forever?

Then Milo asks, softly, Would you ever want to try this—to reconnect with...?

Which one? Arnie scoffs. There are three of them.

Well, I don't know. Is there one you think of—or dream of—more? Or want to, you know?

Arnie works in silence for a while. Milo watches him, wondering if he's said something wrong. Why did he only think to ask him this now? Isn't this the most obvious question, among close friends, from the very beginning? Milo is astonished sometimes at his self-centeredness. But you can only do your best, right, and keep trying? And now the question hangs.

Arnie takes his gloves off and sits back on the floor, looking at Milo. Of course I think about them, he says. A lot of times it's unexpected, like when I smell lilacs or hear a saxophone or step into a bar. And then I feel bad that I wasn't thinking about them the moment before. I worry that I'm not thinking about them as much, which is sort of paradoxical, right, because that's healing? But no, I don't dream. Never. This is probably saying too much, but it stopped after Barb, and I have this theory that it's a defense mechanism. I mean, who has two wives and one partner die by the time they're fifty? I didn't marry Barb because I thought maybe that would break my curse, but a lot of good that did, right? There's just no way to get your head around it so you just fucking shut it down, man. You just shut it down.

Arnie looks at the sterile concrete floor between his running shoes and pauses. Then he looks up with a sad smile and says, But thanks for asking. That means a lot.

I should have asked sooner, man.

Yes, you should have.

Milo feels strangely good to get that mild scolding, like he's come through something. He starts to sweep up. Arnie returns to his laptop to update the modules for the work they've just done, and run a debugger, and fix whatever, and then compile for their trial.

Milo asks, What will you call your paper?

Arnie stops and thinks, looking into the corner of the room, smiling.

He says, I think I'll call it 'Exploitation of the suspension of thermal transfer and sub-atomic action to bridge temporal states.'

Oh, that's good! I'd read that.

Hell of a lot better than *Dreams Manifested*!

Milo brandishes his broom theatrically and Arnie says, Whoa, easy, don't hurt yourself.

Milo drops his arms and exhales.

Arnie says, I'm sorry man. That was uncalled for.

Milo says, I deserve it.

Then it's time for the trial.

Milo pulls a chair up near the titanium tub. It's the next best thing to being inside on a real voyage. Arnie stands at his laptop and types the command to open the circuit to get the magnets running.

Don't get too close, Arnie says. I'm serious.

Milo waves him off. I like to feel the tug, he says. It's like training.

As the electromagnets pulse with current, the surgical steel in Milo's spine turns toward it, pulling the vertebrae along. It's an unnerving sensation, like your body is splitting apart. Maybe it is splitting apart! Milo pulls his chair back a few feet, where he can still see the temperature gauge on the manifold above the tub. The negative number on the simple LED goes steadily upward, as temperature in the chamber descends. The throbbing hum carries on at the heartbeat cadence and there's a whiff of ozone in the air.

Then Milo's eye is drawn toward the window on the other side of the room. Did something move there? He watches. Yes, it definitely moved! That old window, with its leaded panes, and its faulty latch, is definitely cracked open now. Milo gets up and walks to see more directly. In the light there is a figure—a tall and heavy man, it seems, with a red balaclava and a hunter's hat—visible through the gap. Arnie is watching now too, and yells Hey! and cuts the current to the system, which winds down. The bright light of a cell phone camera shines through the gap into Milo's face, training a focus, and then flashes.

Hey, what the fuck?! Milo yells. It immediately sounds dumb, but his adrenaline is surging. He runs to the window as the figure vanishes. Arnie runs to the side door, manipulates the deadbolt and the chain and the clip and the handle lock and finally gets it open, allowing a rush of winter air. He runs into the yard, yelling, Come back here! What do you want! Hey! Hey stop! I'm talking to you!

Then it's silent. And in a few moments, Arnie returns to the doorway, panting, shivering.

Couldn't catch him, he says.

Milo pushes the window shut. Who the fuck could that have been?

Arnie secures all the locks and says, Probably some pissed off neighbor.

Yeah, but he took a picture.

That's not cool. Arnie crosses his arms, thinking.

That is definitely not cool, Milo says. Like we needed any more incentive to get this done. Should we fire it up again?

Arnie shakes his head. Sorry, man. I do not feel comfortable running a trial now. We need to figure out what that was about. Or, at least have better security next time. Seriously, sorry. We'll get there, buddy.

Milo stares into the tub. He says, Okay. You can go. It's late. I'll close up here.

You sure?

Absolutely.

When Arnie is gone, Milo climbs back into the tub, folds his hands on his chest, and stares upward.

He awakens to the buzzing of his phone in his shirt pocket. Without sitting up, he looks and sees a dozen messages from Deloris, all polite but with increasing urgency. All right in there? She asks. Don't mean to pester ya. Hello? Sorry, did something happen? I heard running out on the walk? Or just a squirrel—who knows? Hello? Is Arnie still here? So sorry to bother. Getting a little worried! Milo?

He pulls himself up to the edge of the tub, pauses to let the pain subside, and then gets himself out completely. With blurry eyes, he checks: system down, doors locked, lights off. And then goes to find Ms. Dalyrimple.

She sits at the kitchen table stuffing envelopes for a church capital campaign. Oh! she says when she sees him, and her voice is higher than usual. She pops up to grab hold of his arms and says, You don't look so good, mister. I'll make you some tea.

Milo can't just keep taking all this kindness from her. It was unkind to let her worry, to have ignored her messages. He can't keep playing the role of indulged pre-teen boy, the precious savant, the sulker. He straightens his posture and breathes deeply, pats her hand, and says, No. Have a seat, Deloris. I'll make the tea.

This concerns her. She looks at him, then the table, then toward the counter. You're sure? It won't take me but two shakes.

I'll get it, Milo says. It's the least I can do.

The water heats. He says, I saw your messages. Why didn't you come into the workshop?

Deloris bats her hand at the idea, Oh you don't need me barging in there all the time while you're doing your stuff.

But Deloris you barge in there none of the time. It's fine, you know. I mean sometimes it might be good to knock when we're in the middle of a trial or something but still.

She licks an envelope and tamps it with her fist, then grabs another. She's not looking at him.

I'm just hoping you'll be done soon, she says.

It's a firm statement that doesn't call for a reply. But Milo says, Is that what the meeting with the pastor is about tomorrow?

Ms. Dalyrimple speeds up her paper shuffling, looks serious, and says, Aw how the heck would I know. I mean, maybe. It could be. People get to talking around the church office, you know, and Pastor's so interested in everybody.

It's okay. I understand.

She pauses her folding, but doesn't look up. You do? She asks.

I do. Of course I do. He looks at the back of her head and shoulders, waiting. Should he go to her now? Yes, of course he should. Why is that difficult? This force, that sticks him to the floor, that prevents him from true sincerity, it comes from so deep within.

Deloris continues with the envelopes. The ladies, though, they really love that book of yours! They want you to write a sequel!

Milo feels his throat tighten. He asks, But what do you think of that book? Did you like it, or...

Ms. Dalyrimple turns in her chair and folds her hands in her lap and looks at him. She smiles. It's a great book, dear. Everybody knows that. With all the success and money? But I guess it's just not for me. It doesn't have to be, does it?

To be honest, Deloris, I'm not sure it's for me anymore either. Truth is,

I'm more surprised by anybody how it's come back and sometimes I wish it hadn't. That's another man, who wrote that.

Deloris seems encouraged. Yeah, you know, life just doesn't work that way, does it? Making things come true by just willing it and telling everybody about it and so forth. No offense. But I suppose maybe it's good for some folks, gives them hope. Just not for me. I don't need it, dear. I have you!

Milo starts pulling out cups, saucers, milk. He feels a jolt of realization rush upward—what if Ms. Dalyrimple comes into the workshop while Emily is there?! Would she see them both? Would it frighten her? Would she be upset? It's not like she has any competition with his dead wife, but it could seem like that. It could seem terribly cruel. Is this even possible? Maybe this is a ridiculous worry. But why did he encourage her to come in? It was working fine before. He will have to sort this out.

The tea is ready and he brings the service to the table and sets it down. He pours.

Ms. Dalyrimple stares at him.

What? he asks.

It's for three, she says. Is Arnie still here?

Three?

Yes, she replies, touching one saucer after another. You've brought three cups of tea.

Milo stares. How could he have done this? What a buffoon he is. Poor Ms. Dalyrimple.

She laughs. Silly goose, she says. And that's not the only thing. What else have you done, with your head in the clouds?

He stares, searches, has no idea.

Milo, she says, you know I don't take sugar.

That night, as Ms. Dalyrimple breathes deeply, rhythmically, like a fireplace bellows, Milo returns to Emily in another time. At first he only hears her voice calling through the honey-colored light that we see through our closed eyelids. Let's meet at a memory, she says, Like the time at the school with the boxes and the rain.

You know we can't do that, he says. Not until the machine is working. But I want to—so much it's hard to breathe.

What I mean is, she says, let's remember. Can you do that?

Images appear in the way they do in dreams. If you look straight at them, they disappear, but like the faintest stars, if you look to one side they reemerge as if they had only been shy and then the full idea of the image becomes palpable. There is the elementary school where she worked, and the park beyond it, and beyond that, the lake. There is cut grass and daffodils and fresh tar. Robins call and repeat themselves, over and over, in their drunken serenade.

Yes, he says, I can remember. I am remembering.

You brought all those boxes, she says, in the new station wagon.

They were for the kids.

I know. It was very kind. You had just cashed your royalty check.

Blood money, he says.

You shouldn't judge yourself so harshly. A lot of good came from those ideas.

Okay, I'll try. Are you still there?

Of course I am.

I remember you wore your shop apron, with all the famous buildings of Europe on it. And you had a Cubs hat on, which I thought was strange.

It was a Bears hat. Because it was supposed to rain.

Milo remembers, yes it was supposed to rain. Yes! He remembers so much of it now! Oh thank god some memories still persist—he had cashed the first royalty check from his one and only big book and took some cash to the art supply store and filled two carts with everything he remembered

Emily complained she didn't have, especially for the kids on public aid (the hot lunch kids, whose parents couldn't send them to school with pencils and water color trays and gum erasers and rulers, the kids who maybe needed art the most?). The girls who worked in the shop laughed at him struggling to steer the carts to the register and they rang it all up and he laid down the cash and they helped him bring the boxes into the wagon and oh! that's right, he drove so carefully so things didn't slide around and he brought the boxes one by one and put them outside the school where she was, after hours, cleaning up, while the Mother's Day coffee mugs fired in the kiln, and back then you had to find an actual phone, which he could not, and didn't want to go into the office and arouse suspicion, so he waited on the hood of the wagon hoping Emily would come out, which she did, in her apron and hat, to shake out some cloths…

Was it too sentimental? Did it really happen that way?

Yes, it happened that way, says Emily. It's weird how life seems more sentimental back then and you question it, but it was real, right?

Milo feels the loss, the way the floor of your stomach falls. And he says, Yes, it was before irony. I think that's the main thing. Irony kills sentimentality. Irony is a fun drug, but not worth it.

Like crack, she says.

So they say, he says.

So they say, says Emily.

Outside the school they held each other and kissed and soon the hunger was too great and they felt mischievous and adventurous and ran off, hand in hand, through the park toward the lake and found a sheltered spot and did it. Afterward, there was cut grass on their pants and feet and hands and hair. Rain fell suddenly, unexpectedly. At first it was a charming mist and the scent of the cut grass and the fertility of the Illinois ground— it was overwhelming, combined with the euphoria of sex. Then the rain came hard, and they covered their heads with their hands, as if that would make a difference, and ran back to the school and found the boxes soaked and falling apart. Milo carried two at a time, while Emily held the door, and they got all the supplies inside, mostly unharmed.

Milo said, There! Do you love me now?

I love you forever, Emily said. Since before I met you.

You could smell the antiseptic of the mopped hall. You could smell the kiln cooking clay. You could hear the rain beating the flat pebble roof of the little school that's no longer there.

Now Ms. Dalyrimple turns in her sleep and laughs—a hearty 'whoop!' of a laugh, and she keeps chuckling at some comical dream. The bed trembles with her mirth and Milo is back in the room now. It must be nearly dawn. He is sore and dry-mouthed. The dreadful duties of the day lie just ahead. But in the room there is the fragrance of cut grass.

They sit on kitchen table chairs arranged in a circle in the parlor. Except for the pastor, who sits in Milo's mother's wingback chair, wearing a red hooded sweatshirt and running shoes, one leg crossing the other at the ankle. While they talk, he folds and re-folds a sheet of paper, rocking slightly in his chair, looking at each of them with the interest of a groundhog.

Milo is telling them the story of when he and Ms. Dalyrimple met. It's a pedestrian tactic, to soften them with romance, but they seem like an uncomplicated bunch. Milo says, Then Ms. D—I mean, Deloris comes into the room, takes one look at the IV, and look out! You know when Deloris sees something not right?

The ladies nod with enthusiasm, balancing plates of lemon bars and trifle on their knees, reaching to the low table to accept the coffee Deloris pours, lots of cream, hold the sugar.

Milo continues, In ten seconds, Deloris had torn off that IV and put a neat one in instead. She said 'I just can't stand to see a butcher job.' And my back started feeling better already.

At this, Milo smiles at Deloris and raises his cup in a toast. It's too much, but it works. There is a collective 'awww' among the ladies.

Yeshevsky says, in a voice too bold for the room, Well Ms. D is a rock star, I'll tell you that. A regular ass kicker. The church would be lost without her, praise Jesus.

Everyone looks at the pastor and waits. He has interrupted the flow. Milo is concerned to have lost the floor, but he waits to see the pastor's next move.

Yeshevsky peers at each of them through black eyes, savors their attention, and then blurts, What do you say we get to the matter at hand? I mean, not to be too businesslike about it, or interrupt this nice chitchat, but time waits for no man and God's minutes are precious. Right? Mrs. Castlegate, do you want to take it from here?

The church treasurer, an unusually tall woman with silver hair held back tightly, sets down her cup and folds her hands like you do in a spelling bee. She breathes deeply through her nose and says,

Yes. Well. Thank you, Deloris, for hosting company this week. And your refreshments are, as always... oh my goodness those lemon bars are just ... but to get to the matter—as Pastor says—I think that's how you said it ... I mean, I'm not one for words, more of a number person myself ... not that numbers are a substitute for words ... or The Word ... numbers are, as you've said, Pastor—well, that is, math ...

Then Mrs. Castlegate lifts a tumbler and drinks water while nodding and smiling with her eyes. She breathes again. Yeshevsky makes a rolling motion with his hand to hurry her up. And then Mrs. Castlegate seems suddenly struck with a notion.

Oh! she says, and leans down to reach in her purse. Before I forget... Professor Dudek, would you be willing to sign your book while we're here today?

At this, the other ladies reach into their purses and retrieve their copies of *Dreams Manifested*. They say, Me too, if you don't mind, oh I was wondering the same thing.

To end this hubbub, Yeshevsky says, in the manner of a trumpet hitting notes, Miss - us - Cas - tle - gate! But he keeps his eyes lowered, concentrating on the folded piece of paper. He repeats, Mrs. Castlegate, you were saying ...?!

Oh ... yes, says Mrs. Castlegate. She lowers the book back into her purse as if it might not be noticed. Professor Dudek, she says.

Milo says, Please, just Milo.

Oh yes of course, she says. Milo. We are here as advocates of Deloris, to wish God's blessing on your marriage ... and it's a lovely marriage! That story you told about you meeting just now, well, of course you are a great writer ... and you inspire!

Milo sees the pastor rocking more rapidly in his chair, hears him take the quick breath we take before speaking, and before Yeshevsky has a chance to interrupt, Milo holds up his finger and says, with almost obsequious politeness, Mrs. Castlegate, If I could just ...

Her eyebrows arch high, she glances at the pastor, who lifts two fingers like a judge sustaining an objection, and then she says, Yes? Milo?

Milo folds his hands on his knees and leans forward. He lets the silence hang, as he looks at each one of them in turn with a reassuring eye-crinkled smile. Then he delivers a little speech:

Thank you. I don't mean to interrupt. But I just think it would be good for you to know that Deloris has suggested to me that you're concerned I'm spending too much time on my research—on my project in the workshop, in the garage. You know Deloris is such a loving wife, and such a talented nurse—and church secretary! We shouldn't forget that!—I'm so fortunate—I mean, blessed—to have her in my life. But she's also candid when she needs to be.

Milo lets his gaze rest on Deloris for a pause. She has the kind of eyes-wide expression you see among the audience of a sword swallower, waiting to see if this will turn out. She takes a bite of a lemon bar, automatically, and when she realizes all eyes are on her, she puts a finger over her mouth while chewing and with the other hand, gives Milo a p'shaw wave. He continues his speech:

So, with those concerns in mind, I do want to tell you that Deloris and I have discussed the situation and I have promised to wind down the research. I'll be finished in a few days—a week, max. How does that sound? Does that cover the matter at hand?

Milo gives the pastor a look that says, 'checkmate.' But Yeshevsky's response is not what he's expecting. The pastor extends his lower lip, nods slowly, and begins to clap, so slowly that the first clap makes the ladies jump in their seats. But when he continues, clap, clap, they become enthusiastic and join him. And so in this way, Milo receives applause for his little speech and, presumably, victory for his stalling technique.

Then the pastor waves laterally and ends the applause and says, We can see Deloris isn't the only rock star in this house, am I right?! Bravo, professor. If I didn't know better, I'd think I was looking at a modern-day Paul on the road to Damascus! Hot damn. Well done, dude.

Milo puts his palms together, bows, and replies, Thank you, dude.

There follows another awkward silence. Then Ms. Dalyrimple says, Could anyone use a warmup? I'll get the pot.

And then, almost at once, everyone has somewhere urgent to go. There won't be any warmups. There will be plates carried to the kitchen and chairs returned to the table, and then it will just be Ms. Dalyrimple and Milo and his new promise.

The couple stand at the door in sort of a receiving line, as each of the ladies offer their thanks and get Milo's signature on their books. Finally, they are down to the pastor.

He says, Deloris, I'm so sorry, you have those capital campaign envelopes ready for me?

Oh! Deloris says. I was just going to pop them in the mail, easy as pie.

I got it, Yeshevsky says, no biggie. No biggie at all. I'll do it on my way home. Can you just get 'em?

Ms. Dalyrimple touches Milo's shoulder and jogs down the hall.

The pastor stands close to Milo and looks into his face. Milo notices that when he talks, his lips pull back from his teeth tightly. His breath is sour. Yeshevsky says, Hey bro, so here we are, just you and me.

Milo becomes aware of how much his spine is hurting from sitting. The pastor pulls from his jeans pocket an envelope. Milo's name is printed on it with tape from a label maker.

The pastor shrugs and says, I found this. Thinking maybe it's yours?

Milo stares at the envelope. Is he supposed to open it now?

Go on, says the pastor. Take a look.

Milo looks down the hall—where the heck is Deloris? He opens the envelope, pulls out a photograph, and sees himself, looking terrified in his workshop, illuminated with the harsh light of a cell phone flash. He looks back up at the pastor, who has delight in his eyes.

Yeshevsky says, There are some really interesting things in there, aren't there? In your workshop I mean. Your buddy Arnie, did he get all that stuff? Seems pretty rare, or maybe not something the university wants off site?

Milo sees a tremor in his own hands, which infuriates him, but nevertheless he puts the picture back in the envelope and hands it toward the pastor. He says, quietly, What the fuck is this? Some kind of weird blackmail?

The pastor doesn't take the envelope. Instead he looks down the hall and says, There she is! Oh, we should give you a hand with those boxes!

Ms. Dalyrimple says, No, no, no, it's nothing. I'll put them in your car.

Wait, says the pastor. May I say a blessing before I go?

She stops in front of him and bows her head. Milo continues staring at the pastor, who puts his hands on each of their heads, pressing down slightly, and begins, Dear holy father…

Milo doesn't hear the rest of the prayer. His face is burning hot and his ears are ringing and he can't think of what to do or say.

Next thing, Yeshevsky is walking down the steps toward his car. He turns and calls back to them, Oh snap! I meant to mention: I think we must have lost your latest donation envelope?

Then the pastor shakes his head and adds, Oh, I shouldn't even mention it. Forget I said a word.

Ms. Dalyrimple calls back to him, We'll get you another! ASAP! First thing tomorrow—you can count on us!

The pastor gives two thumbs up, trots to his car, and drives away. Now the street is quiet. The sky is a cold winter blue. A few crows call in agitation.

I wish you hadn't done that, Arnie says. You've committed to an artificial deadline with the sleaziest guy in Middling.

It's after dinner and they're preparing for a big test. Milo presses a button to open the molded plastic canopy over the titanium tub. He says, Look, I had to defuse the situation somehow. I had to act on instinct. But it worked! You should have seen how flabbergasted they all were.

Arnie types at the control panel, and while studying his work, he says, Well the good thing is you have absolutely no commitment to that guy. I mean, I guess he has leverage over Deloris, but what's the worst that can happen? She gets fired? Seems like that would actually be good right?

Milo hears himself say, Yeah, probably. The world would get a great nurse back …

How bad of a lie is this, not telling Arnie about Yeshevsky's blackmail?

It's pretty bad, when you think about it. The pastor called out Arnie specifically, and threatened his career. But if Arnie knew, there's a good chance he'd want to stop the project for a while. Or maybe even entirely! But the right thing to do would be to just tell Arnie everything. That's what good friends do. That's what good people do.

But Arnie seems to have moved on. He walks over to the cabinet and retrieves an old wooden cigar box. He says, Well the good pastor is gonna get what's coming to him one of these days. Are you reading Sheila Fuglesen's blog? She's gonna bring them all down, before she's done—Yeshevsky, Tommy Hinrick—the whole lot of them.

Milo watches his friend walk over with the box. Arnie is probably right. The pastor can't last that long. It'll blow over. They'll make another contribution to Most Redeemed, and that will be that. Or, if the pastor pushes harder, Milo will just give him more money—money from his recent book sales. He'll just be taking money from the Righteous and giving some of it back to them. Who's hurt by that? Money is a made-up thing anyway, right? Like math, ha.

Milo? Arnie says, and waves a hand in front of his face.

Milo spools up the last sentence and says, No I don't read that blog. But it sounds good.

Well, you should, says Arnie. Now, take a look at these.

He opens the box and Milo lifts out two antique pocket watches, the type train conductors once used. They are simple, but the typeface is beautiful and unlike any Milo has seen. Arnie takes one watch back from him.

Arnie says, My grandfather's. One he used and the other he kept for backup. 'To keep the other one honest,' he used to say. They never went out of sync.

They're beautiful, Milo says. And strangely heavy.

Supposedly there's an inscription inside, on the other side of the cogs and coils, which no one can see. When my grandfather asked the watchmaker why, he said, 'Because God can see it.'

Is that true?

Does it matter?

Yeah, Milo says. It's a good story. Who cares if it's true.

A few seconds pass while they stand facing each other, looking at the watches in their hands. With a lot of people, this would be awkward or uncomfortable, but with them it's not.

Then Milo remembers the secret he's keeping and the moment ends and he asks, What are they for?

Arnie says, One goes in the tub and one stays outside. That way we'll know if it worked.

Milo gives him a delighted expression. Really?! he says. We're going to rely on these old watches, and not the time sensors?

Arnie takes the second watch back from Milo and smiles with a sad light in his eyes. You have to have some fun, right?

Arnie places one watch in the middle of the tub, Milo closes the canopy, and they begin the test. The magnetic stabilizer hums in its waves of a slow heartbeat. Milo can feel the harsh tug in his spine. Then Arnie initiates the chilling chamber and the lights dim—even in the workshop. Who knows how dark it is in the neighborhood, but who cares. This is science. They watch the temperature monitor go down—minus 150 degrees Celsius, minus 200, minus 250—down it goes. They get to minus 269, so very close to absolute zero. Then it stops changing.

That's a great result, Arnie says. No hiccups. We're done for tonight.

But we just need four more degrees! Milo protests.

Dude, Arnie says. We just had a very successful test. Let's take it and learn.

But what about the watch? Just, nothing?

Arnie crosses his arms and looks down toward the tub. He lets his jaw slacken, his brows compress. Theoretically, he says. Theoretically, we can still get some malleability at this temp or near it. You know, because there's effectively no heat transfer and therefore no action or reaction and therefore no time. So it could be malleable …

Let's do it! Milo cries. Come on! Can we?

Arnie doesn't respond, which Milo knows means yes. Arnie types into the console.

He says, Okay, go ahead and move the dial. Just five minutes.

There is a dial on the machine. It's the only control not digitally-operated. It has to be, because if the software crashed while you were in a transfer, you'd need an analog control to get out. Or so Arnie says. It might also be because of the satisfaction of having such a dial. It's large, heavy, and smooth—like what you'd find on an expensive audio component.

Actually, Arnie says, make it five minutes and five milliseconds.

Milo looks up curiously.

For perception, Arnie says. We have to compensate for perception.

Milo squints.

Arnie raises his brows and makes his mouth into an 'o,' as he does when he realizes someone needs an education. He explains,

What we perceive is a brief interval after the present. It takes time for things to come through our senses, to be processed by our brain. When something happens, no matter how close to us, we perceive it after it happens. What that means is we all live permanently in the past.

Milo decides he will think about this deeply later. For now, he's confused: But why do we need to do it on the dial? Can't we just subtract the difference? Or add it, or whatever?

It's an experiment, Arnie says. You'll see. He wags his head slowly. Milo concedes.

Milo grips the dial and sees his fingers tremble. Why is that? He feels no anxiety, but there it is. He turns the dial to the prescribed time. Arnie presses Enter.

Then nothing happens. That is, they perceive nothing and Arnie says immediately, It's done.

They look at each other, knowing a result waits for them. So long as they wait, there is the hope that they succeeded. Milo expects Arnie to give in first, to check the watches and the time sensors on the system. But Arnie makes no move.

Then Milo's phone rings. It's Ms. Dalyrimple. She has never called him in the workshop. He answers. She says, I'm so sorry to bother, but it's kind of urgent. Someone is at the door. I didn't know whether to answer. With so much going on, you know? Oh I'm sorry Milo I shouldn't be bothering you ...

But Milo reassures her and goes into the house.

At the front door stands Randy Trundle, president of their neighborhood watch. Randy is from Sheboygan, as earnest as they come.

Hey Milo, he says. I don't mean to bother ya, but some folks are a little concerned what you got goin' on in there. Neighbors, ya know.

Do you want to come in? Milo asks. Get a beer?

Oh, I couldn't bother ya, Randy says, as he walks through the door and heads to the kitchen.

Ms. Dalyrimple offers him some French apple pie. Oh, Deloris, I really shouldn't—well maybe just a little slice. You got ice cream for that?

Randy eats the pie with ice cream. He drinks the beer. They talk about basketball, and Milo pretends to understand by saying things like 'Welp, you never know.'

Finally Randy says, Look, I had some folks wantin' to call the cops. I shouldn't betray confidence in who—but you know, the Klavenders? The Funks? Lots of folks, actually. It's no big deal to me, you know. I mean, I'd love to see your workshop, see what you got goin' on in there, but otherwise, I've got no beef. But some folks. Well, with the lights goin' down you know?

Milo reassures Randy that they're done for the night, and they'll be more respectful in the future. Actually, he says. We're about done. Just a few more days—a week at most.

Randy thinks about this, nodding his head, looking down the sidewalk. Oh great, Milo, he says. That's great to hear. Hey if you ever want to—I'd love to just get a little peek at what you're building in there. I got a nice shop too, pretty good tools and all. You know, maybe you need to borrow something? No problem. I could bring a sixer and we shoot the shit?

Sure thing, Milo says. Just as soon as we're done.

Then Randy zips his coat up to his chin and walks home, pausing to wave at people sitting by their living room windows.

When Milo gets back to the workshop, Arnie is drinking a beer and two empty cans rest on the table beside him.

Milo tries to read his expression and asks, Well? Did you check?

Without you? Arnie says, Of course not. Who was it?

Just Randy Trundle.

What did he want?

Exactly what you'd think—the neighbors are pissed.

What did you tell him?

That we'd be done in a week.

Arnie looks at Milo with a sudden exhaustion. He runs his fingers through his hair. You have to stop that, he says.

Milo takes a beer from the fridge and drinks, trying to look casual. Why? He asks. We're so close.

We're not close, god damn it! It's strange for Arnie to get angry. His eyes fix on Milo, unblinking. He says, Why do you keep saying shit about things that you don't even understand? Why all this pressure? I keep telling you we have to take our time and you just keep ignoring me.

Can we just check the result now? Milo says. I'm sorry. Okay? I'm sorry to push but what are the alternatives? How about we check the result and if it didn't work, we just regroup and take our time and figure out how to keep people off our backs. But if it worked. If it worked, let's keep going, right?! If it worked, let's get me in there tonight and just do it. I'll meet with Emily with real presence, physically, no more of this dreamy telepathic bullshit—I'll actually be there, and that's all I want, okay? That's enough for me. And then we can do more experiments—whatever you like after that, you can see Barb maybe? Or you can get the data you need for your paper and your book and your movie and all that!

Arnie drinks his beer and laughs silently, looking down. He says, Let's check the result. But no matter what it says, we're done for tonight.

Milo says, But …

Arnie scolds, We're fucking done for tonight! Done. Randy was just here. The neighborhood is freaking out. Are you nuts now, Milo? We're done.

Okay, says Milo. Check it.

You check it.

Milo goes to the tub. He lifts the canopy and retrieves the watch. He looks at the outside watch. He compares them together, heavy in his hands.

The first watch shows five minutes ago.

That night Milo wants desperately to dream of Emily, but his perverse mind knows it and works in opposition, waking him abruptly every time he drops into sleep. Although Ms. Dalyrimple is fully out, huffing and blowing rhythmically, she senses his restlessness and throws a heavy arm over his shoulder. She's always the nurse, he supposes, and it comforts him. Her breath smells of sweet yeast and a faint musk drifts from under her arm. But still he can't sleep. Milo extracts himself from her embrace and goes to his study.

He drinks Irish whiskey again to wind down, knowing that's stupid, knowing that will only produce fitful sleep. And it does.

Emily appears while he dozes. She wears an oversized hospital gown and a disposable hairnet. She stands limply, barefoot, her eye sockets dark, her expression vulnerable. The tape and gauze on the inside of her elbow is mostly torn off. She says, so quietly,

Milo? Can you come?

Of course he can! Or so he thinks. But now he is the man he was at that moment, when Emily left her hospital bed in the middle of the night and went searching for him. And she found him, brooding, drafting an angry letter to the Dean of his department. The anger was a kind of medicine, and it masked what he might have actually felt if he had allowed himself to consider Emily's prospects, to share her pain and fear.

Milo feels his anger for the Dean and his compassion for Emily simultaneously. Why does it feel wonderful, pleasurable, but also intolerable, also fatal? Is this what heroin feels like? It seems like it would. Like something horrible and wonderful at the end of everything. Why is he thinking of heroin?

Emily says, Milo, what are you doing out here?

He doesn't respond, because he's not there to respond. This shallow dream is only a recollection, a looping hologram. But he remembers what he did say, how he told her she shouldn't be up and ushered her back into her room and then said he'd go get the nurse, which he did, which was Ms. Dalyrimple, and when she went to reconnect Emily's IV drip, and ease her pain, Milo did not go to the room. Instead, he returned to his yellow pad and his pages of condemnation toward the Dean, accusations he doesn't remember now, accusations he never sent, thank goodness. Or maybe it would be better if he had, and suffered the punishment he deserves.

Milo startles, awakens, looks around through out-of-focus eyes at his study, his books, his stacks of yellow pads. He is surrounded by his bleak friends, Kierkegaard, Schopenhauer, all those sad fucks. No wonder, he thinks. His glass is miraculously still in his hand, and he drinks the rest of it and lets his arm fall to release the glass, which rolls in an arc across the floor. He drops below the surface again.

He is back in Emily's room. The sheet is pulled over her head and there is only the outline of her body—so small now! It's only a twin bed, but there is so much mattress and so little body. It could be a sheaf of dry branches under that sheet. Milo is gripping his fists. His hands! His goddamned hands, they never did what he wanted. They should have been holding Emily's hands when it happened but instead they were just fists, pressing knuckles into his thighs, and beneath his thighs the chair, and beneath the chair, the pile of yellow notebooks that had grown even as Emily disappeared. And now, when the accelerated disordering of Emily's form comes to its conclusion, Milo looks up and sees Deloris.

She wears cheerful teddy bear printed scrubs and a nametag on a yellow lanyard. In one hand, she holds out a tiny, crushable paper cup with two pills. In the other, a glass of water. Milo looks up into her face. Deloris is crying. People cry! It seems impossible, but they really do. In this shallow dream, this static recollection, Milo wants to cry. He feels it pushing up from his stomach, into his lungs, but it's too large to come out. He wants that release. How wonderful it must be to cry!

Is he crying in his sleep in his study now, surrounded by the books and notepads?

Or is he accepting the pills and swallowing them with the water?

Or is Ms. Dalyrimple saying, It shouldn't happen this way, honey.

Is she putting a heavy hand on his neck, the same brusque hand that carried him through the bad surgery?

Yes.

She is sniffling, saying, It just shouldn't happen this way. Christ have mercy. You two kids. Heaven help us. Milo you lay back in that chair now and when you wake up you'll feel better. People will tell you what to do, and every day it will get better, and if you're ever sad or lonely or even just need a slice of pie, you just call Deloris, okay? You know how to find me, hon.

And so he did.

But now that's over and Emily is in the study in her gown except now it's tattered like grocery bags clinging to barbed wire, but still her eye sockets are dark, and still she stands unsteadily and calls to him.

Milo?

Yes! he says, desperately. I'm right here!

But she keeps looking, perplexed. Then she tightens her mouth and drops her gaze and turns to walk away.

He says to himself, For fuck's sake Milo this is your chance for a do-over. Now is the time. Go to her. Use your hands. Smile, or cry, or something.

His consciousness skips a few frames, and then there is a large red spider on the arm of his chair. It has a swollen abdomen and long red-and-black legs. It darts to his hand and he feels its bite. Both his hands swell immediately, until you can no longer see the fingers, so engulfed are they in swelling. Where did the spider go? He wants to kill it before it does more damage. Before it can get to Emily. She is compromised. She can't survive a spider bite like that. But of course, it's no use. Milo can't move. He can only look at his ham-sized fists and wonder where all the fluid comes from. What part of his body shrunk so that these hands could expand so?

The next thing Milo is awake and becomes aware that he's dug his fingernails into his palms. He instinctually stands up to brush his clothes, the chair, for the spider. There is no spider to be seen. There is no Emily.

In the morning Ms. Dalyrimple has a substantial check written out, set on the kitchen counter. Milo accepts a coffee from her and stares at it. He is more tired now than when he went to bed. The check annoys him. So does the bitter coffee and the hum of the fridge and the acute pain in his spine and down his legs. At times like this, he thinks of the accident, and the odds. If he had just waited at that yellow light, brought his bicycle to a stop, none of it would have happened. He thinks of the surgery, the odds. If his surgeon hadn't had a cold, the fuck-up surgeon wouldn't have replaced her, wouldn't have brought in the resident, who liked to party, whose hands shook like a washed-up gunfighter. Of course, all that led to his introduction to Ms. Dalyrimple, who's with him now, who's saying,

I just need you to put your John Hancock on this, all right, dear?

Milo makes a face he knows is ugly. He says, Seems like a lot. The last one—the one Yeshevsky claimed was lost—it wasn't that much, was it?

No, she says. But I feel bad, you know, how that went. And it's for a good cause—can't argue with that.

Milo could definitely argue with that, but he decides not to. Instead he says, How come it has to come out of my account? Why can't you write the check from yours?

Deloris turns to face him and wraps her hands in her apron. She doesn't respond right away and he lets the silence hang.

Well, you know I don't have that kind of money in my little old checking account, she says.

Why not? He asks. He can feel what he is doing now, but he can't help it. It's pointless and stupid, but that's what happens when you don't sleep and your body's failing.

Deloris leans on the counter with one arm and looks into the sink. Then she looks up at him, appealing. Her eyes are wet now. There could be crying. Don't let there be crying.

Well, you know, she says, my job at the church doesn't pay even close to what you make, plus your book and all that. You know all this, Milo.

He says, I do know. And that's the point. Why are you working there, with that creepy prick Yeshevsky, when you could be doing so much good as a nurse?

Milo knows this is true, but it also sounds awful when it comes out, so he adds: You were such a good nurse. The best nurse I've ever known, that's for sure.

Deloris looks at him, searching. She says, Really?

Of course, he says. Of course.

It feels better to de-escalate the conversation. He picks up the pen and signs the check. That was the plan, after all, to buy some time to finish the project with Arnie. To see Emily again. It's just money. Yes, right, you have to stick to the plan and can't let a bad night's sleep ruin that. Deloris watches him sign.

Then she says, Do you really think I shouldn't work at Most Redeemed?

I think you should do what makes you most happy, Milo says. And then he can't help but add, And also what aligns best with your ethics, your purpose in the world.

Deloris brightens, and says, Well that's definitely the church!

Well, there you go, says Milo. Perhaps he'll fight this battle another day. Perhaps it's not worth it. Maybe it's not a battle at all. Maybe it's just the way things are.

Ms. Dalyrimple says, I wish you wouldn't talk about him like that—about Pastor.

You're right, Milo says. That was impolite. But you know I'm not a fan.

She says, He's a work in progress, like we all are. I've told him he could dress better and talk better—more suited to his position and his age. He listens to me.

He does?

He definitely does! Just last week, I suggested that … Ms. Dalyrimple stops there. Probably because she's clever enough to know that her example isn't going to convince Milo.

Never mind, she continues, I'm just glad you took the advice so well at our meeting yesterday and you made that promise. And I'm also glad you said those nice things about me and how we met and everything.

Ms. Dalyrimple holds out her hand and he lets her take his.

Thank you, honey, she says. I really mean it.

She comes closer to him and puts her hands on his shoulders and massages as she talks. It melts his pain. She says, Why can't we just have a simple, happy life? We can do that, right? I take care of you and you take care of me, and that's all anybody can ask for. Nobody knows how many years they have left, or even weeks or days—so let's not waste time bickering over silly things.

Milo puts his hands on her hips and it feels robotic to him. He says, I agree. We shouldn't waste time over silly things.

Ms. Dalyrimple hears the sarcasm and gives him a look of disapproval, but it's the sort of look a precocious student gets from an admiring teacher. So they are okay now, and Milo's thoughts return to the workshop.

Obviously we have to reproduce that result, Arnie says. Several times. At least. It needs to be turnkey before you crawl your sorry ass into that tub. The good news is Emily isn't going anywhere.

Arnie is scrolling through the logs from the last experiment, looking for tweaks they need to make before they go again. Milo sits on a folding chair, drinking a beer. This breaks their rule of not drinking until the work is done, but maybe it will perk him up after the last few nights.

Milo says, To say that Emily isn't going anywhere is a relative statement, and unprovable. What's more relevant is we have a week to get this done.

I reject that artificial deadline, Arnie says, without looking up.

You can't just reject it! It's real! The neighbors, the church gang, all these people have this promise from us now. Plus, we're so close.

Arnie raises his head to look at Milo, but leaves his fingers on the keyboard. He says, We just had that argument. Let's not do that over. Okay? But this is exciting! Today, we're shooting for the big one... 273.15, my man. Right?

Right, says Milo. Arnie's flippancy is irritating. But it shouldn't be, which is also irritating. Milo knows he would see the situation differently if he weren't in such a state. In fact, he can just barely see the situation for what it is, through his fog of fatigue and discomfort.

Arnie says, So don't bum us out with your gossipy business, okay? Let's hit it today! Absolute zero, man! The holy grail, or promised land or whatever.

Why the religious metaphors? Milo asks.

I don't know, Arnie says. He's clearly trying hard to lift the mood, which is unusual for him and so should be touching. He says, You're the philosopher. You're the writer—you make the metaphor.

Milo thinks about it. He drinks some more beer. He's feeling a little better. He says, Absolute zero doesn't need a metaphor to clarify or enrich its meaning. It's absolute fucking zero, after all. It stands on its own.

Fair enough, Arnie says, let's go for it.

He hands Milo one of the pocket watches and keeps the other. They put them in their respective places. The heavy analog dial is still set to five minutes. Arnie starts the process and the system makes its signature sounds and the lights dim sharply and they watch the numbers drop on the temperature monitor. It gets to minus 269—their last best result—and then with barely a hesitation it continues dropping, until it reaches 273.

Arnie's whole face expands as he looks at his friend. His eyes are wide open, his mouth is wide open, his eyebrows push up toward his hairline. Never has he shown such delight, such enthusiasm, such wonder.

Oh my god, dude, he says. That is really, really close. That's like 0.05 Kelvin. He keeps his face that way, unaware of himself.

Milo doesn't feel it. It's so disappointing. Why? All he sees are numbers on an LED screen. It's just too much of an abstraction. But he knows enough to fake it.

We did it! he cries, and throws his arms into the air, like on a roller coaster. And then, as if through this proprioception, the reality sinks in... he may be able to be with Emily, actually.

He says, Should we do the time thing? The malleability thing? You know, the five minutes again?

Arnie pauses, his expression inscrutable.

Ready? Milo asks. Arnie?

Arnie looks at his monitor. He rubs his hands together and looks up through his eyebrows with a sort of leer. He says, This could be the end, you know. Of everything. Right here in this garage in Middling, Illinois, we might rip a hole in the fabric of existence. Maybe it immediately begins to suck everything into itself—just drawing down into another dimension, like the hole they punched in the bottom of the Chicago River. The vortex. Remember that?

Arnie, what the fuck are you talking about? We just did this yesterday and everything was fine.

Yeah but now we're at absolute zero, so the effect could be... exponential.

Are you messing with me? Milo asks.

Arnie smiles, and the old sadness returns. Kind of, he says. I'm not sure. But we are at a temperature where, theoretically, an object can exist at two places at once. So, let's find out...

He holds up his finger to press Enter, flamboyantly.

From just outside they hear a peculiar sound. It takes a moment to process, but Milo places it as the whoop-whoop of a police car warning. He pauses, waits, and looks at Arnie. The car goes whoop-whoop again.

Oh for fuck's sake, Milo says, this is getting like a stupid sit com.

Arnie says, Well, I guess we won't do that test tonight.

No, hold on, Milo says. I'll get rid of them. Ms. Dalyrimple gives them cookies all the time and they love us.

Milo, his friend says. He presses his lips and exhales through his nose. I'm not risking that. He lowers his voice to a whisper and says, Those graphene panels alone could put me in jail!

Just wait! Milo whispers. I'll be right back. No one's going to jail. Have a beer!

Arnie shrugs, but then calls to him, Don't promise anything, okay?

When Milo gets to the kitchen, two police officers are there, and Ms. Dalyrimple is already serving them pecan pie. They're city police, an older man with a grey moustache and a young woman. They stand and hold their plates and forks while they talk. Milo doesn't recognize them, but Ms. Dalyrimple certainly does.

She says to the young woman, We missed you at worship last Sunday. Everything okay?

The older man takes a bite of pie and looks over at his partner.

I'm trying a different church, the young cop says. A better fit—doesn't hurt to try?

The older cop says, One's as good as the next, I figure. You just gotta go.

Then he points his fork at Deloris and says, I got the letter you all sent just now. More money, huh? What's Pastor doing with all of it?

Deloris sets two cups on the counter and says, Well, that beautiful new sanctuary won't pay for itself. Then as she pours coffee she adds, But folks should only donate what they can.

The young woman mutters, Pastor's got a lot of revenue streams, it seems.

Her partner looks at her, says, Hmm?

She replies, as if he were hard of hearing, Good pie, right?!

Milo has been watching this. Is it just a social visit? This late at night? Cops are so weird. He begins to step backward toward the workshop.

Whoa, whoa, whoa, Professor, says the older cop. We're here for a quick word, if you don't mind.

Milo sighs. What can I do for you, officers?

The two of them explain, with the elevated linguistic formality of police officers—They've hit a certain threshold of complaints about disturbance to the peace, and at that threshold they have an obligation to follow up. They don't want to trouble Milo and Deloris, good folks, church-going folks (mostly), they're almost embarrassed to make this call, given the other priorities on the force and the issues the town is facing. But the law's the law and code is code and the neighbors have a legitimate complaint with respect to the reduction in current to the electrical grid on that block, as well as with the peculiar sounds, smells, and bursts of light.

The younger officer says, We're not doubting your work's important, Professor. But maybe you could rent a space near the highway for your workshop? Or is there something on campus?

Milo promises he'll be done within the week. The cops are satisfied. Milo feels a sudden compassion for them. Cops aren't bad people. They're just… regular. People doing their jobs. That job must be hard, come to think of it. This call was probably the highlight of their night. It's good that they had this call and got to enjoy Ms. Dalyrimple's pie and have a little small talk. Now they can go, refreshed, and bust a meth lab or something.

As they walk out, Milo puts one hand on each of their shoulders. I want to apologize, he says, for putting you to this trouble. Maybe next time you can come by for some of Deloris's pie when we haven't caused trouble.

They all have a laugh at this. Ms. Dalyrimple is smiling with her whole face. She is proud. They wave and the cops give a last whoop-whoop and speed away down the street.

As Milo returns, Arnie crushes an empty beer can, tosses it into the recycling tub, and says, That was quick. How'd you get rid of them so easy?

Pie, says Milo.

Ah, says Arnie. That'll do it. So they're gone for good?

Yeah, so now we can do the experiment, right?

Arnie goes to the little fridge and brings back two more beers. He opens them with each hand, gives one to Milo and says, Let's have another and talk.

Milo takes the can but doesn't drink. He says, No, really, we can at least finish the experiment now, right?

Arnie drinks at least half his can at once. It seems too dramatic. Then he releases some air and says, If we fire this system up again now, and bring the neighborhood down again, doesn't that seem like flipping the bird to the cops?

Milo does not like that Arnie is drinking. He never breaks that rule, so the chances they keep going are fading fast. It's irritating. Milo drinks his beer and then goes to get two more. The opportunity has passed, but he can't stop arguing. He says,

The very best time to do our work is just after the cops come. Right? It's like they don't pull you over for speeding right after they give you the first ticket.

Yeah they do, says Arnie. He drinks more. That happened to my first wife. She thought she was clear and she gunned it and it turned out that same cop had just taken the off ramp and got right back on the interstate after her. He was pissed. Just like your friends would be if we pimped them tonight.

It seems like Arnie is talking strangely. But Milo might also just be hearing strangely, seeing strangely. There's no way around your perception, and if you're not sleeping and you're stressed out and you drink, your perception is crap. Milo sits quietly for a minute, continuing to drink because what else is there to do?

Then he shrugs and says, I told them we'd be done in a week.

Arnie crushes his can and throws it in the bin. His expression becomes sharp. He says, You told who?

Whom, Milo says.

Right, says Arnie, who did you tell?

It's 'whom did I tell,' says Milo, And I told the police.

You told the fucking cops that? You promised them? I said don't make any promises.

Milo shrugs and drinks disdainfully. He says, But here we are.

Arnie seems confused. He stares at the floor between his feet. Then he rises, gets two more beers, opens them, and sits back down. They drink without speaking, under the hum of the overhead lights. It's an awful place to drink, when you think about it.

Milo says, I'm going tomorrow. It's quiet, but Arnie hears.

The hell you are, he says, just above a whisper.

Oh yes, says Milo, Yes I am. That's the whole point of all this. And we're ready.

Arnie closes his eyes and wags his head, You have no idea—not the slightest clue—of what it means to be ready.

Hey, Milo says loudly, fuck you.

Arnie snaps his eyes open. Fuck you!

What the fuck? Milo says. Fuck off, Arnie!

No, you fuck off Milo!

Milo's heart races with the acute stress response. Suddenly everything in the room is very clear, but also tinted red, as if a veil of rage has dropped. He says,

Get out of my fucking house, Arnie! How about that?

Suit yourself, Arnie says. He stands up and walks, unsteadily, to the door. The drama of his departure is spoiled by the time it takes him to unlatch all the locks. But then he's gone. Just like that. His coat remains on the hook by the door. His backpack leans just below the coat.

Milo is hazy and confused. How did that escalate so fast? He gets up and walks over to the system, keeping balance by holding on to tables, rails, conduit. He leans right down to the chamber, where the action happens. It doesn't look like much—just a reinforced box about as large as a motorcycle. He leans against it and feels the tug of magnets through his spine.

It occurs to him that he could quit this whole thing. It's entirely up to him. He could call it, dismantle everything. No trouble, no deadlines, no lying. He could put everything back to normal. Everyone would be better off. Everyone except him. Everyone except, maybe, Emily?

Milo leaves the workshop without tidying, without turning off the lights. Back in the house, he can feel how drunk he is. Every action must be methodical to avoid an accident. Don't drop the glass of water. Don't stab your cheek with that toothbrush. Don't bust your toe on the bed frame. Don't wake up Ms. Dalyrimple. Who is it that talks to your drunk self? How can you be drunk, but also have this self that tells you you're drunk and takes care of you? Is that a dialectic? What does dialectic even mean? Why was he so mean to Arnie? Arnie probably really needs some compassion. That guy lost three wives. Who loses three wives? Is Arnie drunk now too?

There will be no sleep tonight.

Arnie doesn't answer his phone, so Milo throws a snowball at his window. He raps sharply on the storm door. Arnie appears in his robe and brings him inside.

For Pete's sake, Milo, it's the middle of the night.

I know Arnie, I'm sorry. I just... Milo loses his train of thought. What is he doing again?

Come on in, says Arnie. Come on. I'll make some tea or something.

They sit at the kitchen table. It's a small room in an old house, and the table has a formica top and chromed steel tubing. Milo tells Arnie about his last visit with Emily. Or, the flashback, really. And also about the spider.

I'm just so full of regret, Milo says, I feel like I can't hold any more. And I'm sorry about the argument we had—that was my fault. I'm all strung out, but it's no excuse. I was really rude, and I apologize.

Arnie nods, sips his tea, and looks at the table. Clearly, he's thinking, as he always does, but he also seems fuzzy. Of course he is—he went to bed drunk and angry and someone woke him up two hours later. Milo searches for his purpose in coming there. He lacks the energy, but digs deeper. You can't keep going like this—something has to be done.

I have to go to her, he says. Tomorrow night. Or maybe even in the morning.

Arnie looks at him wearily. You just need some sleep, he says. When's the last time you got a decent night's sleep?

I have to go, Milo says. I'm serious.

Let's talk in the morning. You want to stay here? I can set you up on the couch. I'll text Deloris and let her know.

Suddenly Arnie's resistance is intolerable. Milo yells at him, Arnie! He stands to make his point and bumps the table with his thigh and both cups of tea rock on their sides and spill. The two professors watch the liquid flow gracefully across the table, pool up temporarily at the chrome edge, and then cascade over to the floor. It moves so quickly. They stare.

Milo rights the cups. He says, Arnie, I beg you.

This is what people say in dramatic literature or movies. He says again, I beg you. I am begging of you. I beg of you.

Maybe one of those will work.

Arnie looks around the kitchen. He rolls his head around, like he's searching, or working kinks out of his neck. Then he draws his face toward his friend and smiles the sadness of an old hound.

Milo, he says. Milo.

What?

Arnie exhales greatly. He says, You know it won't work. Come on, you know this. We're just playing.

This can't be true. The words won't soak into Milo's consciousness—they just run off.

Milo says, What are you talking about?

Arnie says aloud, as if to the room, He doesn't know. Aw, shit.

Arnie stands up and shoves his hands in his pockets and says

Look, man, I really need to level with you. I've let this go too far. I figured it was like a hobby, something therapeutic for us. But this thing doesn't work. I mean, it works in the sense that we're getting close to absolute zero. That's good but not new. But the concept of transfer—the magnetic manipulation of the fabric. That's not real. Or, not anywhere real enough you should get in that tub. You know? Come on Milo, you know this.

As Milo listens, an explanation appears. Suddenly, it's all very clear. But he has to confirm.

So all this, he says, this plan for re-connecting me with Emily—it's all been a kind of prank? Just a deception?

Arnie winces. Well, those are pretty harsh words. But I guess that's accurate, yeah.

And you did it to help me? To keep my spirits up, to distract me?

Yes! says Arnie, pleased. Exactly. I wanted to keep it going because it was fun, you and me working on this secret thing together. It was good for both of us, I have to admit. You know, you're not the only lonely person.

This is probably true, but Milo knows the rest of it is a lie. Arnie wasn't lying before—he's lying now. This is the deception, this denial of their project.

Milo says, What about the watch? That happened. I saw it.

You saw the second watch after I took it from you each time. Arnie holds up his hands and wiggles his fingers. I'm a dexterous guy, he says.

And what about the 5 milliseconds?

Well, the perception part is true. We do live in the past. But the adjustment made no sense—I was just seeing if you were paying attention to the logic of all of it. When you didn't call me on it, I could tell you weren't interested in that. I could tell you were hooked. I'm sorry, Milo, this was so horrible and manipulative. I'm a terrible friend.

Don't say that, Milo says.

But it's true. And it's worse. The cops—it was me who called them.

Gosh, Milo says. You put yourself at risk with that.

Maybe. I doubt it. I also called Randy Trundle.

You did? Milo didn't expect this. How about the pastor? Are you in cahoots with him?

Arnie shakes his head disdainfully, No, that asshole is on his own. Come on—I wouldn't do that. But the other two, yeah—I called them to slow us down. To buy more time, just you me, two old run-down professors having a little fun in the lab. Is that so bad?

Milo looks at his friend across the table. This poor guy. Look what this is doing to him. What kind of friend would pull him deeper and deeper into this? And now poor Arnie is hooked on the journey and doesn't want to see it end. He'll do anything to keep it going, obviously. It's horrible to have put him in this situation. Milo doesn't deserve a friend like Arnie. Maybe he doesn't deserve any friends—or any wives, for that matter. He should be on his own.

I should let you go, Milo says.

Really? Arnie studies him. Just like that?

Yeah, Milo says. I understand. He manages a smile. This is a wake-up call for me, this whole little crisis we've had. I get it, Arnie. Let's be done. We can start dismantling the system this weekend. We'll figure out how to get the materials back to your lab—maybe I take the fall for that? And then we'll find another hobby we can do together.

Arnie stares at him. He says, Let's talk about it in the morning, okay?

In the morning, Milo says.

Mrs. Dalyrimple is waiting for Milo in the kitchen when he gets home. He can't remember the last time she woke from her deep and reliable sleep. Her robe sleeves are rolled up and she's scrubbing the inside of the sinks with some abrasive cleaner. When she sees him come in, she grabs a towel and faces him with this expression of someone dreading bad news. Her face is puffy and tired; her temples are wet with perspiration. The room smells of cleaner and vanilla candles.

Where have you been? she asks. In the middle of the night?

Arnie's, Milo says. He had a little crisis—he needed a friend. This is true, technically.

Ms. Dalyrimple puts a fist on her hip and tilts her head. She seems relieved he hasn't brought bad news, yet. She says, You're a good friend. Now take off all those coats and come to bed. Or do you need a little bite of cake first?

You go to bed, Milo says. I'm just going to finish something in the workshop.

What? What could you possibly need to do right now? Her tone has changed to incredulity. Milo is on thin ice.

I need to wind down some systems. That takes time. Might as well get started now if I'm going to have everything put away by the weekend.

She speaks slowly, searching his face, You're really going to do that? Stop the whole thing?

I am.

Because of Pastor's visit.

No, Deloris, he says. Despite his visit.

She shrugs, as if to say 'I have the answer I want and don't care to know more.'

Don't be long, says Ms. Dalyrimple.

Good night, he says, and turns before she can come closer.

Milo remembers every step. He has seen Arnie do it so many times. He brings the system back to temperature. He goes to the small bathroom in the shop and relieves himself, smooths his rumpled hair. It occurs to him that, with the delay of light bouncing off the mirror, and with the lag in his perception, he is looking at himself from the past. It's funny and he smiles, wondering what kind of man he'll be in the future, which he exists in now, but cannot perceive. He looks younger when he smiles. He should smile more often. Maybe he will.

He returns and climbs into the titanium tub. He can feel his heart beating through his sweater, hammering with urgency. He feels no shooting pain from all the compromised joints in his spine. He feels strong, vital, alert. His brain and organs are making this happen, creating chemicals, and his heart is pumping them into every cell. His heart is in command.

It occurs to Milo that the dial is on the outside of the tub, and so is the button to open and close the canopy. This is a design flaw. Maybe it's true Arnie never intended this to work. Or maybe he thought if it ever did work, he'd be the one controlling the outside. It's too late to worry now—Milo will do what he can. The great dial controls an LED screen that can show any moment in time. Before, he left the default to 'today' and only rotated it for five minutes. But now he spins the date and time way back, to the day before Emily first felt signs of illness. A day they went out on the lake in a canoe. Then with no hesitation, he presses the canopy button and holds it until there is just enough crack to retrieve his hand and then with tremendous relief he sees the lid finish its process and form a seal over him.

The system does its work.

We are in the canoe facing each other in the soft light of morning in late summer. Fog hovers over the water. Our paddles drip audibly. Mallards cackle and mutter nearby, leaving wakes on the smooth water. In the shallows under some hanging maples, wood ducks dart. A turtle surfaces and releases bubbles. Fish rise in pops and quickly submerge.

Our legs are touching in the center of the canoe. I can feel the wetness of the lake water on her smooth calf. It's now that I realize the transfer has happened. It worked. I can feel, and Emily is here. But, strangely, there's no sense of excitement. The heart has resumed its mundane job of keeping time. Rather, there is a feeling of relief. Large gladness. A release of pressure. I reach out and touch her knee—it's a little awkward, because only my fingertips get there, almost like I'm poking, but Emily reaches out and hooks my fingertips in hers and makes it all right.

Interesting, she says, that we came back here. Somehow I expected we would meet in your time. Like when I appear in your dreams.

I take a hearty stroke with the paddle, press my calves outward with the effort, and she presses her calves against mine to brace me.

Were they dreams? I ask. I thought of that more as … visitations?

Like I'm a ghost? She laughs and her eyes compress.

I laugh too. I guess, I say. Call me crazy, but …

I suppose I am a ghost, of a sort. But doesn't that also make you one, to me?

Does it seem sometimes like we always were?

Ghosts?

Or, at least our time was borrowed—we were from different places or times, just stealing moments together we knew wouldn't last? All the songs we liked and shared—they were all about the end of something. Isn't that strange? Why would we do that? Unless, of course, we are just ghosts. That seems like what ghosts do.

She leans back in the canoe and puts her bare ankles up on my thighs. She closes her eyes and looks into the sun. I paddle a while, careful not to upset her feet in my lap.

You're a handsome old grandpa, she says.

You say that like it's a surprise, I say.

No. It's what I would have expected.

A breeze picks up, carries the fragrance of lilacs over the water. The canoe rocks gently and I let it drift.

Should we have had kids? I ask.

Of course we should have, she said.

Why didn't we?

Because I died. Emily keeps her eyes closed, lying back, but she chuckles and I can see it in her belly.

No, I mean before that. We could have.

We tried.

We did?

I did.

I take her foot in my hand and massage it. I'm sorry, I say. What did I do? Did I say no? I don't remember.

We never talked about it. It was like this untouchable object in the room—like a golden idol from biblical times, just sitting on the kitchen table and we refused to look at it. We wouldn't even acknowledge it was there.

I'm sorry.

You should stop saying that.

I'm sorry.

I mean it.

Okay.

Because it doesn't let you off the hook, you know? Emily sits up with effort, steadies herself with a hand on the gunwale and the canoe rocks. I steady it with a paddle out on the water.

I understand, I say.

She leans forward toward me, elbows on her knees and peers into my face. Now I can see the color of her eyes, the softness of her cheek and most delicate transparent hairs along her jawline. I see the pink of her lower lip, always just a bit puffier than the upper. I feel her breath, its warm, humid, sweet animal vitality. In and out, she breaths, and her heart keeps time. As she looks at me.

You can love people, she says. Or you can love the idea of them. But you have to learn which one is happening to you.

Because she is so alive right now, and our faces are inches apart, fixed in place even as the horizon rocks back and forth, I feel comfortable saying, Are you wiser now? Since …?

Am I smarter dead, she laughs.

I raise my eyebrows, waiting.

Definitely, she says. One day you'll see.

We move closer. We hold each other's hands and let our foreheads touch.

I say, What did you mean? At the end. The last thing.

I feel her wag her head, as if to say 'no.' After a while she says, Do you still not know?

I still don't know.

What did I say?

You said, Don't follow me.

And now, now that we're finally together again, conjured up by yours and Arnie's contraption—what do you think it means now?

Well, I say. I thought at first maybe you were worried I might do something horrible, I might just end things violently.

That's true, she says. But it's not what I meant.

I suppose I think now that you meant I shouldn't... Well, that I should carry on with life. I should keep your memory but not cling to it.

Emily lifts her face, now just an inch from mine, and smooths my hair. Looks back and forth between my eyes. Very good, professor, she says.

I say, I should be kinder to Ms. Dalyrimple.

You should, she says. You can save her soul, you know. And she can save yours. You just have to invest.

Let's not talk about that. I shouldn't have brought it up.

She leans her head back against mine. We let the boat drift. She says, Milo.

Yes?

I have to go.

No, you don't. How do we know? Maybe we can just stay here. Maybe we found a rare place of stasis. Maybe this is what it feels like in absolute zero.

Milo, I know you understand. I can just feel it. Can't you?

I take a long breath. It comes out in a sort of shudder. I say, Yes. I do. But not just yet.

No, says Emily. Not just yet. I will come to you.

She brings her legs over my bench in the canoe, one on each side of me, and rests on my thighs. We press our bodies together as if we're trying to fuse them. She is soft, light, immutable. There is not enough of her to satisfy this longing but I try in that embrace. There is sadness and gratitude and joy.

Then she pulls away, so she can look in my eyes and at my mouth.

We kiss.

And that is enough.

Now there are sirens, all at once, and all around, shrieking like the sound pinched nerves would make, if nerves could make sound, and someone is striking the outside of the canopy lid, and Milo is trying to catch his breath but can't, perhaps because his cells are disordering too rapidly, but there is enough for him to hear someone calling his name, Milo! Milo! Milo! What have you done! This is a good question, his rational mind observes, because he's not sure what he's done, but it's strangely wet and sticky on the contoured floor of the titanium tub. That has to be blood, that wetness, and it must be related to some malfunction or injury to his spine, because his arms and legs don't respond to his efforts. But it's good he can feel wetness and stickiness—that's something to build on, isn't it, that basic sense of touch—he can work with that, and every day make a little more of that sense, and bring in the other senses, if that siren would just stop, please, if he could just get a little peace, he could make it up to Arnie and he could be good to Ms. Dalyrimple and still, still he could love the things or maybe just the ideas of things, gradually working up to things, but still sometimes when he's tired of trying so hard, sometimes, maybe, he could dream of Emily.

DOWNRIVER

After 17 days of thunderstorms, the skies finally clear, and I see the old farmer Hanacek floating over the nettles at the edge of our field. He floats because he's a ghost, of course, and so are his two mules. All that rain drowned the crops we planted—everything's pretty much dead now. Not to complain, I mean, I guess it could have been worse. But the most frustrating thing was that Hanacek, that stubborn son of a gun, didn't show himself the whole time. Through all the storms, and the river flooding, and the trash piling up, he was just gone. I actually thought he'd abandoned us. But now he's here, thank goodness, just in time to save my marriage.

I need to run back to the house to get Morgan so she can see our ghost farmer has returned, on a beautiful, clear morning. So I give him a one-finger gesture, like Hold on a second, I'll be right back. He hooks a thumb in his overall strap and nods once, tipping the brim of his felt hat below his eyes. One mule shudders his skin against ghost flies and the other mule flaps her ears. I figure they're not going anywhere soon, so I jog up toward the house.

On the way, I do a quick scan to see if any junk showed up overnight. It's not uncommon for us to find, say, oil cans, or punctured tires, or baby cribs—that sort of thing—in our yard or on our field. Mostly the neighbors leave these things for us because our little 6-acre farm used to be their collective dump. I haven't caught anybody doing it yet, but still I asked about it one time at the Rural King and the cashier said, I wouldn't make a stink about it if I were you—around here people value their freedom. When I pointed out that was maybe not how I'd define freedom, she shrugged and handed me my receipt and said, Suit yourself. You ain't the first and you won't be the last.

Sometimes, though, I think the junk comes right up out of the ground, especially with all this rain, and a lot of times you see it first thing in the morning, like a chunk of food on a baby's chin. But regardless of the source, Morgan doesn't like it. In fact, to be accurate, she hates it, and she's at her wits end having her dream home treated like a dump. So I get up early and try to tidy as best I can.

This morning things look pretty good except for one beautiful old tractor transmission emerging from a field where we tried to grow corn. It's rusty red among the yellowed corn stalks. Morgan is definitely going to notice this. While Hanacek waits, I grab a shovel to pry it from the muck. The shovel handle splits, so I reach down and try to roll the transmission out so I can get it with the tractor bucket. I'm still in my jammies, though, and my slippers don't hold well in the mud and my arms are bare, and when I hug the transmission a rough edge makes a nasty cut near my wrist and I start bleeding. I stop by the garage and tie up the wound with some yellow hazard tape and scoot back to the house.

Morgan's still in our bed, where I haven't slept for 16 days. I pull back the cover from her head, carefully, and she smells like warmth and honey. I want to slip in there with her, but I don't because that move has not gone well recently. Also, Hanacek is waiting! Morgan grabs the cover back and buries herself.

Sorry, sweetie, I say. But you have to see something.

She doesn't reply. The outline of her ribcage rises and falls with her breathing.

Seriously, honey, I say. We got to go right now—you have to see this.

After a pause, Morgan drops the covers and shows her face. She blinks and rubs her eyes and squints at me. Her voice is a little croaky when she says, Can we not make today any harder than it has to be? Okay, Arthur? Let's just get through it.

She is talking about moving out, which is of course ridiculous. That can't happen and that isn't going to happen, and especially now the skies are blue and the morning is gorgeous and Hanacek is back.

I reach down, very cautiously, and brush her hair back from her forehead. Her expression is a lot like when she sees junk in the field—like there's no fight left in her.

You love me, I say. This is what we say.

Arthur, she replies.

Come on … I say.

She closes her eyes and waves a hand and mumbles, You love me too.

I want it to be a surprise, but I can't help it, so I say, Hanacek is back! It's a beautiful day. That's what I have to show you—sorry, I can't help spoil the surprise. So let's go!

She exhales loudly and begins to argue, but then she sees my arm. Secretly I'm glad, I have to admit, because I know she can't stop nursing even when it's not her shift, and this will get us past the snag. It's worked before. And sure enough, in a minute my cut is properly bandaged and I've brought her a coffee and rubber boots and we're ready.

I'm doing this, she says, as a good faith gesture. Okay? Do you understand what I mean?

She takes my wrist and secures a piece of tape over my bandage.

Of course, I say. Of course.

Outside the sun makes purple highlights in Morgan's hair and the breeze presses her nightgown against her legs. Six turkey vultures wheel above us, probably looking for kill from all the rain. Morgan stops to sip her coffee and sees the transmission. She winces, sighs, and shakes her head.

You know, she says, you don't have to stay here. You could find another place too.

But not with you …

Well, like we talked about …

Why would I do that, I ask. Just abandon everything we have here for some random rental place somewhere?

Forget it, Morgan says, and turns into the bright sun.

We're having the same old conversation again, which was certainly not my goal, so I return to my goal.

Come on, let's hurry while he's still there. Isn't it gorgeous out? You look nice in this light.

I take her free hand and it's limp, but doesn't pull away. That's progress.

We march down the slippery path along the field toward the woods and the river. Half way there, Morgan sees something under the honeysuckle bushes along the path. I missed it this morning. She covers her mouth with both hands.

Oh, Arthur! Why?!

It wasn't me, I protest. Not this time.

There is a pile of rabbit carcasses heaped under the bushes, maybe a dozen tumbling over to the edge of the path. Their leg meat has been stripped, but the rest remains, like bloody hand puppets. Flies gather on their eyes. This is what the vultures are after.

Who would do this? Morgan asks. Why would they just kill all those rabbits and then come over here and dump them? It's just not … logical.

Maybe the vultures dropped them, I suggest. It sounds dumb when I say it out loud. We both know that's not how vultures work.

Morgan turns once again to the sun and closes her eyes. She mutters, as if to herself, Why am I bothering? This isn't my problem anymore. Not my problem. I'm done.

Then, apparently recovered, she turns back to me and says, Okay, I promised, so show me your farmer and then I'm going back to the house to pack.

We walk, separately now, toward the trail into the woods where I saw Hanacek over the nettles. We slip on the wet grass. No one speaks. This is not going how I planned.

When we get to the edge of the field, the farmer and his mules are gone.

On this very spot, where the path into the woods begins, on our first day at the farm, we saw a doe and two spotted fawns. Ten minutes after that, we saw a red fox strut along the edge of the field, and then we saw a barred owl staring from the crook of a white oak. That was a little more than a year ago. Morgan had a huge sketchbook and colored pencils, to draw a map of where all the crops and livestock would go. It's a beautiful illustration—now crumpled from when I pulled it out of the garbage— because she drew the chickens in their yard, and the goats on top of a garden shed, and rows of corn and pumpkins, and a grove of pines we'd plant, near another grove of oaks and hazelnut and prairie flowers. At the end of that morning, Morgan sat down in the grass with her sketchbook on her lap and added to the map the three deer in the woods, and the fox along the hedge, and the owl in the tree and said, Oh my god Arthur I don't think it could be any more perfect. And I said, You mean your drawing? And she laughed and said, You know what I mean. I leaned down and kissed her and she kissed me back and then she stopped abruptly and said, Later! We have work to do! She raced up the hill in her blue dress with her sketchpad and tin of pencils and I watched, not knowing how to cope with the gratitude I felt.

It's been a rough year for those animals. The chickens disappeared, one by two, despite our best attempts at fencing. It might have been the fox, but he appeared later on the road with a tire track through him. The three goats died from eating car batteries someone dumped here. We haven't heard the owl call in months. Only the deer remain, now large enough to wipe out a row of beets in one night. So, you could say it's been a challenge—for us and the animals! But still.

For those first few weeks, we realized we weren't reading books or watching videos about simple farming—we were living it! Every morning we'd get up before dawn and walk right out of the house to our projects, not because we felt bound but because we loved it. We fell asleep each night looking forward to the morning. Twice I found Morgan gone from the bed in the middle of the night. She was outside standing at the edge of the field under the moon just looking. Just looking, you know?

Well, now as we stand, this spot brings back all kinds of unproductive memories for Morgan. We can't linger here or things will really go south.

Hanacek! I say, He's killing me. He must have drifted back into the woods. You know he's usually right along the river bank, like we saw him that one time.

Morgan starts to say something and then stops herself. Instead, she says, I'm not going back there.

Oh, sure you are, I say. I just mowed the path. It'll be fine.

I smile, but I know I'm blinking too much. She notices these things. I keep talking.

I just want you to see him again, like that time, because it's been a long time and I know things have been a little … tricky. I mean, I listen to what you've been saying. I know. But this is something really good, right? I mean, who else has a little farm with a ghost farmer, like a real ancestor who haunts the woods sort of benevolently? Right?

This all sounds strange, as I hear myself speak. But you can't deny your senses—that's all we have.

I'm not going back there, Morgan says. We came down here, like I promised. But he's… your, um, farmer is not here. And I don't really like being in this spot, as you know, so I'm going in now, okay?

She gives me a weak wave and then wraps her arms around her torso and marches up the hill in large strides. I stand still, groping for a new strategy.

It was dusk when we saw Hanacek together, just a week into our new life. We sat on a bench swing I'd repaired and perched on the bluff that overlooks the river. The rusted chains groaned as we moved back and forth. The wind came from the north and you could barely hear the interstate. A wood thrush called from across the river. I had my arm around Morgan and she was playing with my hand absentmindedly. We just sat.

She broke the quiet, whispering, What is that? Somebody, right over there.

I saw it too. There were lumpy forms moving among the trees along the bank. I could feel Morgan's pulse race. I could feel my own, just as quick. These shapes moved steadily, but so slowly, as smoke drifts through woods on a still night. The moon was out, and there was urban glow from Middling, but this little light seemed to have no effect on these creatures. What was visible about them came only from themselves. Unlike the trees they passed, they cast no shadows. It was like a photograph you know is wrong but don't know why.

But then as they moved down the bank, they appeared to grow brighter, and it was plain there was an old man leading two harnessed mules. The man wore striped overalls and a felt hat and Wellington boots. They came down to the water and entered the river, in the shallows that form at the bend. But their feet made no ripples.

I felt Morgan's breath on my ear as she whispered, Should we say something?

I wasn't able to speak. When we first saw the shapes, I thought it might be neighbors. That was good, because we hadn't met anyone yet—no one had come to welcome us with some home baking, as is usual in this part of the country. I thought perhaps this was how we'd meet our neighbors, who were maybe just giving us some space. But now, as the farmer and his mules became more visible, it was plain that they were spectral forms, not members of the living. Ghosts. I had a strong physical reaction, in which my blood surged to my head and my throat seized up and my arms and legs got cold.

Morgan, now looking at the side of my face, said, Are you all right?

I managed to nod. She turned back to the forms. Just then, Hanacek looked up and his gaze fell on us. Even at that distance, you could see in his eyes the weariness and sad amusement. I looked back at him and we remained that way for who knows how long and in those moments I came to understand. Later, in the library and on the county website and in the archives of the historical society, I confirmed it all. But it seems to me Hanacek told me everything that very first night.

What the heck was that, Morgan said. It broke me out of my trance.

They were spirits, I said. Ghosts. I don't know what's the right word, but you know.

Morgan shuddered and leaned into me. Come on, don't be silly, she said. It must have been some neighbors. It's getting cold. Let's go in.

You saw them, right? I asked.

Morgan looked into my eyes, first one and the other. Sure. Yes. Of course. Let's go in okay?

But if you saw them, then you saw how they didn't have shadows and didn't disturb the water. So, not just neighbors?

I don't know, she said. She stood up and rubbed her arms vigorously. Let's make some tea.

Also, no one has mules any more. We don't have neighbors with mules.

Morgan's chin darted back in surprise. Mules? she asked. And then, before letting me reply, she grabbed my arm and interlaced my hand and led me out of the woods and up the path toward the lights of our kitchen.

Afterward, she never said exactly what she thought happened. And she says she never saw Hanacek again.

I have seen him a dozen times, at least.

When I get back to the house, Morgan's muddy boots are on the deck and through the open door I can see her pulling books down off the shelf.

I say, That's my copy of Blood Meridian.

She looks at the cover, shrugs, and puts it back on the shelf.

I'm kidding! I appeal to her. You can have it. You can have anything you want. In fact, if you stay, you can leave it all where it is.

This sounds better than I had planned. Morgan lets her arms drop and stares at me, her face distorted and suppressed.

Just as I'm about to build on this success, a horrible sound comes from back in the woods. It's some tremendous motor, maybe an unmuffled truck and it roars like someone tearing a hole in the sky. Then we hear a man's voice yell, rapidly, Go-go-go! And then the motor roar carries away and then turns and continues to fade on the county road. Strange how sound carries here.

What the fuck was that? Morgan asks.

This is another opportunity. I say, We should go see.

It was right in the back of our property, she says. She's looking out the window now.

Yeah, it was really close.

What would someone be doing back there? There's no reason to be back there.

I am remembering how she said, just this morning, 'Not my problem,' and I'm thinking please don't say that again. But she's concerned now. When there's an emergency or a threat or a wound, she can't help herself. It must be triaged and treated.

Let's go, I say. And we do.

We walk quickly, trying not to slip, Morgan takes a course around the spot where the path opens into the woods. I wonder if she'll ever forget about that spot, the moment 16 days ago, when it was littered with dead grackles—all black on green grass, like a fabric pattern. All shot with a single blast of a 12-gauge, which I can still feel in my shoulder. The birds were gorging on strawberries, the only crop still living, the only thing not drowned by rain. (And who knew another 16 days of rain was yet to come?) I would like to forget that spot, too. After the boom, when the maddening chorus stops, when the ravenous beaks hang limply beside yellow eyes in a contortion of feathers —immediately the rage vanishes and you're left with something else. I can't explain what that is. It had to be done, I said, it's the reality of farming, and that's true, but Morgan disagreed. I'm hoping it all passes in the flow of time, washes downstream, for both of us.

I follow Morgan down the path into the woods toward the river, where the old gravel road dead-ends into our place, just short of the river. I scan the banks for Hanacek. Morgan stops and I bump her back. She breaths in hard and grabs my arm and I turn to see where she's looking.

A human body lies in the mud just past the end of the old road. He is face-up on his back, but his hips are twisted and his legs are curled sideways. Like a yoga pose. His face has an ancient look to it, sharp facial bones and copper skin.

No, Morgan says. No, no, no. She turns and bumps back into me and I try to gather her in my arms but she pushes away. That's fucked up, she says. That guy is dead.

Well how do we know, I say. I start moving to get a closer look but she stops me.

Don't be naïve, she says. I know what a dead body looks like. Look at the contusion on his face and he's got a broken clavicle bleeding right through his shirt. We got to go.

Okay, but don't we have to do something? That's our property, where he's lying.

I don't know, Morgan says. She puts fists to her eyes and says, We just have to think. And then she flaps her hands like they're wet and asks the sky, Why today? Just one day is all I need. Why this now?

I look at the man and then at Morgan. Is it bad that I'm thinking maybe this will help? If Hanacek won't come then maybe this incident will connect us, give us a common goal. People die every day—150,000 they say, every day. This is just one, who happened to die here. It could be worse, right?

I say, We should check if he's really dead. You're the expert, I know, but you can't really tell from over here, right?

Morgan has her arms crossed in thought, her head down. She glances at the man, then down again.

I ask, Don't we at least need to call someone?

Who are you going to call, Arthur?

The cops?

Which cops?

I don't know. Middling?

They don't cover this area.

Then the Sheriff? The county police?

And that's worked for us before? With the shooting? Or all the junk and the dumping?

Not exactly, but this is a dead man.

You said maybe he's not dead.

Maybe not! We should check.

Now Morgan raises her palms up, outward, like a dancer and says to the woods, No! No, no, no! I didn't see this. You hear me, Arthur? I will swear under oath I did not see this and I am walking back to the house. I'm supposed to pick up the trailer. I have to pack. You said you'd help me.

I know, but we can't just leave him there, I say. Priorities have changed.

Morgan drops her arms and says, Actually, we can. We can just walk away. Because priorities haven't changed—not for me.

She stops abruptly and half turns, draws a finger precisely under each eyelid. I go to her but she keeps me away.

I'm leaving now, Morgan says. I'm walking back to the house. Are you coming to help?

All I can do is shrug. She turns and walks with big strides.

I look toward the river. God damned Hanacek's never there when you need him.

The first time I saw Morgan walk up to the house like that was last summer on our fifth anniversary. We had brought a picnic down to the old bench swing. I remember our white wine glasses balanced on the boards between us. In the surface of the wine reflected the leaves of the canopy overhead. A woodpecker rapped and a wren sang. When the first gun shot fired, Morgan jumped and the wine glasses fell. It might have been all right, but the shots continued, not far into the woods across the river. These weren't hunters, or farmers taking a shot at a varmint, or sportsmen sighting in a rifle. These were people shooting for the sheer thrill of shooting—dozens of rounds from semi-automatic weapons. After five minutes, when I said,

Maybe they'll stop soon, Morgan left me with the picnic set and made that first march up to the house.

I ran after her while the gunfire continued and, sensing an emergency, I led her to our car and drove to Middling and checked into the hotel where we'd had our reception and booked a suite on the top floor. We drank two bottles of champagne and finally Morgan's face relaxed and she lay against the pillows looking at her bare feet and said, God it's nice to just be in Middling. Some kind of civilization. Just where there's … you know, reasonable people. And no flags! I'm so sick of all those god damned flags.

Then she closed her eyes, and I took the glass from her hand and covered her in the blanket. Later, we woke up and drank water and stared at each other in the vague light of the town below and Morgan said, Thank you for bringing me here. And later, when she was asleep again, I stood at the window and looked past the lights of the town, beyond the lights of the grain elevators, toward the river and wondered what was happening on the farm.

Standing in the woods as Morgan leaves again, an inspiration strikes me.

He's breathing! I call out.

Morgan stops half-way to the house. She turns and tilts her head and squints.

He took a big breath! I say, and wait. I can see her shoulders slump in defeat, but then she jogs back toward me.

How many times, she asks, did he breathe?

Before I can respond, a vulture descends through the canopy and lands on the gravel road. Three more follow, and the first one hops on the dead man's chest.

Oh god! Morgan turns away. Did you just lie to me? Did he really breathe?

I run a few steps toward the vultures and clap my hands to scare them off. We can hear their wings rustle in the silence.

I'm done, she says. I'll tell you what—this is your problem. I don't have to fix this. I don't have to do anything. You discovered the guy...

Actually, you did, I say.

What?! Her voice is elevated.

You saw him first. You discovered him.

Why are you saying that? Are you trying to trap me somehow?

Without considering, I say, Well yeah of course I'm trying to trap you. I'm trying anything I can to keep you from leaving.

Morgan holds her hands up in a kind of deflection and says, not exactly to me, That is messed up. You just said you are trying to trap me into staying in this horrible, horrible place, by lying to me about a dead man who some redneck murderers just dumped on our property. That's what just happened, isn't it? Oh my god this is unbelievable.

Now Morgan begins to walk away for the umpteenth time, saying, I'm not the one losing it. I have to remember, I'm not the crazy person here.

I call out to her. He might have breathed! I'm going to check his pulse.

She turns abruptly and yells, Stop! Don't touch him! Your DNA for fuck's sake!

She has raised a good point. I look down and see a line of blood running from my bandage.

A wave of emotion comes over me and it's extremely difficult to view it constructively or philosophically. I say to her, What am I supposed to do if you leave? What am I supposed to do?

Morgan makes fists and stamps a foot and says, Exactly! You don't have to be left! You can recognize this for what it is and cut bait and come with me and we start over. In fact, we probably hide that dead guy so the police report doesn't show up on our property listing and we get what we can for the place and start over. Not to be morbid or calculating, but that's surviving, right? That's all we can hope to do out here—it's a fucked up place with fucked up people who are unredeemable. It's not our job to fix them.

Then she pauses, breathing hard, and says finally, This is it—your last chance. Are you coming with me?

I look at the dead man and the vultures, who have returned, and then up at the canopy of leaves, and then down toward the river and then back toward Morgan. But I can only look at her boots.

I say, Maybe it's not our job to fix these people but isn't it our job to fix the land? Like we said we would? I mean, if we give up on that aren't we admitting that it's all a wash and who can live in a world like that? Who can love in a world like that?

I'm too agitated to know how logical this sounds, but it's all I have.

Morgan leaves, holding her face in her hands. I don't follow her.

Now Hanacek has returned, that old bastard. He stands facing me between his two mules just across the river.

Too late, I say to him.

He crouches down, with an arm on his bent knee, and studies the ground. I'm guessing he's looking for mushrooms. Although I don't suppose he could eat them—maybe it's out of habit? Honestly, I don't know a thing about ghosts. There are lots of mushrooms back here in the damp woods—morels, puffballs, coral fungi, hen of the woods. Hanacek would know. It was his farm originally. You can see a photo of him at the historical society museum. He was the last farmer in the county to stick with mules when tractors became *de rigueur*. He wrote a little book about it, which he printed and bound himself. He fed six kids and seven grandkids on what he grew on ten acres, including our parcel, and made enough profit to put half of them through college. You might say that backfired on him, because the college-educated kids wanted nothing to do with this place.

So when he died, they collectively sold the land to a tractor dealer, who sold it to a trailer park builder, who let the neighbors use it as a dump and subsequently sold it to a lawyer who never set foot on the place and quickly flipped it to a family who ran a religious day care, who didn't last a year before selling it to us. But Hanacek? He never left.

What am I supposed to do? I ask.

Hanacek, still in his crouch, turns his head to look downriver, where the trees make a long corridor until the next bend. This river winds in countless turns like an intestine through a narrow strip of trees and brush. Beyond those trees, just thousands and thousands of acres of corn and beans. This river is a little remaining oasis of wildness. Abraham Lincoln canoed on this river, no shit. He wanted to make it navigable, and it's probably good he failed, because that left it wild, though at this point, I don't know if it matters. If you walk the bank of this river, as I have, sometimes with Hanacek walking nearby, you see all kinds of things people have left. There was a whole motorcycle buried so deep in the mud all you could see was the crankcase. There was a bunch of barrels and heating elements where someone cooked meth. There was a dilapidated ferry still hanging from cables. There was a miniature gallows complete with noose. And there is, always, gathered in every snag, along every curve, piles of plastic trash compressed in neat designs along with all the driftwood. I don't mean to paint a gloomy picture. I mean, still, there's lots of wildlife.

A south wind picks up, bringing high wispy clouds and I feel the barometer fall. More rain is coming. I look at the dead man, still twisted in his yoga pose, spotted with flies, and he seems to be flattening. Eventually, the vultures and coyotes will take care of him. But like Morgan said, there's still a chance someone will discover him, and then it will become a thing that needs explanation. It will become a recorded incident. Morgan always knows. When I look back, Hanacek has vanished with the mules.

Up at the house, she's gone already. Piles of books remain on the living room floor. A trailer rental contract lies on the counter. A single wine glass from last night remains in the sink. I don't know whether this is bad, because she left so suddenly, or good, because she'll have to come back. But for now, the house is silent.

The tractor engine drowns out everything in the woods, including my thoughts. When I try to slide the bucket under the man, it just pushes him away. I lower it and scoop up a couple of inches of mud with him, and then he comes up easily. I tilt back the bucket and see him in there, folded like a bug in your palm. I drive through poison ivy and nettles along the bank until I have the bucket high over the water. It feels like there should be some ceremony, but those kinds of things seem strange now, small and pathetic in a world like this. I just push the lever and tip the bucket forward until the man drops into the river.

He splashes, submerges, and then floats to the surface. His body swirls, dancing extravagantly in the swift current and then straightens out, like a canoe, and bumps around a snag, and floats downriver beyond where I can see.

THE AD MAN AFTER DARK

Through the patio window I can see the councilman at his kitchen table sorting pills on a sheet of steel. He separates a few and pounds them with a mallet. Then he cuts the powder into lines and sniffs them clean. He slouches forward with eyes closed and a shudder moves through his body. Then he raises his head and smiles beatifically, looking straight at the window where I lurk. He can't see me, of course, because it's after dark. In the reflection in the glass he sees only himself, Tommy Hinrick, still handsome despite the jowls, despite the marine-cropped orange hair. He straightens up and points at his reflection, winking, as if to say, Giddyup.

Oh Tommy, have I got a surprise for you.

His wife, Lisa, lies in the recliner in the adjoining family room with a glass of white wine, a phone, and a remote control. She's watching a group of ladies on television, whose caustic grins are framed by lines of 'breaking news.' She might be sleeping, but I hope not, because I'm waiting for her to leave. Tommy turns toward her and calls out something, his chin extended. Rather than reply, she waves her hand to shoosh him and drains her glass.

Tommy shakes his head and begins to tidy the table. Lisa's phone flashes a message, just like clockwork.

Now she will switch the channel to a nature show, put away her things, kiss Tommy on his glowing forehead, and step upstairs. Now a white Silverado will park at the road and a man will emerge in camouflage clothes and run to the corner of the house, scale the downspout to the balcony off Lisa's bedroom, and disappear inside. Now Tommy will take a bottle of bourbon over to the recliner, lower himself with a groan of satisfaction, and raise the volume on the television. He won't hear what transpires upstairs. You might wonder if this is intentional, whether they have an arrangement so common among couples with their influence, but that's not likely, because Tommy cannot tolerate anyone taking what he has acquired.

I am wearing the image of Tommy's dead mother. It's a kind of radiant husk left behind when she rejoined the universe without regret. Fortunately, she was not among the troubled ones who roam this county after dark. Instead, she left this elegant husk, which was easy to find, just outside the Hinrick mausoleum in the Middling Memorial Cemetery, where it flickered and bobbed alongside the remains of other untroubled Hinricks. I slid the husk over my own spectral form and although the fit was tight, in a matter of minutes I was walking and talking just like Peggy Hinrick, the old firebrand herself. Having successfully borrowed Peggy, I gave my best to her family, and dashed to Tommy's mansion. And here I prepare to conduct my first haunting in more than a month.

Today is my deathday, by the way, and although I'm here on this particular night for other reasons, it does seem nicely timed. A perfect way to get back in the saddle and do the honest work of the damned. Kidding! No such thing, of course. But Tommy doesn't know that, which works very much in my favor.

Looking at the unsuspecting councilman, I consider how I'll make my entrance. There are so many ways to do it. The thing is, you want the emphasis to be on the people, rather than on some phantasmagorical trick. Emerging through walls, for example, or dragging chains or whipping around like a zephyr—these are all fun but typically distract your beneficiary from the point of your visit. I want Tommy's wicked heart to melt from the warmth of his mother's tough love. I don't want him shrieking and wetting his pants because his dead mother just dropped from the ceiling. Substance over style, as we say.

Also, I have learned the hard way that you can't control the radiance of these husks when you're wearing them. It's not like your own form, which modulates so nicely. The husks are basically 'on,' making stealth a real challenge.

I slip into the room through the patio door, behind Tommy, and glide toward him until I'm just off his right shoulder. It's show time. I'm ready to be his mom, to flow with her strength and wisdom and deliver a message that will change Tommy forever. Or at least knock him off his game for a few days.

So here goes.

Nope, not yet.

Tommy nods off in his recliner and his glass of whiskey splashes on his leg, waking him.

Oh for christ's sake! He says and hurls his body forward from the clutch of the chair.

As he gets to his feet and turns, I dart out of the room and take cover in the pantry. You have to pick your moment.

The pantry is stuffed with packaged food from SnackTyme, the chain of stores Tommy inherited from his father. That's it—just stacks of cookies, cakes, chips, soup—all in plastic-wrapped boxes bearing the SnackTyme logo, a sort of Celtic cross rotated a few degrees to make it look 'fast' and stretched across a field of stars to make it look 'American.' I should know: I managed that branding when I was an ad man. I might say, with due humility, when I was THE Ad Man of Middling County. SnackTyme, just like every other decent company around here, used my little agency to make a small fortune. Who would have thought I'd be hiding in the pantry of the son of Adlai Hinrick, surrounded by all this immortal food product that I promoted, wearing the image of Adlai's wife? But here I am, and I'll tell you, things don't get any less weird after the dark of your life. I mean, they get much weirder, of course, in a spectral sort of way, but you don't really shed any of the weirdness of mortal life. Which you'd think you would.

I am thinking of Sheila, my granddaughter. She would groan to see all this 'poison' stacked up neatly, and she would probably laugh to think that the royal family of this junk are eating their own product. To that I would say, junk food is the least of their problems. And Sheila, using the stare she has perfected as a reporter, would reply, Is it? But this conversation has not taken place, because Sheila has never met me, in life or after dark. I've never met any of my grandchildren. I didn't make it that long.

Nevertheless, I have a gift prepared for Sheila and one day, if I ever earn the right to contact her, she might thank me. Because when she meets with Tommy tomorrow, to interrogate him about his questionable voting record and the whole sidewalk shenanigan—when that interview happens, Tommy will be softened up. He'll be eating out of her hand. That is, thanks to me and the surprise I have in store for him. So, here we go.

The councilman is back in his chair. He levels his eyes toward the television and raises his glass. I can hear the slurp of his lips and see his thick ears wiggle with the movement of his jaw. All is quiet. Now it's show time. I glide into the room, stand next to the television, and say to my mortal beneficiary, Hello Tommy. We need to talk.

He is completely still. The glass remains just below his lip, his shoulders slumped forward, his eyes fixed. Then those pink-rimmed, pale blue eyeballs rotate toward me. He blinks. I was expecting more response. The silence is uncomfortable.

Can you see me, Tommy? Your mom? As I say this, I'm questioning my voice impersonation, which comes from the husk but requires some effort to get right, like tonguing a reed on a clarinet.

He whispers, Good christ.

But still he barely moves. His eyes flick to the television, and then back to me.

Perhaps we should switch that off, I say. I cross my arms and drop my chin like Peggy would.

Tommy takes his glass with his other hand, holding it from the top, and places it on the side table. He grips the arms of the chair and pulls himself up, glances back at me, and then takes measured steps into the kitchen.

Tommy! I say, Can't you hear me? Your mom?

He makes a high-pitched 'hooo' sound, and then says, Oh I can hear you, mom. That's why I'm gonna fix some coffee and then I don't know maybe take a little walk until my head's right?

I move toward him as he scoops coffee and say, It's not the whiskey, Tommy, or the drugs. Yes, I saw you doing that earlier. They might make you a little foggy, but what you're seeing is real. It's your mother. It's me, Mom. I'm back from ... Well, let's say I'm 'visiting' you, in this life, because it's important. Okay? I need your attention.

Tommy loses count of the coffee scoops, dumps the filter out, and starts again. He mutters, You have my attention. That's the problem.

Then he looks up toward the ceiling and asks, Why would this be happening? There must be some reason. I'm not dreaming, right? Maybe a lucid dream? Is this what they mean by lucid dream? That's pretty messed up ...

Tommy, turn around this instant and address your mother with respect!

This doesn't sound right when I hear it out loud. Peggy was formal but she didn't spew clichés. Tommy continues, hands in pockets, staring at the coffee maker.

He says, I'd think it was some kind of prank, or like a hack. But no way those dandelions could pull off something like this. I mean ... look at her. Super real.

He steals a glance back at me as I stand, hands on hips, head tilted. I try a different tack, recalling one of the speeches Peggy made in the march on the courthouse back in the day.

Son, I want you to know I'm here because I love you, and I want to help you. Difficult times call for extraordinary measures. I go to this length because it's important.

Tommy pours coffee into his cup and sips it methodically. He blinks, smacks his forehead a few times, drinks some more, and then turns to face me.

Sorry, mom, he says, but to be honest you were always sort of full of shit, so this doesn't really surprise me. Okay, I've talked with you. So now can you go away? Is that how this works?

He drinks the coffee as he stares at me.

This isn't some trick, Tommy. Stop that.

He shakes his head and puts a hand over his heart. Look, he says, whatever you are. I'm a man of faith, and that tells me that you are nothing but a test of that faith. So you can keep talking and ... glowing or whatever. But I call thee an evil vision and I know with faith you will go away in due ...

Save the bullshit, Tommy, I interrupt. I know you too well. This has nothing to do with faith. This is science. Well, sort of. I mean, science will eventually catch up. But, okay never mind that. Um, what was I saying?

Tommy narrows his eyes and watches me. This is not going well. I can tell the voice sounds funny to him and my word choice is probably off too. That's a crack in the illusion, and once there's a crack … I need to take bolder measures. I decide to cross a line we are advised not to cross.

I look toward the pantry and summon my energy. Realizing that the channeling of energy will increase the radiance of my own form, possibly glowing through Peggy's husk, I command Tommy, Look into the pantry and tell me what you see!

He frowns with skepticism, maybe a little disdain.

The pantry! I yell, and move a few more feet toward him.

He shrugs, sips from his mug, and looks over. At this moment, I summon the energy … up! Up, up, up it comes from all the fields that surround us and I feel the old authority, the phantom's drug. I direct it toward the pantry and before Tommy can look away, the stacks of food burst from their shelves and drop to the floor in a mess.

Tommy staggers back, sets his cup on the counter, and says, Jesus F—

And then the front door bursts open.

Both Tommy and I turn to see. He no doubt thinks it's part of the haunting and I'm thinking, Now what?

Jess, his teenage daughter, stands in the foyer. Her lovely hair is matted on one side and contains a few sticks. There's sand on her knee. She's holding her phone.

Oh hi Dad, she says. What's up?

I dart into the pantry before she can see me. No wait! This mess will attract her attention. I improvise and ascend to the ceiling so I can zip into the living room out of her sight and then drop back beside the television.

Unfortunately, Tommy sees this trick, because he's switching his gaze between his daughter and me, and he's looking very unstable and unwell.

Oh god, Dad, are you wasted already? What the heck happened here?

She strides into the kitchen, pockets her phone, and begins to pick up the packages of food. Where's mom? she says, Is she still up, because I really need to talk with her about the campus visits—I think we need to reschedule because something's come up and don't ask what it is because I'm sure you'll think it's trivial but it's a big deal to me and I care about relationships even if nobody else does around here or at least most people don't seem to anymore, so …

Jess pauses in a crouch, holding a pack of SnackTyme brownies, and looks at her father. She draws out her words saying, And … no one … is … listening, as usual.

Tommy pulls his stare away from me and shakes his head. Sorry! He says. I'm sorry, Jess. Your mom—yes, she's upstairs. In bed early I guess. Maybe a headache.

He steals a glance at me and then looks back at her. I think: come on, Son, where's your discipline. If you look, she'll look. If Jess just turns her head, she'll see the radiant ghost of her grandmother. That is definitely not part of the plan. But instead Jess stands up, crosses her arms, and peers into her dad's face.

I think you need to go to bed early too, she says. You look super sick. What's with the coffee? You're gonna be hurting tomorrow. Go up and I'll bring you some water and a Xanax or something. Okay? I'll play mom tonight.

Tommy shakes his head vigorously. Oh no, he says. I don't need anyone playing mom around here tonight. I'm fine, thanks. Glass of water would be good though.

As Jess pours him one, she says, Speaking of … what is this bullshit I'm hearing about sidewalks? You want to tear out sidewalks now? Why is that again, Dad? Tell me it's a rumor.

Tommy gulps from the glass and sets it down. I can tell he's using all his effort not to look over at me. He says, breathlessly, Sidewalks are socialist.

Jess laughs and blurts, No really. What's the story?

Tommy makes this gesture, striking the side of one palm into the other hand, like he's slicing something, and recites, Sidewalks are a socialist scheme to encourage the random milling about of shiftless people and vagrants and to promote the assembly of violent, Earnest mobs. Decent people don't need sidewalks! So we are tearing them out. I've got the votes, almost, and we're going to get this done for the Righteous people of Middling. So help me, God.

Jess pulls from the fridge a hard seltzer and pops the top. She looks at her dad like you might consider a child's creepy drawing. She says, If you say so. But TBH it does sound pretty shitty to me and also a waste of money maybe? She pulls out her phone and studies it as she speaks.

Tommy changes the subject, How's that boy Donnie Martin? I haven't seen him around lately.

Jess doesn't look up, but replies. Me and Donnie broke up ages ago. I've got a new boy now. You'd hate him. He's super nice.

Tommy sneaks a glance, drops his chin in disappointment to see I'm still there, and looks back at Jess. Well, you'll have to tell me all about it. Right now I need to sit down in my chair and catch up on a few things. You heading up?

Jess is already walking away, looking at her phone. Yeah, she says. I'll see if Mom's up.

Tommy turns to look at me. His arms drop to his side and his mouth hangs open, slightly.

Now what? he asks.

Upstairs we hear the slam of a door and Jess yells, Oh Mom, really?! Oh my god that is so gross! With Dad right downstairs …

Tommy looks toward the noise, shakes it off with his head, and looks back at me, waiting.

I suppose it's worth reviewing some of my failures. That's how we learn, and I've been on a real learning streak. Let me start at the beginning—or you might say, the end. At the height of my career, I had landed a client in the lucrative corn syrup trade, and we were shooting a commercial in a field a few miles outside Middling. This was before the age of irony, when you could appeal to people's unspoiled sense of nostalgia.

A local farmer had agreed to appear in the ad and run his thresher at dusk, during the golden hour. The shot began with a wide-angle view of the vast field and sky, then zoomed in to a close-up of the combine. There, behind the wheel, we saw the farmer in ball cap and overalls. Seated next to him, his mature-but-gorgeous auburn-haired wife and between them his even-more-gorgeous blonde 19-year-old daughter, laughing and pointing with wholesome enthusiasm at something off camera. A voice-over read the tagline: 'Savor the Sweet Life.' And then we wrapped with images of all the delicious foods enhanced with the syrup of that corn. And although I now regret the grave consequences of that trade, and the role I may have played, I still shudder with pride at the pure genius of the spot. I am a work in progress.

After the filming, we catered a big party at the farm and I spoke with Kelly, the farmer's daughter, and discovered that she had remarkable potential for the ad business. We took a little walk after dark, with a bottle of dandelion wine, to discuss job opportunities and—one thing leading to the next—found ourselves asleep in the middle of the field, surrounded by 7-foot corn under a meteor shower.

I suppose my tone is a little off here, because the unfortunate consequence of this tryst was as follows: At first light, the farmer returned to harvest his corn for real and unwittingly threshed Kelly and me into the dark.

The next thing I remember it was night again, now on a barren field of stubble, with the lights of police cars flashing on the horizon and a strong southerly wind blowing. After I became aware of my own radiant form, I saw that Kelly was not far away. Or rather, the husk of Kelly's mortal energy, just bobbing and flickering like a Christmas decoration on the front lawn. I went to her and found, through a process of investigation and out of sheer curiosity, that I could assume her form.

Wearing this spectral disguise, I felt an overwhelming sense that I had to do something. It was my first encounter with that sentiment we call 'remorse.' A 19-year-old girl was dead, and I was to blame. It was impossible to imagine the grief her parents suffered. They must be recalling the last words they had with Kelly (perhaps 'don't be late now!' or 'skeeters are nasty—you want some bug spray?'). They must regret not saying something more profound or sentimental. Maybe I could help them wash away that regret, maybe allow them to have some final words. It was the least I could do. So I went to them in Kelly's husk.

I could see through the kitchen window, Mr. and Mrs. Farmer sat at the linoleum table drinking coffee. The police were gone and the place was quiet except for the shudder of their frame house in the wind. I drifted up the poured concrete steps, went right through the front door, and stood beside them at the table. Mr. Farmer leaped from his chair, tipping over the coffee cups. Mrs. Farmer rose too and came to me (in the form of Kelly) and said, Oh, honey is that you—I just knew it couldn't be true! Then she wrapped her arms around me and came up with nothing. She stumbled in the lack of resistance and then staggered away and screamed. Mr. Farmer reeled backward with a look like he had just seen a ghost.

It only got worse after that. The farm sold in three days (to Adlai Hinrick) and no one ever heard the true story because we don't talk about things like that in places like Middling County. The Courier just ran a feature story called 'Death by a Thresher,' mourning the loss of Kelly and calling for better safety precautions with farm implements. They didn't mention me in that article, to spare the reputation of the Farmers. But the next day, they ran an obituary about me, which was quite flattering, except for a few poor choices of words—like 'shill,' and 'huckster,' and 'snake oil.'

So. That was my first failure. But in the process, I discovered this unique form of haunting. The premise of the trick is this: You assume the identity of someone who, while they were living, had great influence over your mortal beneficiary. In that guise, you haunt the beneficiary, open their mind in a state of terror, and put into that open mind some wisdom— some seeds of better living. This is the hypothesis I've been trying to prove. And some day, I hope, I'll do some good with it.

But it's hard to call my subsequent efforts good. For example, there was the new editor-in-chief of the *Courier*, who was hired out of Knoxville after an English media company bought the paper. I visited him with the husk of his late journalism professor, and tried to convince him to stop predicting 'all-out war' in Middling over zoning disputes. Despite my protestations (or, those of the professor) he took the visit to be a sign that the end of days was nigh. He cut all news reporting and replaced it with nothing but inflammatory editorials and opinions, plus sports and weather. Not long after, there was the school board president, whose seven children did not, technically, attend Middling schools. I visited her with the specter of a child lost to violence, hoping to convince her to endorse a weapons ban in school neighborhoods. Instead, she called me (as the child) a messenger of demons sent by some Earnest sorcery. Instead, she launched a program to subsidize semi-automatic pistols for crossing guards and lunch ladies.

That's just two examples. Haunting is hard.

After each failure, I confess, I sulked a little. I spent a lot of time at the cemetery, walking aimlessly among the monuments and glowing husks of all the lucky so-and-sos who went into the dark without regret, with no open issues. Some nights, especially when the moon was bright, I would drop to my shimmering knees and press my fists against my eyes and scream things like What am I doing wrong?! Or Can I just get a break here—I'm trying to do some good!! And then I might sob a little and say, Oh, who am I even talking to—this is ridiculous, I am ridiculous.

A few times, stoned college kids witnessed my tantrums, and pointed with delight, covering their astonished mouths, thinking they were keeping quiet which they were not. These were my worst moments, because I had been reduced to a clown, whose messages were nothing but a thrill for wayward youth. I had a much higher purpose in mind, needless to say, and I was falling so horribly short of it.

I had known failure in life too, and this made my haunting debacles even more painful. I've told you I was THE Ad Man of Middling County—which is true—but you wouldn't have to look hard to find embarrassing failures too. I mean, when I convinced our local pet food company to release a brand of snacks called 'Doggie Style,' what was I thinking? Or how about the 30-second spot for our Chevy dealer, where he painted his family's faces red, wore feathered bonnets, and proclaimed to the camera, 'We make fair trade!'

I sulked after those disasters too.

In life, I drank. But now, after dark, there's no booze. So I find comfort and inspiration by visiting my grandchildren. They don't know I'm there. In fact, no one has seen my true spectral form—the ghost of the Ad Man. I worry it might ruin my whole scheme. But more important, a visit from me would only be useful to someone who respected me in life, who might listen to my advice—and I'm not sure there are any such people. My best hope is my grandchildren, who never knew me, but might fondly recall a story or a photo. But first I need to master this haunting trick. Meanwhile, I like to see the kids doing their lives in the un-self-conscious way young people do. I like to watch my grandson Felix walk along the river, recording song lyrics into his phone. I like to see his cousin, Nick, doing odd jobs, staying busy to drive away his demons. But most of all, I like to see Sheila in all her controlled and benevolent fury, facing injustice like a heroine stands against the hot breath of a dragon.

Mostly, I see her typing. On her laptop, on her phone, on a terminal at the library—she types and types, posting stories to her independent news site, holding officials accountable, exposing criminals in power, celebrating the achievements of the good-hearted. But sometimes I catch her in the field, intercepting legislators at lunch, photographing schemers in warehouses, climbing fire escapes and silo ladders and bell towers—always climbing toward the truth. She runs and stalks and climbs and types.

And those failures I mentioned? She cleaned them up. She exposed the *Courier* chief for faking letters to the editor, and now he's back in Knoxville. She caught the school board president paying for test scores, and now she's running a quilting shop down state. I haven't told you about my tragic run-in with Pastor Yeshevsky, but now he's in prison, thanks to Sheila. Here in Middling people love her or fear her. And she's only 28!

I like to think Sheila inherited some of her admirable traits from her grandpa. We both made a living telling stories after all—it's just that hers are true and don't pay much. And she falls into gloom now and then, but always gets up afterward, with even more resolve. And we both have a temper. I wish she hadn't taken that from me. I wish she were more like her old man or her brother Felix—calm, analytical, controlled. But my anger gene didn't disperse—Sheila got it all. And that worries me.

So I'm going to help her.

Sit down, Tommy, I tell him.

He sits in the recliner, still holding his cup, and peers at me. I lower my form to the coffee table, sitting like I imagine Peggy would —this balance between elegance and motherly compassion.

What are you? Tommy asks, more to himself than me. Maybe some kind of hologram? I know they're doing that shit over at the research park now.

Then he looks to the corners of the ceiling and says, But there would have to be little projectors or something, right? Freaking dandelions must have broke in here—or maybe Lisa let them in accidentally?

Tommy, I'm your mother, I say. I'm not a hologram, or prank, or a dream. I'm really real and right here, and I've come to help you. I want to talk about the sidewalks.

Tommy gestures violently and spills coffee on his shirt. Freaking sidewalks! he exclaims. Okay now I know you're an Earnest trick. Everybody with their obsession with sidewalks, for crying out loud. I'm going to bed.

Tommy leans close, looks into his mother's spectral eyes, and says, You can tell whoever's behind this, whoever's watching or recording or whatever, that I'm not having it! Ha ha ha, I get the joke. Great job, you nerds. Now it's over!

He thrusts himself out of his chair.

I can't even convince this jackass that I'm a ghost, much less change his mind about public policy and soften him up for Sheila. This was supposed to be an easy one! I abandon my script and improvise.

Tommy! I say, When you were eight you had a black-and-yellow checkered cape you wore to do bad magic tricks! You put on a show at school and the Radecki brothers dragged you around by that cape at recess and you came home and cried and I washed your face and let you eat a whole box of SnackTyme brownies!

He pauses, not quite standing up yet, and stares at me.

How do you know that?

Because it's me, Mom! I say. What I don't say is that the brownies were a lucky guess—the rest of the story I heard from my son Winston, who was Tommy's classmate.

Those god damn Radeckis, Tommy says, I had the last laugh with them—ran their auto shop right out of town.

And you cried the night you pulled their loan, didn't you? Because it brought back all the memories. (Now I'm going way out on a limb.)

Tommy nods, his eyes focused in the middle distance. I did, he says, I did, Mom. But you were already gone. Did you see me?

(It worked!)

I always see you, Tommy. I am always watching over you. And usually, I don't want to meddle, but this time …

Oh, Mama! Tommy sobs.

I was not expecting this. His face is wet and he leans toward me, his arms wide. I move away from the table.

Get a hold of yourself, Tommy, I say. You're a grown man. Not that it's bad for grown men to cry. Of course, they should get comfortable with their emotions. I mean, emotional repression is what's behind all sorts of problems these days …

I'm rambling …

I say, But you can cry when I leave! We need to make the most of my visit.

Okay, he says, sniffing, pawing his wet cheeks. He clears his throat, crosses his arms, and returns to his voice, Okay Mama, what do you want me to do? Just say the word. I own this town. I can do anything I want.

All right, I say. Here's what you want …

Then the doorbell rings.

Tommy stares at me with an exaggerated look of terror. We pause, motionless.

The doorbell rings again.

Tommy looks toward the hallway, though there is no line of sight to the front door, and then looks back at me. I hold up a finger for him to be calm.

The doorbell rings a third time.

From the stairs, Jess says, Doesn't anybody answer the door around here?

Tommy calls out to her, in a kind of croak, Tell them I'm not home!

Jess opens the door and says, Oh hi!

There is another voice. It's Sheila.

It's Sheila! If I had a heart it would pound; it would swell with sadness and worry and excitement. But my lack of physical heart doesn't matter—strangely, I still feel all those feelings. What do I do now? I know only one thing: I can't let her see me. Not the husk of Peggy, certainly, but especially not the sad grandpa inside.

Hey Jess, is your dad home? Sheila asks.

Umm…. Jess says.

Can you get him?

There's a pause and Jess says, I think … he's busy right now?

I can wait, says Sheila.

Tommy tosses his arms in frustration. I motion for him to stay calm. Meanwhile I'm not calm, but that's my business.

Or maybe he's out right now? Jess says. I can check?

Sheila asks, Jess, are you dating my little brother now?

This is signature Sheila—the abrupt disarming question.

Well, I don't know, Jess says, I mean, we went out today.

Are you going to be a bitch to him? Cause he's a nice kid and I don't want to see him hurt because you're a bitch to him. Make sense?

I guess, Jess replies. Her tone is irritated but compliant. I mean, sure.

Then there's a pause that feels awkward, and Jess continues, Hey, I always wanted to say I love your work, Sheila. Your writing. You're kind of inspiring to people you know? If that's not too weird to say.

Oh no, thanks. Thanks for reading. Can you get your dad now? Better yet, how about I just show myself in and save you the trouble?

Sheila begins to walk down the corridor. I can tell by the sound of her boots. She likes to wear these tall-heeled black zip-up boots, which add a few inches to her otherwise diminutive frame.

Tommy mouths to me, She's coming! And he makes a shooing motion.

I retreat into the massive entertainment cabinet, surrounded by shelves of superhero movies and war-play video games. I summon a shot of energy and draw the door shut. From inside, it's easy to hear.

Sheila's boots stop nearby and she says, So you are home.

Sheila Fuglesen! Tommy says heartily. Great to see you. What can I do you for?

I was thinking we might do that interview.

Kind of late, Sheila. But it's on my schedule for tomorrow! Looking forward to it!

Councilman, Sheila says, how many times have we scheduled this interview?

Oh, we might have had to reschedule once or twice—things have been—

Seven. We have scheduled this interview seven times. I've been to your office seven times, and each time you were indisposed. So how about we do it right now? That'll clear your schedule in the morning. Make sense?

Well, Sheila, I'll tell you—now's not a great time.

It seems like a perfect time for me. If you don't mind, I'll take a cup of that—

I said now's not a great time! Tommy barks.

Inside the cabinet, I'm not thrilled by his sudden change in tone. He sounds unstable.

Sheila says, No need to raise your voice, Mr.. Hinrick.

He mocks her, saying, No need to raise your voice, Mr.. Hinrick.

Now that's just childish.

He mocks again, Now that's just childish!

I can feel Sheila struggling to keep her composure. I have seen this before, and it looks a lot like me. It breaks my heart, the one I don't have. I want to tell her to keep it together, and then for a moment, it seems like she will.

Look, she says, I came here to do my job. I'm a journalist and you're a public servant. We're supposed to work together. It can work to your benefit, you know?

Tommy says bitterly, You're not a journalist. You're a hack. A fabricator. You're a pawn for the Earnest machine.

And you're a pawn for the Righteous machine.

I'm guessing Sheila wishes she hadn't said that.

I am the Righteous machine! Tommy exclaims. I run this town and don't you forget it!

Now we're getting somewhere, Sheila says.

Tommy says, What the heck is that? Are you recording this?

Of course I am. But trust me, it's off the record until now. I'll just set it on this coffee table while we talk, okay?

Are you fucking joking? Get the fuck out of here! You can't just barge into my house—

Your daughter invited me in.

And I'm inviting you out!

Councilman, do you have a financial interest in the demolition company you want to hire to rip out all the sidewalks?

There is a beat of silence. Then Tommy says, Sidewalks! All anybody wants to talk about is sidewalks!

Well, Sheila says, You kind of started it. No one talked about sidewalks until you called them a socialist plot.

That's beside the point!

How, exactly? That is the point, right?

Don't you talk circles around me! Do you know who you're talking to?

Then there's another pause in which I can hear Tommy breathing. He is calming himself down. Then I hear a movement.

Give me my phone back! Sheila says.

I'm confiscating it.

That's ridiculous. You don't have any authority to confiscate that. Give me my phone!

I am standing my ground, Tommy asserts. It's my house and I can confiscate.

Do you even understand how the law works? Seriously. Give it to me.

I hear Tommy walk around the room. He speculates, I bet I could learn all kinds of interesting things with this phone—

Then there is a thud, like a sack of potatoes hitting the floor, and Tommy lets out an Oof!

This is getting bad, so I crack open the door to see.

Tommy is bent over, clutching his gut. Sheila stands solidly, facing him, pointing her phone camera at him. Then Tommy uncoils and makes a move toward Sheila with open hands. She darts behind the recliner as he bangs his shin on the coffee table. Tommy curses and goes after her again, and Sheila escapes his grasp, and then they have a standoff with the couch in between them.

I'm calling the cops, he says. Assault and battery.

I have a right to retrieve my stolen possession, Sheila says. Her lips are compressed and her eyes wide.

I have seen this face before. I have worn that face many times. Don't do something you'll regret, Sheila. Please.

Tommy says, The cops don't like you. Sgt. Medina doesn't like you. You're screwed.

Sheila holds up the phone. Are you saying you have influence over the Middling police? Are you saying, councilman, that the police may take action based on their personal opinions about me?

Record all you want, you little bitch, I'm calling Medina and we'll get that phone and everything on it. And then, if I'm not feeling satisfied, we'll go after your father and pull the lease on that research space he's renting from me, and then maybe we'll see about getting your brother kicked out of the marching band—

Sheila lunges to the table, grabs the remote control, and flings it at Tommy. It strikes his glistening red forehead, and a seam of blood appears. He brings up his hand, sees the blood, and his expression becomes dangerous. I have to do something. It will be okay. I can handle this. I step out of the cabinet, radiant in the husk of Tommy's mother.

Hold on! I say. Hold on, you two. Let's all keep our cool.

Tommy looks at me, then at Sheila, then at me. His face holds a peculiar tangle of emotions. He puts his hand to his head and says, Mama, I'm bleeding. Tell her to go.

Sheila's expression fades from rage to wonder. Whoa, she says. That looks like Peggy Hinrick …

It is Peggy Hinrick, dear, I say. And if I'm not mistaken, you are Sheila Fuglesen.

Then I can't help but add, I truly admire your work.

Sheila stares inquisitively and replies, Thanks. Though … I'm not sure how you'd know that?

Now that I'm in the same room with her, she looks so small. Formidable, but small. I wish it were just the two of us and we were up on a hilltop over a lake flying a kite. I could have taught her some things, I reckon, if it weren't for that damned thresher. Now they are both staring at me. Ghosts aren't supposed to daydream.

I say, Although I've passed, dear, I still keep my eyes and ears on things. Now, I think it's best you go, so everybody can cool off, and then you two can have your interview in the morning? Sound good?

I clasp my hands in front of me, hold my ankles together, and smile with all the grace Peggy Hinrick showed in life.

Sheila has pointed her phone camera at me and takes a step backward.

Tommy, Sheila says uneasily, Who is this?

It's my Mama, he replies. Put your god damned phone down.

Well, that can't be, because your mom died a while ago.

Sheila starts to circle me, to film at different angles.

Have you touched her? Sheila asks. To see if it's an illusion?

I begin to say, No, no, let me tell you why—

But Tommy interrupts, pointing at Sheila saying, It's none of your business! And don't call her 'It!' I tell you what: I'm calling Medina now and we'll take this to Judge Murray and get that rag of yours shut down.

Sheila has turned to film him now. Well if that is your mom, she says, it seems like she likes me better than you.

Tommy strides toward her again.

Stop it! I say. Leave her alone!

But Tommy catches her this time, smacks the phone from her hand. It skitters across the hardwood floor. As Sheila reaches down to grab it, Tommy shoves her and she falls. He grabs a cushion from the couch and drops down on her, holding her against the floor. Sheila kicks backward, trying to inflict some pain on his legs with her boots.

Stop moving! He says. Stop moving!

Sheila shouts, Get off me you fat fuck! and reaches toward the hearth where a set of brass fireplace tools hang.

I feel as if I'm watching a horrible movie. Or better yet, one of my failed ads, after a focus group tore it to shreds. I suddenly see what I've created—what once was genius is now grotesque and banal, with all the filthiness and asymmetry of regular life. A result exactly the opposite of what I intended. What do you do?

I summon the phantom's drug. I draw up energy from the fields that surround us, until I am glowing with potential. Then I release it all toward Tommy, launching him into the fireplace and away from Sheila.

He looks back at me. Sheila looks at me. Their faces—it's like they're in shock. I look down at myself and understand. My spectral form—the ghost of the Ad Man—is glowing brightly through the husk of Peggy Hinrick. We are two dead persons fused as one, each fighting against the other's light. This is too much for my mortal beneficiaries. It's too much for me!

I tear Peggy's husk off myself and we float beside each other, just above the coffee table.

I say to Sheila, Do you recognize me?

My voice sounds meek. I realize what's happening. I am revealing myself to my grandchildren—to Sheila! This is not the way I wanted it to happen.

I say, Do you? From pictures, maybe?

There is a pause, in which I think perhaps Sheila might say, Oh Grandpa!

But instead, Sheila and Tommy scream.

I feel out of myself. As if I'm a camera slowly pulling away. I have thoughts like: these primates are opening their mouths and forcing the most unpleasant sound to express their vulnerability. And then I think, Oh Sheila, honey, please don't scream. And then I think shit! In a few seconds, Jess, and perhaps Lisa, and Lisa's lover, will all be downstairs to witness this horrible scene. That can't happen, or the whole town will know and I'll never haunt again. And also, Sheila shouldn't see more of me—maybe it's brief enough that she'll forget.

But still, I might be able to do just a little good …

I begin to say, Before I go, can I just give you guys a little advice—

But they have scrambled to their feet. Tommy brandishes the couch cushion toward me. And Sheila has drawn the fireplace poker.

Whatever you are, Sheila cries, please go!

Get out! Tommy yells.

I say, I am only here to help—

Go! they yell in unison. Then they look at each other, surprised, and then face me fiercely.

I hear Jess call from the stair, What's happening?

It's over. Every second I stay, I make it worse. Sheila's on her own, but it's clear she's better off that way. So I grab Peggy's husk like you might grab a jacket, and I flee. I pass directly through the walls, because we're long past good manners, and find myself on the front lawn. I would be out of breath, but there is no breath after dark.

Outside, the town is quiet. I hear crickets and then the distant wail of a train heading north. The moon is nearly full and there's a halo around it—weather coming. In the hedge I see a raccoon scale the trunk of a white pine and pause to look at me, its eyes reflecting the street light. I become aware that I'm still holding Peggy in a manner of haste, so I right her husk so she looks respectable again. It's the least you can do for the departed. Then I realize we are visible, and so I take cover in the hedge.

A shape drops from the bedroom balcony, and slides down the downspout—a man in camouflage, holding his shoes. He runs toward the white Silverado and pulls himself inside. Through the front door comes Lisa, running in a sheer robe toward the truck—she jumps in as he rolls away. I suspect she hasn't thought this through, but who am I to judge?

Then Jess comes out from the open front door and takes a few steps down the sidewalk. She sees the taillights of the truck, hears the bark of its tailpipes. She looks back at the house, then back toward the street. She raises her arms and drops them in exasperation.

Jess says, to no one, Are we all just … insane?

Then she brings up her phone, which illuminates her face, and she dials and says, Felix? Sorry. I know it's late. Can I come over?

She jogs away across the lawn.

The house is still and I sense a peculiar calm. I should go. I should return Peggy to her mausoleum and then … well I don't know. But I can't go. Because Sheila's inside and I just have to know. I leave Mrs.. Hinrick's husk floating in the hedge and glide around the house to the patio doors.

They can't see me, of course, because it's dark. But I see them, Sheila and Tommy. They sit on the couch, not far apart, leaning forward, their elbows on their knees. They are both looking into full glasses, and there's a bottle of bourbon open on the table. Tommy keeps shaking his head. Sheila says something, then stops, and resumes looking into her glass. Tommy mutters something and takes a drink. Sheila thinks, smiles briefly, and drinks to that.

And …scene, I whisper. Not bad for a night's work.

LETTER TO MY MORTAL WIFE

Dear Helen,

Thank you for your last letter. I read it over your shoulder as you wrote. I know I should not have been there. If you had but turned around and seen me, glowing in my husk after dark, without a body to touch, it would have given you an awful fright—perhaps too much even for your stalwart soul. Certainly too much after the ordeal you had just suffered and were writing about. So I apologize, but come to think of it, I do not. I miss you terribly, and wanted to throw my arms around you in your chair and smell your neck and comfort you. For that, I cannot apologize.

On my way into our house, I heard screaming from the Fallendini place next door. I didn't realize it then. I will try to get to that before the end of this letter. But at the time, the screams must have blended into the overwhelming assault on my senses. You'll remember that after the storm, a hot wind blew up from the south, bringing more trouble for everybody here in Middling. I could hear all their suffering—feel all their suffering—all at once. I had been wandering around for days, not knowing what to do. That is probably the worst part of being after dark—the interminable awakeness, the restlessness and absolute weariness with no promise of sleep, ever again. It's hard to come up with things to do, especially after you've tried and failed a few times, which happens to all the troubled ghosts, as far as I can tell. So eventually the only thing I could think to do was to come see you. And so I read your letter as you wrote it with that pen you're still using even though it should have long run out of ink, even though the cap is lost and the clip is broken and the logo of that seed company is worn off. You wrote it with your fingers that I know you don't like, because they are knotted at the joints like burr oak branches, but in those fingers I still see the mild and milky hands I held as we walked on autumn nights when we could barely contain our desires. How long ago was that? My sense of time fails, as the ratio of my days shifts in the direction of dark. I might be ancient. I might be prehistoric.

And that reminds me: Yes. I have seen the mastodon, and the giant sloths, and the passenger pigeons and all the phantoms of the beasts we've destroyed. And yes, you're right, they are not resting in peace. They are sometimes full of rage and when it gets to be too much to bear, they burst out in one of those tantrums. People call them 'storms,' as if they were nothing more than a reminder to close your window and turn up your television. If only they could see, well, maybe things would be different. I hear there's a ghost up north, along the highway, a woman, who takes rides with men infected with fear. She uses phantom energy to drain their fear, for just a little while, so they can see the world as it is, and as it might be. I have heard sometimes she is successful. That there are men who remain liberated from fear after they meet her, that afterward they do good deeds and spread the word of her legend. I can't say. But I hope it's true.

I am so glad you lifted your head out of those flood waters. It is such a relief that you got up, and you helped the chickens back into their house, and you thought to write me, and you held your ground against despair. It's too soon to join me anyway. We can't say whether we would be together, if you just let go. I hope we will. But it's a risky choice, if you haven't finished your mortal obligations. I want to say that I am proud of you, for your spirit and compassion and temerity.

But I was also sad, when I left the house, after you finished the letter and folded it in thirds and sealed it up and then, for so long, stared at the envelope knowing there was no address to write. I was sad because of all the things you don't know—all the things that if you did know, maybe you wouldn't have lifted your head from that water. It seems contrary, doesn't it, that I would tell you I'm glad you made a decision because you didn't know the things I'm about to tell you. That's what it sounds like. And it's true but also not true. I wish I could write as well as you and explain this properly. Maybe I used to write better? Everything fades, all your senses, from the moment you pass into the dark. I don't know how it ends, though I do see many husks just floating in peace over grave sites and along wooded river banks and in the bottom of meadows where the fog gathers and the lightning bugs flash. That sounds nice.

Those things you don't know! I can tell you now, because there's more to come, if I can get to the end of this letter. You remember that young couple who moved to the country outside Middling a few years back, who bought the place along the river that everyone used as a dump. They couldn't have known how bad it is. We were excited that young people would want to move out here and try to repair the land. But I suspect it's only the boy there now, as the girl has gone. It's true what they say, that Hanacek still haunts that land, and that boy probably will too someday, because he's given in to it. If you'll pardon my language, Hanacek is a cruel bastard, and he should have scared those kids away before they dumped the body and became accomplices. Maybe Hanacek has a perspective broader than mine. But it would have made you sad, Helen, to see how it went. You might have given in to the despair.

I would have, but it's pointless for a ghost. You can despair all you want, you can lament, as Dickens would say, and it doesn't do a bit of good, so instead, eventually, you find yourself trying to fix things. This is what I see most often—these poor, sad phantoms roaming around this town, meddling with the ones they love, straining to prevent the same stupid decisions they made in life. You should see John Fuglesen, the old Ad Man—everything he touches turns to shit, if you'll excuse my language. The best thing he could do, in my opinion, is nothing at all, and let Sheila do her earnest work, one fierce day at a time. How they share the same blood is beyond my comprehension. But none of us can do nothing—who am I to judge? There's just too many waking hours. But still. John Fuglesen. That starry-eyed dandy.

It's a bleak and comical dance you see every night. Well-intentioned phantoms chasing kids from gun-crazed madmen, spooking pickups from gas stations, shoo-ing birds from giant windmills, cutting power during cable news hours, scaring Righteous judges on the eve of mad decisions. It never seems to amount to much. But we do it anyway! You can't help yourself—have I said that already? I don't like to go back and read. I used to. It gave me such pleasure to read what I had written—why is that? It must activate the neural pathways that lit up when you wrote, and so you get the same neurochemical high. Oh, I understand now! I no longer have neural pathways, so that's why I don't bother to read what I've written. But then how do I write? Why am I saying all this? Oh for Pete's sake. Let me get to the point, dear Helen. Let me at least try.

When I left you in the house, after you had put the unaddressed letter in the drawer with all the other letters, as I drifted across our lawn through the row of spruce we planted to block the brutal southerly winds, I was struck again how I no longer look for roads or sidewalks, how I just glide in any old direction (and lately, I've learned how to drift upward, when that seems necessary). And so in my wandering course I came closer to the

Fallendini place and heard the screams again, but this time they registered in whatever serves as my neural pathways, whatever computing part of the apple of light that was once my brain.

How I ramble! I guess it was like that at the end, my incoherency, after all the years I had ingested all the miraculous chemicals we sprayed year after year, overflowing the grain elevators, jamming freight trains and semi-trailers, who spilled corn along the tracks and highways from here to Chicago, stockpiling cash, investing wisely, not knowing we were incurring a debt of the worst kind, a debt that can only be paid by life itself. We were growing a debt that killed me—that thrives in the tender, fertile soil of the brain and grows recklessly like ragweed and honeysuckle until all the cells have caught the disease and there's nothing left. Nothing but a lovely husk, and some new kind of residual existence no one can explain.

Are you with me? Only you, dear Helen, would still be reading now. Bless you. Do we still say that? I guess we decide who or what does the blessing, and so it works all right.

So I heard the screams at the Fallendinis and went over to see what was going on. That little schoolhouse was never the same after the shooting, as you know, but they've fixed it up, haven't they? I suppose Caleb was always handy—you can say that much, and that's about all you can say. The last I saw, he was headed north with his friend and his Daddy, toward the highway phantom who heals men. I'm sure you must have checked on Susan now and again, even after I was gone, even though she never wanted help. Poor dear. She's a hard one to love.

Well, I noticed how the place was fixed up, and all the bullet holes had been filled, and there was fresh paint, even on the old bell. But also, the windows were boarded, I suppose because of the storm, but who boards windows before a storm anymore? Susan must have stopped worrying about what people say. Or maybe she was frightened in some new way.

When I got to the front door, the screams were plain. They weren't all screams, exactly. It was shouting, hollering, and banging on boards. The spirits of all the murdered children were all about, of course. They will be there for a long time, with all the moxie of country kids, pranking whoever's brave or dumb enough to live there, playing games on the lawn just like mortal kids, looking for friends, just like mortal kids. They made a racket, all these children after dark, and their little husks glowed brightly, buzzing around the house like yellow jackets around a dumpster. But even through the racket, I heard the hollering inside the house, and so I shooed away the ghost kids, who made some catty remarks, but then did as I said.

I opened the door, because that's just good manners, rather than barging right through the wall, and as soon as I was inside I could tell there was trouble. A bureau was pulled on top of the door to the cellar, and from that cellar came the hollering, and now it must be obvious what I discovered that night. But before I go on, please don't blame yourself for not doing something to prevent this crime. A person can only take on so much, and if you're at the point where all you can eat is eggs from hens who barely lay—well, you're in no position to save a crazy family next door when they've rejected your offers again and again.

(Which reminds me, you should be seeking help yourself, Helen. There's no shame in that. There are people who will help, I assure you. Oh hush now, I know, I would never have asked for help, but since when is my stubborn foolishness your model for behavior? That's right: never. I have some ideas about this. But that will come in another letter. Or maybe it will just come, and you will believe it's a change in fortune, which happens like phases of the moon—yes it's better if you think that.)

My energy is amazing now, I must say. I can say it, without bragging, because it's just so. It's not exactly a controlled power yet, it's jerky, kind of like the old Farmall. But it took just a second before I had that bureau moved aside and tipped against the wall. And then I focused my energy on that locked-up cellar door and flipped it open, like a roof shingle in a windstorm.

Then, there was a whoosh of horrible air—smokey and rank. I could not smell it of course (I guess you don't know we lose the sense of smell after dark). But I could see the smoke and feel the dampness of the rank. There must have been a fire down in that hole, and I reckoned it was the kids cooking something in the three days they were trapped. I heard chickens croak when the beam of light burst down the cellar stairs and I surmised those kids must have cooked a chicken or two. But why were chickens even in the cellar with them? I suppose that was Susan too, in some convoluted logic. Be that as it may. Clearly, these kids were resourceful, and willing to do difficult things to survive in this difficult world, which is not how people talk about kids their age—least not as I remember. So I thought, Huh. I'm going to find a place to hide, so as not to further upset this poor family. And I'm going to see if they're all right—or even, still alive—and then I'll see what they do and whether they need anything else.

The first to appear was Rebecca, the youngest one, clutching a filthy stuffed rabbit, borne up by the hands of her oldest brother, Eli, who emerged just after her. He set her on the floor beside the hole, and then reached down and helped up Mary, who was carrying a bucket of bones and feathers. Mary staggered for a moment as her eyes adjusted to the light, but she recovered quickly and went to Rebecca and wrapped an arm around her and spoke quietly. Then Noah appeared through the hole and reached for Eli's hand, but he missed it and fell back down the cellar stairs. Someone must have caught him, because there was no sound of crashing, and in a moment Noah came up again and found Eli's hand, and he ran to the door and peered out. Finally, Sarah came up, carrying two chickens by the legs, upside down. The chickens remained calm this way, as they do. But when Sarah set them on the floor they ran off to the corners of the room and hid.

Poor things, said Sarah. And all five children stared at the chickens for too long, with exhausted gazes, like a shipwrecked captain might look at the sea.

Eli took a deep breath, and said, Come here. Let's talk.

The other four came and they stood in a circle. Rebecca dropped to the floor on her bottom and her head rolled. Sarah grabbed her hand and pulled her up.

Don't sit down, Sarah said. Not yet.

Water, said Eli.

Yes, said Sarah. You get it and I'll hold Becky.

Eli went to the sink and returned with a milk bottle full of water. They passed it around and he said, Not too much.

But Noah kept drinking and walked away with the bottle, gasping between gulps. And then in a burst he vomited—first the water, then some green bile, and he convulsed and retched.

I told you, not too much, Eli said.

Do you see, Helen? These kids are resourceful. It's a shame about Noah, but how about Eli? The young people know things.

And then Sarah said, Does anyone's phone still work?

They searched their pockets and found phones and all of them had blank screens, except for Mary, who said, I turned it off when it wasn't going to do any good.

Sarah seemed about to cry when she heard this, and that seemed uncharacteristic for Sarah, but we all have our breaking points. She said, Oh my god Mary, you're the fucking best—try to turn it on.

Mary pushed the button and after a moment the screen flashed and they looked.

Three days, said Mary.

My god, said Eli. He put a hand to his mouth, then he looked around the house keenly, as if something should have happened—or needed to happen.

Sarah kept looking at the glow of Mary's phone and said, slowly, The fucking bitch.

No, Eli said. He stepped over and brought his face close to Sarah's. Let's not do that.

Then Sarah drew air in, like a sob, and fell toward Eli, and buried her face in his chest. As he hugged her, Sarah said, You're right. You're right. But still I want to kill her.

Okay drink some more, everybody, said Eli, But slowly.

Have I told the story well enough, Helen? You see, I did a good thing, didn't I? I'm just as pathetic and confused as any restless spirit, but even so I freed the Fallendini kids from their prison, where they surely would have perished. I know I'm putting too fine a point on it, but sometimes we have to, don't we? Don't we need to sing out when we do some good against all the odds and obstacles? I think so, but I will let you make up your own mind, while I finish what remains.

The kids rested a long time. They found places to charge their phones and then sat beside them. They drank more water, and ate apples that remained on the counter. Then, as their young bodies revived, they began to look around the house, as if seeing it for the first time, as if they were some rear guard showing up at a battle that was lost days ago. And then they began to discuss a plan, in a sort of perfect coordination.

Eli said, I'll go find her. I can go by myself. I'm going to try to get her to the hospital.

He saw Sarah shake her head slowly, and Eli added, Even if I have to trick her into it.

Mary said, Noah and I can fix the satellite dish. She must have cut it or something.

Eli said, There's a box of tools under the boot rack.

Mary smiled, as you do when you're patronized without malice. And

Noah said, No shit.

Watch your fucking language, Noah, said Sarah.

And they all laughed and the laughter seemed to do something for their spirits—I don't know what to call it exactly, but it has the quality of energy that becomes the husk after dark. Oh, that sounds superstitious or occult when I say it, Helen, but that laughter was like rain on parched fields, rain that runs off at first and into the cracks of drought, but rain that later softens everything and makes the lovely scent that I can smell no more.

Well, finally, Sarah said, I'm going to find Sheila Fuglesen. I want her to come and take pictures and write this story first. Don't tell me not to do it because I'm going.

Eli grabbed his elbows and lowered his head and said, Come on, Sarah, we don't want to be famous for this. We don't want to be those people.

Sarah turned and looked at him with this intense sincerity and resolve. She said, We're already famous. For all that shit. It's too late. And we are those people. But I want it to stop with us, which I know it won't, but maybe there will be just one family who changes—or gets changed—because of our shitty fame. You know we'll be some gross meme anyway—that's fucking inevitable. But at least if Sheila writes the story first there's some hope some people will get it and maybe we'll stop just one fucked up …

And then Sarah stopped talking, and wiped fingers under her eyes, and shook her head as if to rattle her brain into clarity.

Okay go, said Eli. It makes sense.

Rebecca came to Sarah then, and dropped into her lap, and put her rabbit up to her ear and whispered, Can I go?

Sarah looked at her, and her gaze became severe, and then it softened into the image of an idea, and she smiled. She said, Yes, Rebecca. You can definitely go. Bring your bunny. And let's not wash up first.

Eli watched this. He said, Sarah …

They looked at each other.

Sarah said. I know. Only the truth. That's all we'll need.

I left then, fading backward through the wall, and found myself in the field behind our house. The sun was getting high and the shadows were short and steam rose from waters receding back to the river. I could see you through the kitchen window, over the stove, boiling some eggs I suppose. And I thought. And I am thinking now: Thank you for getting up from that mud, Helen. Thank you for saving those birds. I am overcome with gratitude that you made that choice, and it is the right choice. Because tonight I'll go out again and look for where I'm wanted. Because you were right when you said those beasts shall not have died in vain.

Because there's still so much good work to do on this earth.

Printed in the USA
CPSIA information can be obtained
at www.ICGtesting.com
LVHW052002160823
755462LV00004B/45